Heinrich Preschers

The Gift

A Book of Tales and Pencillings in Poetry and Prose

Heinrich Preschers

The Gift
A Book of Tales and Pencillings in Poetry and Prose

ISBN/EAN: 9783744685665

Printed in Europe, USA, Canada, Australia, Japan

Cover: Foto ©Andreas Hilbeck / pixelio.de

More available books at **www.hansebooks.com**

A BOOK OF

Tales and Pencillings in Poetry and Prose.

ILLUSTRATED BY GREAT ARTISTS.

Keep thou this token that I send,
  A trifle though it be;
The humblest tribute from a friend
  No trifle were to me.

LONDON:

T. NELSON AND SONS, PATERNOSTER ROW;
EDINBURGH; AND NEW YORK.

1866.

PREFACE

N giving this book to the Public little requires to be said by way of preface. It is one of those works which, without pretending to anything original, embraces much that is interesting, and calculated to turn a leisure hour to good account. It commends itself to our attention at times when the mind, not disposed to vacuity, is inclined to unbend itself from the severer duties of life, and when it may receive such gentle impulses in new directions as may help its elasticity while it invigorates its powers.

Milton has celebrated the happy union of Music and Poetry—

"Sphere-born, harmonious sisters, Voice and Verse;"

but it has been left for this age to add a third Grace to the harmony, and to link Art in Painting with the other two. This is a very prominent feature of the present work; and it is confidently believed that the Illustrations which it contains, (being after the works of great Artists,) will be found to be in all respects worthy the attention of the most cultivated and refined.

The "Pencillings" are characterized by elegance and variety. They have been selected with care, holding in view the diversity of tastes which prevails; and it is fondly anticipated that very few indeed will take up the volume without finding in it something to soothe, to interest, or to instruct.

CONTENTS

THE GIFT.

The Hall of the Castle.

OTWITHSTANDING that the Castle of Kilkenny generally held a strong garrison, upon an October evening, in the year 1390, its bastions, towers, and other points of defence, were almost unmanned; its courts almost silent; and but a few very old or very young domestics sat in its great hall, with arms in their hands, and with doubt and anxiety impressed on their features. It had sent out its last regular soldier, together with all of its able-bodied serfs, to support their lord, James, Earl of Ormonde, in a battle against the Desmond, touching the rights and bounds of certain lands; and intelligence of the result of the fray was, upon this evening, every moment expected at its gates.

The lady of the fortress knelt in her private chapel, at "the altar of the holy stone," in fervent, but not faltering prayer. The pride of name, the pride of feudal animosity, and the pride of her love of her martial husband, equally kept her heart unconscious of fear. The utmost condescension of her anxiety was to doubt; but nothing did she, or would she, doubt upon the subject which engrossed her soul, so far as regarded its issue by mortal means. Uncontrolled by a superior power, the Botiller, the Ormonde, the lord of her heart and her life, ever commanded success against a Desmond; and she knelt, therefore, only to pray that the will of God might not, on this occasion, fight against her and hers.

Her orisons ended, she slowly arose, and after bending her head, and crossing her calm and high forehead before the altar, paced along the solitary chapel, and issued from it through a low, arched door. Many flights of narrow stone steps, twining upward from the foundations of the castle, upon a level with which was the chapel-floor, then conducted her to the suite of small rooms leading into her sleeping-chamber; then she gained a lobby, which gave entrance to what was called "The Long Gallery," of the edifice; where, finding herself alone, the lady of Ormonde blew a shrill and loud call upon the little silver whistle which hung from her neck.

But no person answered her; and while her commanding brow assumed a severe expression, she was again about to put the whistle to her lips, when the notes of a trumpet, sounding the signal for defence, reached her from, as she believed, the embattled wall which faced and fell down to the Nore, full forty feet, although its top was still much lower than the foundation-stone of the fortress it helped to defend.

The point from which the martial strain seemed to arise was fully commanded by the spacious end window of the long gallery ; and thither the lady of Ormonde now repaired, with a more rapid step than was habitual to her.

Arrived at the window, she boldly flung open its casements, and gazed directly downward. Two figures only met her view, those of the individuals whom she had reckoned upon meeting in the gallery after her return from the chapel ; namely, Simon Seix, the half-witted foster-brother of her only son (and only child, too), and that only son, himself, mounted on Simon's shoulders, who galloped, or pranced, or curveted, along the terra-plane of the wall.

"The poor born-natural!" she muttered ; "again will he disobey my commands not to leave the castle with his young lord? and leave it for such antics, too, and to be played upon that perilous wall ; and doubtless it was he who erewhile mimicked the sound of trumpet which so challenged us!"—

The lady recollected Simon's talent for imitating the tones of all the instruments of music which he had ever heard played, as well, indeed, as of the voices of many animals ;—and even at the moment her surmise was confirmed ; for, after he had exceedingly well performed the loud neighing and snorting of an enraged battle-charger, as an accompaniment to a devious and (still the lady thought) perilous caracole, she saw and heard him blow a second trumpet blast through the hollow of his hand, which might well be mistaken for the martial music it faithfully copied. It was a strain of victory and triumph ; and Simon seemed enamoured of his own execution of it, for he prolonged the sounds, as though he would never end them, until, at last, they suddenly stopped, breaking off in a ludicrous cadence of terror as the overmastering shrillness of his lady's whistle cut them short.

Turning up his large gray eyes to the open window far above him, he saw the awful figure of his offended mistress half bending from it. Her arm was raised, her hand clenched, and she stamped her foot, and pointed to him to re-enter the castle. The Lord Thomas—so was called the little boy of seven or eight years on his back—looked up also; but while Simon assumed a face of the utmost fright and affliction, he only laughed merrily and graciously, in answer to his mother's signs; and then, resisting his foster-brother's preparations to place him on his own feet, he obliged Simon still to bear him on his shoulders.

In a few moments the little Lord Thomas appeared before his mother, in the gallery. Her first look towards him was one of grave reprehension; but when, presuming on her love for him, as well as prompted by his own love for her, the boy came bounding forward; his perfectly amiable and intelligent countenance wearing smiles, which at once deprecated her anger and admitted error, but made light of it; the stately lady's brow relaxed, and, thinking of his father, she opened her arms to receive him.

"But where tarries Simon Seix, boy? with him, at the least, the overgrown adviser and contriver of all thine antics, I shall call a strict reckoning," she said, after some previous words between them.

Lord Thomas made a gleeish signal to his mother of a con-

fidential understanding sought at her hands, and then com-
posing his features, spoke in a voice of mock solemnity, as
he turned towards the door by which he had come in, "Enter
Simon, and face my lady mother."

The ill-contrived figure of Simon, short, thick, and bandy-
legged, dragged itself through the doorway, and stood still a
few paces past the threshold. His long arms dropped at his
sides; his jaw fell; his crooked eye-brows became propor-
tionately elevated; his heavy-lidded eyes turned sideways
upon the floor; and altogether he presented a very ludicrous
caricature of repentance, fear, and self-abasement, of which
one half was, however, only affected; for, with his young
lord for advocate, he really apprehended no bad consequences.

"So, knave," the lady began, "neither your respect for
my commands, nor your love and fear of the lord of Ormonde,
exposed, at this moment, to utmost peril, can keep you within the castle, with Lord Thomas, sage and sedate, as the
time requires him and you to be ?"

Simon whiningly, yet with a certain sly expression of tone
and manner, replied : "I wot not, gracious lady, wherefore,
at this time, aught is required from Lord Thomas, his
father's son, or from me, his poor, simple servitor and body-
man, save the bearing which bespeaks joyousness and trouble
past."

"And why, sirrah, wot you not ?"

"Because, by this hour of the day, our good battle hath surely
been fought and won, and a Botiller's foot again planted on
the neck of a Desmond," answered Simon, confidently.

"Say you so?" continued the lady, her eyes brightening; "and whence come your tidings, sir?"

"From our common thought of whatever must be the fortunes of the Ormonde against his present foe, lady," said the reputed fool; and while he spoke, he gave his noble foster-brother an anxious sign to second his interested sycophancy; in consequence of which, as well, indeed, as in assertion of what he really felt, the boy answered:

"True, Simon; and it would, in sooth, ill become the Ormonde's only son to show, by wearing of a sad face, this even, a doubt of his own gallant father."

"List, excellent lady!" adjured Simon; "his nobleness repeats the very words which drew me from the castle by his side."

"Peace, knave!" said the lady, her face, voice, and manner suddenly changing into great energy as she heard the well-known sounds of lowering the draw-bridge before the principal gate in the walls of the castle: "Nay, by my holy saint!" she went on rapidly, while a burst of wailing voices reached her from the hall below—"here I have been sinfully bandying words with an idiot, at the moment that I should have bent my knee to Heaven! Who comes to greet us? who waits below? she cried, pacing towards a side-door of the gallery; and she was about to issue through it, when the sound of many feet echoed on the lobby without. She paused, and grew pale. Presently old John Seix, the father of Simon, clad in complete mail, and looking jaded and agitated, presented himself before her: the few servants left in the castle crowded at his back. Her eyes met his, and during their short but eloquent glance, she drew in her lips hard, crossed one hand over her bosom, and with the other, extended at full length, motioned him to speak.

"The noble Ormonde lives, dear lady," answered the old man; and there he paused.

"But the battle is lost, John Scix?" she said, apparently with calmness. Evasively he replied, that his lord, in quick retreat upon Kilkenny, close pressed by the Desmond,. had despatched him to bid his lady summon the citizens of the town to arms; that some of them might help to garrison the castle, and some hasten to join his army at Green's Bridge, a mile up the river, where he purposed making a last brave stand against his old foe.

"All things shall be tried," answered his lady : and thereupon she despatched one domestic to the civil authorities of the town, over whom the house of Ormonde held despotic sway; and another to the steeple, which held the great clock, in the court-yard, with orders to ring the alarum. "John Scix," she resumed, walking up and down the gallery —"however may betide this last struggle at the bridge, I give way to no fears for the dear and precious life of the Ormonde; supposing him a war-prisoner at the present moment, Desmond hath never lived who dares to harm a hair of his head."

"Nor ever shall live to but think of it, mother," said the almost infant Lord Thomas, coming to her side and taking her hand; his childish tears, which had flowed at John Scix's first news, being now almost dried up. She raised him in her arms and pressed him to her bosom, but she did not weep. After setting him on the floor again, she continued :

"No, old and faithful servant, I fear not the poor Desmond on my lord's account; but should he a second time prove fortunate at yonder bridge, and afterwards break his rude way into our castle, here—then, John Seix, ungarrisoned and lone as we are—then would I fear him on mine own account."

"And wherefore, mother?" demanded the boy at her side, while old Seix sighed heavily and assentingly.

"It needs not that I inform you of the broad grounds of my fear," she resumed, still addressing her old house-steward: "before my marriage with my noble lord, you remember his bold pretensions to my favour—they were plain to all the world: nathless, no living creature, save myself, can now tell you the especial reason why—woman, wife, lady and—mother, as I am"—her accents trembled, she stopped her rapid walk, and put her hand on her son's head, while he looked up into her face most intently, though not as if he comprehended her present discourse—"the especial reason why my soul begins to shrink before the Desmond."—

"Hark to the noise which comes faintly down the river, lady," said, to her great surprise, Simon Seix, the half-fool, speaking seriously and steadily, as he gracelessly moved from a corner in which he had hitherto been standing unnoticed, though, perhaps, not without noticing all he saw and heard; and edging round by the wall, approached the end window of the gallery.

"Ay, and so it does!" exclaimed his mistress, hurrying to

the point of observation before him; "and, for the nonce, Simon, well have you spoken."

She gained the open window. Quick as a flash, her glance shot at once up the river, to the bridge, and there fixed itself. The October evening began to close in, and it was sunless and heavy; yet the twilight did not so much prevail as to hinder her from distinguishing the general features of things at a good distance.

The faint shouting and uproar still came down the Nore; but nothing to interest her as yet occurred upon the bridge. In a very short time, however, the wild tumult growing louder, she saw a large body of armed men pour over it, rapidly and in disarray; and some rallied at the country side of the bridge, some between its battlements, and some at its town side. The lady of Ormonde knew that these were her husband's men, hotly pursued by the Desmond; and that they now prepared to make the last stand of which old Seix had spoken to her. Nor were they allowed much time to prepare themselves; nor did they long resist the fierce attack of their assailants. The particular incidents of the struggle she could not see; but in the furious shouts of the Desmond, at first confident and insulting, and then cruel and triumphant; in the haughty blasts of their trumpets; in the gradual receding from the bridge of her lord's bands, as those of his enemy thronged thick upon it; and in the frequent plunge of men and horses into the river, at that point evidently possessed at first by her friends;—in all these occurrences the unhappy lady saw, too plainly, signs of discomfort and of woe to her husband, his child, and herself.

Old Seix, watching her from the interior of the gallery, needed nothing but her action, and the expression of her countenance, to tell him the issue of the fray, and to impart to his own bosom the successive emotions which agitated hers. When she first looked out from the window, he knew by her bending attitude, extended neck, and unwinking eyes, that, as yet, she saw nought which she had expected to see. Suddenly, in answer to the rush of the Ormondes over the bridge, she stood upright, and clenched her hands at her sides; then she bent low again, and her fingers grasped her knees; and then she started a second time to her full height, stamped with one foot, waved an arm round her head with a quick, chucking action of impatient command; and, finally, in observance of a termination which has not been described by us, she threw up her hands, locked them together, and dropped her head between her arms.

"All is over, lady of Ormonde?" demanded Seix.

"It is, John," she answered; "our base hinds fly like the poor deer they are only fit to tend, scattered and wild, over the distant country."

"Do the Desmonds pursue?" again asked the house-steward.

"Gallantly!" replied the lady; "and all in a body—not a man stays on the bridge."

"Then we have some pause, dear mistress; since none of them hasten this way."

"Ay, I grant you, if our townsmen enter the castle in time. But where linger they? false, burgeois churls! Begone, thou, John Seix, and assay to rouse their sluggish spirit! But no—hold an instant—it may—it may be so!" She interrupted herself, by speaking these last words in a joyous, hopeful tone, as she again looked up the river.

"The Ormondes, lady?" questioned the old man.

"I do believe it is, John Seix! Some five or seven mounted men have parted from the confused body of pursuers and pursued, beyond the bridge—and now regain it— now spur fiercely over it—and one keeps ahead of the others—and now I lose him and them as they turn into the town. Quick, quick, John Seix, and mount the turret over the grand gate—thither they repair, whoever they be—quick, old man! I wait you here."

The house-steward did as he was commanded. In a short time after he had taken his position in the turret, seven horsemen galloped up the ascent which led from the near end of the town to the castle; and one, of noble bearing, led the rest. But as it was now deep twilight, and as the riders kept their visors down, he could not, at a first look, pronounce whether they were friends or foes. Coming nearer, he fixed his glance upon a banner which they bore, and his heart beat with joy, for it was the banner of the Ormonde. He challenged them, as they pulled their reins before the gate; they, one and all, shouted the gladdening word; and he hastened from the turret to admit them within the walls of the castle.

Meantime, his lady impatiently, pantingly, awaited his return to the gallery. Leaving the window, she cast herself at first into a seat; then quickly arose, paced the gallery, stopped, listened, took her son's hand, and rapidly walked with him to the door at the remote end.

She had again heard the unbarring of the gate, and the lowering of the drawbridge. Now she distinguished hasty steps ascending through· the castle to the gallery. A few paces from the end door, she stood still: a knight clad in full armour entered. In height and figure he resembled her husband; but his visor was down. Upon that she fixed her eye. An instant passed in silence, neither moving. The knight slowly raised his hand, and put up his vizor— it was the Desmond!

She did not scream nor start, nor ˙even step back, for her heart had misgiven her, and spared her a surprise which might have betrayed the heroic lady into some weakness which she would have scorned to show.

"I know you, Desmond," she only said, nodding her head, and endeavouring to look down his deep and fearful stare; "ay, and I knew you before you put your hand to your casque."

"You did, Petronilla?" he asked, in a low voice.

"Call me by my own name, here in mine own castle, Desmond;—the lady of Ormonde is that name; none other have you license to utter; and then tell me, what would Piers Gerald of Desmond with the lady of Ormonde—with her, and with her son, whom she holds by the hand?"

"It pleasures me," he answered, evasively, "that you know me, as you say."

"And wherefore should it?"

"Because the knowledge so little angered you towards

me, when I feared far otherwise of our meeting, lady of this castle."

"And is that all? Then I tell you, Desmond, build nought upon such a seeming. Learn, rather, that there be some in the world who deeply feel, though they despise much outward show of *what* they feel; and who leave actions in the stead of words to decide between them and those they love or hate, honour or spurn."

"And 'tis well, passing well, that thus calmly we *do* meet," he resumed; "for it hits the fashion of the time, and the change of—"

"Of what?" she interrupted, for a woman, almost sternly —"the change of what? what change? Think you, Desmond, that, for an hour's mishap—the first he ever knew from *your* hand, at the least—the lord of Ormonde, or I, his wife, will brook that word? think you that spirit bends or snaps so soon? think you that the cowards who fled from you on yonder bridge make a tithe of the Ormonde's truer and loyaler vassals and fighting men? or, granting that he stood alone to-night, in some nook of his own wide lands, think you no other friends may be near, although come from far, to take his part and give you back to him, hand to hand, and foot to foot?"

"What other friends?" asked Desmond.

"Hark in your ear—true English friends! ay, Desmond, and with one who loves the Ormonde to bid them on— with England's King to bid them on!" she continued, exult- ingly.

"Who hides behind this arras, to witness our discourse?"

demanded Desmond, striding to the place of which he spoke, his hand placed on his sword.

"Harm not my poor jester, black Desmond!" cried the little Lord Thomas, springing after him from his mother's side; "none but he, Simon Seix, the half-witted, is there, and he has only crept behind the arras to sleep."

The child pulled aside the arras as he spoke, and discovered, indeed, Simon Seix, sitting behind it, his clumsy, bony knees crimpled up into his mouth, and his whole figure curiously twisted into the smallest possible size, while he seemed, at least, to sleep profoundly.

"Bid him awaken, and to the hall with you, for pastime, my brave man," said Desmond, shaking Simon with his mailed hand till he opened his eyes, uttering a strange cry, and starting to his feet. "May they not leave the gallery, lady?" resumed Desmond: "our speech grows of import."

"But surely of no value to an infant and a simpleton," answered the lady of Ormonde; "wherefore, Desmond, they may not leave the gallery for the hall."

"Dicken Utlaw, my proved body-man, will there do service and ward upon your fair son," continued Desmond.

"And *is* he there? *he?* Dicken Utlaw, your *proved* body-man?" asked the lady. "I know of him; in my days of un-wedded youth, I had a reason to know of him, the which you can tell; and, oh! Heaven forgive you, Desmond, the intents in furtherance of which you bring that stony-hearted Dicken into this castle!"

"If the child and the fool are to rest here," rejoined

Desmond, "I pray you let it be at the end of the gallery, out of hearing."

To this she assented, and the young Lord Thomas and Simon Seix accordingly withdrew to the window.

"And now, lady, touching your wild speech of the English King's coming to Ireland—"

"He lands to-day, at Waterford, Desmond: 'tis as wild as that—England's second Richard—at Waterford."

"Hush!" cried Desmond, as he perceived that Simon had again drawn near them, alone, so cautiously that his steps were not heard: "now, sirrah, do you dare to pry into the discourse of your lady and myself?"

Simon humbly and earnestly denied any such bold and sinful design; and reproved and chidden, he again withdrew, while Desmond went on with what he had to say.

"Lady, 'tis passing strange I should not have heard of this: but, let the King be at Waterford; I shall have loyal friends to wait on him there before midnight; you can have none—"

"The Ormonde may think of having some there before midnight, Desmond."

"Alack the day, lady!" said Desmond, sighing.

"Ha!" she cried, receding from him, "when *you* put on that seeming grief, there must be a black tale for me to hear, in good sooth! Speak, man! you have jumped upon his body—laid prostrate by thousands for you—and then passed your coward knife through his noble heart."

"The Ormonde forced me to the field, lady, in just defence of my bounds of lands; but, otherwise, I bore him no ill blood: his life I never sought; and, had I seen it threatened, would have saved it: but the last melée was fierce upon the bridge, and he fell ere I knew that—"

"Dead! my Ormonde dead!" she cried, clasping her hands, and fixing her eyes on Desmond.

"I bore his banner to your gate—please you to see it in the hall? Could he have drawn living breath when that was done?"

"I think, no," she answered; "and you have reached him, then? And now, Desmond, 'tis in your mind that all looks clear for the fulfilling of an old oath." Stern despair was in her tones, as she uttered these words.

"Sweet lady, pass we that worthless matter—an error of mere youth, and nought besides—unless we add an outbreaking of passionate love, as pure and true as—"

"Insolent fool as well as villain!" again interrupted the lady: "where are you, boy? Come hither to my side, and hold fast by my hand—hither, hither! Ha!" as she turned round, and looked towards the end of the spacious and dusky apartment,—"my child hath left the gallery—with his poor fool, too! and left it, for what company!—for what chances! Desmond, I leave you to go seek him; and aid me in the task; and promise not to part us, when I find my boy, and I will kneel down to bless you."

Terrible fears of Desmond's designs began to press on her mind, and she scarce knew what she said. Her unwelcome visitor earnestly promised to do as she requested of him; and they left the gallery by different doors. Desmond hastened to the hall, where, taking Utlaw aside, he said to him in a whisper—"Dicken, if by some secret outlet the young spawn of the Ormonde hath evaded us, we nearly lose our present game. Search well the courts and out-buildings—"

The calls and cries of the afflicted mother, echoing through the castle, interrupted his speech. She rushed in-to the hall, still uttering the name of her child. "You have murdered him, too!" she exclaimed, wildly, stopping before Desmond. "Ay, you! even while we spoke, above, some devils in your service spirited him away. Give place!" She darted past him, and left the hall, to engage in another search.

Desmond followed close in her steps to receive the child, for himself, if he should be found. His confidential follower explored every hiding-place out of doors. None of them succeeded : and then Dicken and some trusty comrades mounted their horses to ride to the town, and through all the surrounding country.

Half an hour before the lady of Ormonde missed them, Simon Scix, stealing on tiptoe to the nearest side-door, had carried the child out of the gallery in his arms. By private and obscure passages, which, as he whispered to his young charge, the Desmond's men would not be found to have yet mounted guard upon, they then gained nearly the same spot, under the window of the long gallery, where, some hours before, he had enacted, together, the parts of battle charger and of trumpeter to the little Lord Thomas. Here he put the boy on his feet, and stooped down upon the terra-plane of the wall. "John, the father of Simon, showed it to me more than once," he said : and, while speaking, he contrived to loosen a small stone, and extract it from the surrounding ones. A ring appeared : he tugged at it with all his strength, and a square portion of the smooth, small flags, moved, were displaced, and discovered narrow steps winding down in darkness through the thickness of the wall.

"Now, noble son of the noble Ormonde, and most noble foster-brother of a born natural, remember all you promised me while we whispered together at the window over our heads," resumed Simon. "Here be the steps which will free us of the castle ; and, though it seemeth somewhat dark a little way downward, still trust to my guidance ; for the sake of thy dear lady-mother, and of thy—"

"I am not afraid, witless," interrupted the child ; "take my hand, and lead me after you."

Without another word, Simon safely conveyed him to the bottom of the turning steps. Here they stood in utter darkness ; the misnamed fool groping with his two hands over the rough surface which temporarily opposed their further progress. A joyful exclamation soon told, however, that he had found what he sought ; and the next moment a part of the wall (here but of a slight thickness), framed in iron, moved inward on hinges, and they saw, through a low arched opening, only a few feet from them, the river whose rapid dash and chafe had come on their ears as they descended.

A rugged bank, often interrupted by eddies and little coves of the river, fell from the foundation of the wall into the Nore. Along this, his back turned to John's bridge and the town, and his young foster-brother once more astride on his shoulders, Simon was soon hurrying. The wall made an abrupt turn, striking off at right angles, inland: he turned with it, and still pursued its course.

"There is the paddock, truly; but where is my lord's favourite horse for the chase?" he said, after having made considerable way—"nay, I see him—and now for a hard ride, without saddle, and a *suggaun* bridle in hand."

Some hay was piled in the paddock: from it he adroitly and quickly spun his *suggaun*—fastened it on the head of the fleet courser—placed the child on the animal's back—vaulted up behind him—and a few minutes, over hedge and ditch, brought them to a highway.

"For Waterford, Raymond!" cried Simon, shaking his hay bridle: "and we have need to see the end of the twenty-and-four Irish miles in little more time than it will take to count them over!"

"'Tis well to be a fool, ay, and a sleepy fool, too, at times, Simon, else neither Raymond, nor his riders for him, would know the road so well," said the child.

"There be tricks in all born crafts, your little nobleness," replied Simon; "else how would fools, or even wise men, win bread? In sooth, I deemed I might catch a needful secret behind the arras; though I wot not of the road till I bethought me of treading lightly back from the window to hear another word."

It was night—but a moonlight one—when the hoofs of their courser beat hollowly along the banks of the Suir: they had avoided the town, and followed the widening of the river a little distance beyond it. Unpractised as were his eyes to such a sight, Simon soon was aware that a great many ships floated on the moon-lit water ; that boats moved to and from them ; and that large bodies of soldiers, destined for taking the field against the formidable young Irish chief, Arthur MacMurchad O'Kavanah, were every moment landing.   While he looked, a sentinel challenged him.   He reined up his foaming horse, and answered, by giving the name of the Lord Thomas of Ormonde, and demanding to see the King.   The soldier scoffed at his request ; and, as Simon insisted, his words grew rough and high.   A group of noble-looking men, who, from a near elevation of the bank, had been watching the disembarkment, were attracted towards the spot ; and one, a knight completely clad in splendid armour, advanced, alone, from the rest, saying, " The Lord Thomas of Ormonde to have speech of the King ?—where bides this Lord Thomas, Master mine ?"

" I am the Lord Thomas of Ormonde !" answered Simon's little charge, spiritedly, and as if in dudgeon that he had not been at once recognised.

" Thou, gramercy, fair noble ?" continued the knight, good-naturedly, as he touched his helmet. " And on what weighty matter wouldst thou parley with King Richard ?"

" An you lead me to him, like a civil knight and good, Richard himself shall learn," replied the child.

" Excellent, well spoken," whispered Simon to his charge ; " abide by that fashion of speech."

" By our Lady, then, like civil knight and good, will I do my devoir by thee, Lord Thomas of Butler," resumed the knight ; " little doubting that the King will give ready ear to thy errand, for passing well he affects one of thy name, the Lord James, Earl of Ormonde."

"Which noble Earl is mine own father," said the boy.

The knight showed real interest at this intelligence; and commanding the horse which bore Simon and the child to be led after him, walked towards the town of Waterford.

Half an hour afterwards, mounted on a fresh steed, and accompauied by their patron and a body of well-armed soldiers, our adventurers galloped back to Kilkenny. The knight had pressed their stay till morning; but Lord Thomas and Simon convinced him that for the sake of the lady of Ormonde this ought not to be. She required not only to have her son restored to her, but also to be protected against the Desmond, who, ere morning's dawn, might work her irremediable harm. Finding these reasons good, the friendly knight resolved to bear them company.

Upon the road, he arranged with Simon various plans of proceeding; and upon a particular point was wholly governed by the simpleton's advice. Simon said that there was but one vassal of the Desmond in Kilkenny Castle who, after the tidings they had to communicate, would at all hazards attempt to spill blood. "Then can ye not make free with his, before I enter the castle hall?" demanded the knight. Simon demurred, but proposed an alternative. "We will make him drunk with wines, till he sleep soundly," said Simon; "and then, upon hearing of my signal, a child may enter the hall."

The knight assented, but added, "Good success still rests upon the chance of the Desmond's army not having yet marched from the field to greet their lord in the Ormonde's fortress; for, though our liege comrades here may well suffice to master the knaves already within its walls, they could not withstand thousands."

Notwithstanding this chance against them, the travellers held on, however, and by midnight gained the secret door through which Simon had escaped from the castle wall upon the rough and scanty bank of the Nore. Previously, all had dismounted, and, conducted by him, were now ushered, stealthily, into the interior of the castle; and their hopes grew high, when it appeared evident that Desmond's army had not yet come to garrison it.

Few moments then elapsed until Simon entered the hall of the castle, leading his foster-brother by the hand. By the light of a lamp, suspended from the arched roof, he saw his old father stretched on the tiled floor, mournfully support- ing his head upon his hand, and guarded by a soldier; at the oak table, immediately under a Scottish broad sword and buckler, won by the Ormonde, some years before, in a battle against the Bruce, when that chieftain made preten- sions to the crown of Ireland, sat Dicken Utlaw, the man whom Simon had meant when he spoke of the single follower of Desmond whose hand would be prompt to shed the blood even of his liege King, in defence of his lord, or in revenge of his discomfiture. A wine cup and a flagon stood at the ruffian's hand, by means of which he had already anticipated, half way, Simon's designs upon him.

Utlaw's voice was high and angry, as the two truants appeared before him: and in fact, he was roundly expressing his wrath against them for the useless chase they had led him over all the neighbouring roads, and from which he had only lately returned. So soon as his eyes met theirs, he started up, roaring forth commands to the armed man who stood guard over old Seix, to secure the door of the hall.

"It does not need," answered the boy; "we come hither to be your prisoners, good Dicken."

"Ay, thou vagrant imp! and whence come ye so suddenly, after all our chase, as if ye grew out of the ground, or were blown in upon a wind?" asked Utlaw.

"Perchance even as thou sayest, we come," answered Simon; "for, all this evening, we have footed it merrily with the fays of Brandon Hill; and be patient now, sweet Dicken Utlaw," as the bravo raised his sheathed sword, "and but suffer us to enact for your pleasure one of the good dances they taught us; and I will bribe my father here, the house-steward, to whisper thee in what corner of the cellar thou mayest chance on a magnum of such renowned wine as has scarce filled to-night the empty flagon at thy hand."

Dicken became somewhat soothed; and growling an exhortation to the sentinel to guard all his prisoners well, strode off to avail himself of the ready instructions of old Seix. During his short absence, Simon studied the features of the soldier who rested on his tall spear near the door, and drew comfort from their tranquil, and even benevolent expression. Utlaw returned to his seat at the oak table, called the wine good, and gulped it down rapidly: it was of great power, and Simon knew the fact well. But it also seemed capable of making him obliging, for he consented to see the fashion of the dance practised by the hill-elves; and accordingly, Simon, with a whisper to the child, performed a vagary so grotesque that the drunken savage laughed hoarsely in his cup, and the guard smiled quietly on his post.

Simon continued his frolics till the critical powers of Dicken began rapidly to desert him. Very soon afterwards, he slept profoundly, snorting like the swine he was. Simon now preparing for his most important feat, proposed that Lord Thomas should take a war-horse, namely, an old weapon at hand, and ride it about the hall to the notes of the trumpet. The boy was soon mounted, and Simon taking up a useless scroll of parchment, and rolling it loosely, applied it to his mouth.

Before he would blow his signal blast, however, he glanced into the face of the sentinel, and afterwards to the half open door of the hall. The man was still smiling good-naturedly at the gleeish gambols of the little Lord Thomas; and, in the gloom without the hall, Simon caught glimpses of armed men; one of whom presently entered, unseen by the soldier, and bent watchfully over the snoring Dicken. "Now to the charge!" cried Simon, addressing his foster-brother; and to the astonishment of the sentinel, of the knight who had just stealthily come in (Simon's friend at Waterford)—and of every one in the castle—a perfect trumpet sound rang through the spacious building.

Dicken sprang to his feet, half conscious, and was instantly felled to the ground by a blow of the knight's battle-axe, who had been watching him. Old Seix arose, and seized his sword. Simon armed himself with the weapon upon which the child had been astride, and placed himself spiritedly, though grotesquely, before him. The sentinel quickly brought his spear to his haunch, and stood on the defensive, regarding the stranger knight (who wore his visor down) with a threatening look; but a second knight now gaining that person's side, rendered his hostility vain. Almost at the same moment, an uproar and a clash was heard through the castle—presently the lady of Ormonde ran shrieking into the hall—and she shrieked wildly again, though not in the same cadence, as she caught up her child to her bosom. She was quickly followed by Desmond, now the prisoner of some of Simon's friends. The bold lord had fought desperately, and bled from his wounds, though the rage which was upon him did not allow him to think of them.

"What treachery is this? and what villains be these?" he exclaimed, as he came in—"who calls himself chief here?"

The knight who wore his visor down raised his arm, and touched his breast in answer.

"Then call thyself by such name no longer!" continued Desmond; and with that he suddenly freed himself from his guards, snatched the sentinel's long spear, and aimed a thrust at the knight.

"Traitor! stay thy hand!" exclaimed his antagonist, in a voice of high and dignified command; "thou knowest not what thou doest—nor that indeed thy feudal sceptre is here broken in pieces.   Look at me now!"—he exposed his face.

"Richard!—the King!" faltered Desmond, dropping on his knee, as the lady of Ormonde and all in the hall knelt with him.

Chacun a son Gout.

————

WHEN dandies wore fine gilded clothes,
   And bags, and swords, and lace ;
And powder blanched the heads of beaux,
   And patches graced the face :

When two o'clock was time to drive
   To flirt it in Hyde Park ;
And not the finest folks alive
   Took morning drives till dark :

When people went to see the plays,
   · And knew the names of players ;
And ladies wore long bony stays,
   And went about in chairs :

When belles with whalebone hoops and tapes
   Defied each vain endeavour
To trace their forms, and made their shapes
   Much more like *bells* than ever :

When chaste salutes all folks exchanged
  (A custom worthy, such is),
And ladies to be served stood ranged,
  As kings would serve a duchess:

In those good days, a widow rare
  Astonished half the town ;
So gay, so sweet, so blithe, and fair—
  Her name was Mistress Brown.

This widow Brown had diamond eyes,
  And teeth like rows of pearl,
With lips that Hybla's bees might prize,
  And loves in every curl.

And more; this beautéous piece of earth
  (And she could make it clear),
Had stock and property, quite worth
  Four thousand pounds a year.

As syrup in the summer's sun
  The buzzing fly attracts,
So Mrs. Brown—the lonely one—
  Was subject to attacks ;

And tall and short, and rich and poor,
  Pursued her up and down ;
And crowds of swains besieged the door
  Of charming Mrs. Brown.

Among the rest a worthy wight
  Was constant in her suite;
He was an alderman and knight,
  And lived in Fenchurch Street.

He wasn't young—if he's called old
  Who fifty-nine surpasses:
He sugar bought, and sugar sold,
  And treacle, and molasses.

But he was rich, dressed fine, was gay,
  And mighty well to do;
And at each turn was wont to say—
  Ha!—*Chacun à son goût.*

This was his phrase—it don't mean much,
  He thought it rather witty;
And, for an alderman, a touch
  A bit above the city.

Sir Samuel Snob—that was his name—
  Three times to Mrs. Brown
Had ventured just to hint his flame;
  And thrice received—a frown.

Once more Sir Sam resolved to try
  What winning ways would do;
If she would *not*, he would not die,
  For—*chacun à son goût.*

He sallied forth in gilded coach;
  And in those heavy drags
No stylish knight made his approach
  Without his four fat nags.

But gout and sixty well-spent years
  Had made his knightship tame;
And, spite of flannel, crutch, and cares,
  Sir Sam was very lame.

" Is Mrs. Brown at home ?" said he.
  The servant answered " Yes."
" To-night, then," murmured he, " shall see
  My misery or bliss."

And up he went—though slow, yet sure,
  And there was Mrs. Brown :
Delightful!—then, he's quite secure !
  The widow is alone.

Close to the sofa where she sat
  Sir Snobby drew his seat;
Rested his crutch, laid down his hat,
  And looked prodigious sweet.

But silence, test of virgin love,
  A widow does not suit ;
And Mrs. Brown did not approve
  Courtship so mild and mute.

The man of sugar by her look
  Perceived the course to take :
He sighed—she smiled—the hint he took,
  And on that hint he spake.

"Madam," said he—"I know," she cried,
  "I'll save you half your job;
I've seen it—though disguise you've tried—
  You want a Lady Snob!"

"Exactly so, angelic fair!
  You've hit it to a T.
Where can I find one—where, oh! where,
  So fit as Mrs. B.?"

The dame was fluttered, looked aside,
  Then blushingly looked down ;
But as Sir Snob her beauties eyed,
  He saw no chilling frown.

At length she said, "I'll tell you plain
  (The thing of folly savours)—
But he who hopes *my* heart to gain
  Must grant me two small favours."

"Two!" cries the knight—"how very kind!
  Say fifty—I'm efficient!"
"No," said the dame, "I think you'll find
  The two *I* mean, sufficient."

" Name them !" said Snob.—" I will," she cried ;
  " And this the first must be :
Pay homage to a woman's pride,
  Down on your bended knee !

" And when that homage you have done,
  And half performed your task,
Then shall you know the other boon
  Which I propose to ask.

" Comply with this," the widow cries,
  " My hand is yours for ever !"—
" Madam," says Snob, and smiles and sighs,
  " I'll do my best endeavour."

Down on his knee Sir Snobby went,
  His chair behind him tumbled,
His sword betwixt his legs was bent,
  His left-hand crutch was humbled.

He seized the widow's lily hand
  Roughly, as he would storm it :
" Now, lady, give your next command,
  And trust me I'll perform it."

She bit her fan, she hid her face,
  And—widows *have* no feeling—
Enjoying Snobby's piteous case,
  Was pleased to keep him kneeling.

A minute passed :—" Oh speak ! oh speak !"
   Said Snob : " dear soul relieve me !"
(His knee was waxing wondrous weak)
   " Your *ne plus ultra* give me !"

" One half fulfilled," says Mrs. Brown,
   " I shall not ask in vain
For t' other favour—now you're down,
   Sir Snob—*get up again !*"

Vain the request—the knight was floored ;
   And—what a want of feeling !—
The lady screamed, while Snobby roared,
   And still continued kneeling.

The widow rang for maids and men,
   Who came, 'midst shouts of laughter,
To raise her lover up again,
   And show him down stairs after.

They got him on his feet once more,
   Gave him his crutch and hat ;
Told him his coach was at the door—
   A killing hint was that.

" Such tricks as these are idly tried,"
   Said Snob : " I'm off—adieu !
To wound men's feelings, hurt their pride,
   But—*Chacun à son goût.*"—

" Forgive me, knight," the widow said,
    As he was bowing out:
" Your '*Chacun à son goût*,' I read
    As ' *Chacun à son* gout.'

" That you could not your pledge redeem
    I grieve, most worthy knight:
A nurse is what you want, I deem ;
    And so, sweet sir, good night."—

He went—was taken to his room—
    To bed in tears was carried ;
And the next day to Betsy Broom,
    His housekeeper, was married.

The widow Brown, (so goes the song,)
    In three weeks dried her tears,
And married Colonel Roger Long,
    Of the Royal Grenadiers.

Thus suited both, the tale ends well,
    As all tales ought to do ;
The knight's revenged, well pleased the belle—
    So—*Chacun à son goût.*

The False Rhyme

N a fine July day, the fair Margaret, Queen of Navarre, then on a visit to her royal brother, had arranged a rural feast for the morning following, which Francis declined attending. He was melancholy; and the cause was said to be some lover's quarrel with a favourite dame. The morrow came, and dark rain and murky clouds destroyed at once the schemes of the courtly throng. Margaret was angry, and she grew weary: her only hope for amusement was in Francis, and he had shut himself up—an excellent reason why she should the more desire to see him. She entered his apartment: he was standing at the casement, against which the noisy shower beat, writing with a diamond on the glass. Two beautiful dogs were his sole companions. As Queen Margaret entered, he hastily let down the silken curtain before the window, and looked a little confused.

"What treason is this, my liege," said the Queen, "which crimsons your cheek? I must see the same."

"It is treason," replied the King; "and therefore, sweet sister, thou mayst not see it."

This the more excited Margaret's curiosity, and a playful contest ensued: Francis at last yielded: he threw himself on a huge high-backed settee; and as the lady drew back the curtain with an arch smile, he grew grave and sentimental, as he reflected on the cause which had inspired his libel against all womankind.

"What have we here?" cried Margaret: "nay, this is lêse majesté—

> 'Souvent femme varie,
> Bien fou qui s'y fie.'

Very little change would greatly amend your couplet:— would it not run better thus—

> 'Souvent homme varie,
> Bien folle qui s'y fie?'

I could tell you twenty stories of man's inconstancy."

"I will be content with one true tale of woman's fidelity," said Francis, dryly; "but do not provoke me. I would fain be at peace with the soft Mutabilities, for thy dear sake."

"I defy your grace," replied Margaret, rashly, "to instance the falsehood of one noble and well-reputed dame."

"Not even Emilie de Lagny?" asked the King.

This was a sore subject for the Queen. Emilie had been brought up in her own household, the most beautiful and the most virtuous of her maids of honour. She had long loved the Sire de Lagny, and their nuptials were celebrated with rejoicings but little ominous of the result. De Lagny was accused, but a year after, of traitorously yielding to the Emperor a fortress under his command, and he was condemned

to perpetual imprisonment. For some time Emilie seemed
inconsolable, often visiting the miserable dungeon of her
husband, and suffering on her return, from witnessing his
wretchedness, such paroxysms of grief as threatened her life.
Suddenly, in the midst of her sorrow, she disappeared; and
inquiry only divulged the disgraceful fact, that she had
escaped from France, bearing her jewels with her, and accompanied by her page, Robinet Leroux. It was whispered
that, during their journey, the lady and the stripling were
often too familiar; and Margaret, enraged at these dis-
coveries, commanded that no further quest should be made
for her lost favourite.

Taunted now by her brother, she defended Emilie, declaring that she believed her to be guiltless, even going so far as
to boast that within a month she would bring proof of her
innocence.

"Robinet was a pretty boy," said Francis, laughing.

"Let us make a bet," cried Margaret: "if I lose, I will
bear this vile rhyme of thine as a motto to my shame to my
grave; if I win—"

"I will break my window, and grant thee whatever boon
thou askest."

The result of this bet was long sung by troubadour and
minstrel. The Queen employed a hundred emissaries—
published rewards for any intelligence of Emilie—all in vain.
The month was expiring, and Margaret would have given
many bright jewels to redeem her word. On the eve of the
fatal day, the jailer of the prison in which the Sire de Lagny
was confined sought an audience of the Queen: he brought

her a message from the knight, to say, that if the Lady Margaret would ask his pardon as her boon, and obtain from her royal brother that he might be brought before him, her bet was won. Fair Margaret was very joyful, and readily made the desired promise. Francis was unwilling to see his false servant, but he was in high good humour, for a cavalier had that morning brought intelligence of a victory over the Imperialists. The messenger himself was lauded in the despatches as the most fearless and bravest knight in France. The King loaded him with presents, only regretting that a vow prevented the soldier from raising his visor or declaring his name.

That same evening as the setting sun shone on the lattice on which the ungallant rhyme was traced, Francis reposed on the same settee, and the beautiful Queen of Navarre, with triumph in her bright eyes, sat beside him. Attended by guards, the prisoner was brought in: his frame was attenuated by privation, and he walked with tottering steps. He knelt at the feet of Francis, and uncovered his head; a quantity of rich golden hair then escaping, fell over the sunken cheeks and pallid brow of the suppliant. "We have treason here!" cried the King: "sir jailer, where is your prisoner?"

"Sire, blame him not," said the soft, faltering voice of Emilie; "wiser men than he have been deceived by woman. My dear lord was guiltless of the crime for which he suffered. There was but one mode to save him:—I assumed his chains —he escaped in my attire with poor Robinet Leroux—he joined your army: the young and gallant cavalier who delivered the despatches to your grace, whom you overwhelmed with honours and reward, is my own Enguerrard de Lagny. I waited but for his arrival with testimonials of his innocence, to declare myself to my lady, the Queen. Has she not won her bet? And the boon she asks—"

"Is de Lagny's pardon," said Margaret, as she also knelt to the King: "spare your faithful vassal, sire, and reward this lady's truth."

Francis first broke the false-speaking window, then he raised the ladies from their supplicatory posture.

In the tournament given to celebrate this "Triumph of Ladies," the Sire de Lagny bore off every prize; and surely there was more loveliness in Emilie's faded cheek—more grace in her emaciated form, type as they were of truest affection—than in the prouder bearing and fresher complexion of the most brilliant beauty in attendance on the courtly festival.

The Dark Lady.

PEOPLE find it easy enough to laugh at " spirit-stories " in broad daylight, when the sunbeams dance upon the grass, and the deepest forest glades are spotted and checkered only by the tender shadows of leafy trees; when the rugged castle, that looked so mysterious and so stern in the looming night, seems suited for a lady's bower; when the rushing waterfall sparkles in diamond showers, and the hum of bee and song of bird tune the thoughts to hopes of life and happiness; people may laugh at ghosts then, if they like, but as for me, I never could merely smile at the records of those shadowy visitors. I have large faith in things supernatural, and cannot disbelieve solely on the ground that I lack such evidences as are supplied by the senses; for they, in truth, sustain by palpable proofs so few of the many marvels by which we are surrounded, that I would rather reject them altogether, as witnesses, than abide the issue entirely as they suggest.

My great-grandmother was a native of the canton of

Berne; and at the advanced age of ninety, her memory of "the long ago" was as active as it could have been at fifteen: she looked as if she had just stepped out of a piece of tapestry belonging to a past age, but with warm sympathies for the present. Her English, when she became excited, was very curious—a mingling of French, certainly not Parisian, with here and there scraps of German done into English, literally—so that her observations were at times remarkable for their strength. "The mountains," she would say, "in her country, went high, high up, until they could look into the heavens, and *hear* God in the storm." She never thoroughly comprehended the real beauty of England, but spoke with contempt of the flatness of our island —calling our mountains "inequalities," nothing more—holding our agriculture "cheap," saying that the land tilled itself, leaving man nothing to do. She would sing the most amusing *patois* songs, and tell stories from morning till night, more especially spirit-stories: but the old lady would not tell a tale of that character a second time to an unbeliever; such things, she would say, "are not for make-laugh." One in particular, I remember, always excited great interest in her young listeners, from its mingling of the real and the romantic; but it can never be told as she told it: there was so much of the picturesque about the old lady—so much to admire in the curious carving of her ebony cane, in the beauty of her point lace, the size and weight of her long ugly ear-rings, the fashion of her solid silk gown, the singularity of her buckled shoes—her dark-brown wrinkled face, every wrinkle an expression,—her broad thoughtful brow, beneath which glittered her bright blue eyes—bright, even when her eyelashes were white with *years*. All these peculiarities gave impressive effect to her words.

"In my young time," she told us, "I spent many happy hours with Amelie de Rohean, in her uncle's castle. He was a fine man—much size, stern, and dark, and full of noise—a strong man, no fear—he had a great heart, and a big head.

"The castle was situated in the midst of the most stupendous Alpine scenery, and yet it was not solitary. There were other dwellings in sight; some very near, but separated by a ravine, through which, at all seasons, a rapid river kept its foaming course. You do not know what torrents are in this country; your torrents are as babies— ours are giants. The one I speak of divided the valley; here and there a rock, round which it sported, or stormed, according to the season. In two of the defiles these rocks were of great value; acting as piers for the support of bridges—the only means of communication with our opposite neighbours.

"'Monsieur,' as we always called the Count, was, as I have told you, a dark, stern, violent man. All men are wilful, my dear young ladies," she would say; "but Monsieur was the most wilful: all men are selfish; but he was the most selfish : all men are tyrants—." Here the old lady was invariably interrupted by her relatives, with, "Oh, good Granny!" and, "Oh fie, dear Granny!" and she would bridle up a little and fan herself; then continue— "Yes, my dears, each creature according to its nature—all men are tyrants; and I confess that I do think a Swiss, whose mountain inheritance is nearly coeval with the creation of the mountains, has a *right* to be tyrannical; I did not intend to blame him for that: I did not, because I had grown used to it. Amelie and I always stood up when he entered the room, and never sat down until we were desired. He never bestowed a loving word or a kind look upon either of us. We never spoke except when we were spoken to."

"But when you and Amelie were alone, dear Granny?"

"Oh, why, then we did chatter, I suppose; though then it was in moderation: for Monsieur's influence chilled us even when he was not present; and often she would say, 'It is so hard trying to love him, for he will not let me!' There is no such beauty in the world now as Amelie's. I can see her as she used to stand before the richly carved glass in the grave oak-panneled dressing-room; her luxuriant hair combed up from her full round brow; the discreet maidenly cap, covering the back of her head; her brocaded silk (which she had inherited from her grandmother), shaded round the bosom by the modest ruffle; her black velvet gorget and bracelets, showing off to perfection the pearly transparency of her skin. She was the loveliest of all creatures, and as good as she was lovely; it seems but as yesterday that we were together—but as yesterday! And yet I lived to see her an old woman; so they called her, but she never seemed old to me! My own dear Amelie!" Ninety years had not dried up the sources of poor Granny's tears, nor chilled her heart; and she never spoke of Amelie without emotion. "Monsieur was very proud of his niece, because she was part of himself: she added to his consequence, she contributed to his enjoyment; she had grown necessary ; she was the one sunbeam of his house."

"Not the *one* sunbeam surely, Granny !" one of us would exclaim ; "you were a sunbeam them."

"I was nothing where Amelie was—nothing but her shadow ! The bravest and best in the country would have rejoiced to be to her what I was—her chosen friend ; and some would have periled their lives for one of the sweet smiles which played around her uncle, but never touched his heart. Monsieur never would suffer people to be happy except in his way. He had never married ; and he declared Amelie never should. She had, he said, as much enjoyment as he had: she had a castle with a drawbridge; she had a forest for hunting; dogs and horses; servants and serfs; jewels, gold, and gorgeous dresses ; a guitar and a harpsichord ; a parrot—and a friend ! And such an uncle ! he believed there was not such another uncle in broad Europe ! For many a long day Amelie laughed at this catalogue of advantages; that is, she laughed when her uncle left the room— she never laughed before him. In time, the laugh came not ; but in its place, sighs and tears. Monsieur had a great deal to answer for. Amelie was not prevented from seeing the gentry when they came to visit in a formal way, and she met many hawking and hunting; but she never was permitted to invite any one to the castle, nor to accept an invitation. Monsieur fancied that by shutting her lips, he closed her heart; and boasted such was the advantage of his good training, that Amelie's mind was fortified against all weaknesses, for she had not the least dread of wandering about the ruined chapel of the castle, where he himself dared not go after dusk. This place was dedicated to the family ghost—the spirit, which for many years had it entirely at its own disposal. It was much attached to its quarters, seldom leaving them, except for the purpose of interfering when anything decidedly wrong was going forward in the castle. 'La Femme Noir' had been seen gliding along the unprotected parapet of the bridge, and standing on a pinnacle, before the late master's death; and many tales were told of her, which in this age of unbelief would not be credited."

"Granny, did you know why your friend ventured so fearlessly into the ghost's territories?" inquired my little cousin.

"I am not come to that," was the reply; "and you are one saucy little maid, to ask what I do not choose to tell. Amelie certainly entertained no fear of the spirit; 'La Femme Noir' could have had no angry feeling towards her, for my friend would wander in the ruins, taking no note of daylight, or moonlight, or even darkness. The peasants declared their young lady must have walked over crossed bones, or drunk water out of a raven's skull, or passed nine times round the spectre's glass on Midsummer eve. She must have done all this, if not more: there could be little doubt that the 'Femme Noir' had initiated her into certain mysteries; for they heard at times voices in low, whispering converse, and saw the shadows of two persons cross the old roofless chapel, when 'Mamselle' had passed the foot-bridge alone. Monsieur gloried in this fearlessness on the part of his gentle niece ; and more than once, when he had revellers in the castle, he sent her forth at midnight to bring him a bough from a tree that only grew beside the altar of the old chapel ; and she did his bidding always as willingly, though not as rapidly, as he could desire.

"But certainly Amelie's courage brought no calmness. She became pale ; her pillow was often moistened by her tears ; her music was neglected ; she took no pleasure in the chase ; and her chamois not receiving its usual attention, went off to the mountains. She avoided me—her friend ! who would have died for her ; she left me alone ; she made no reply to my prayers, and did not heed my entreaties. One morning, when her eyes were fixed upon a book she did not read, and I sat at my embroidery a little apart, watching the tears stray over her cheek, until I was blinded by my own, I heard Monsieur's heavy tramp approaching through the long gallery ; some boots creak—but the boots of Monsieur !—they growled !

" ' Save me ! oh save me !' she exclaimed wildly. Before I could reply, her uncle banged open the door, and stood before us like an embodied thunderbolt. He held an open letter in his hand—his eyes glared—his nostrils were distended—he trembled so with rage, that the cabinets and old china shook again.

" ' Do you,' he said, ' know Charles le Maitre ?"

" Amelie replied, ' She did.'

" ' How did you make acquaintance with the son of my deadliest foe ?'

"There was no answer. The question was repeated. Amelie said she had met him, and at last confessed it was in the ruined portion of the castle! She threw herself at her uncle's feet—she clung to his knees: love taught her eloquence. She told him how deeply Charles regretted the long-standing feud; how earnest, and true, and good he was. Bending low, until her tresses were heaped upon the floor, she confessed, modestly, but firmly, that she loved this young man; that she would rather sacrifice the wealth of the whole world than forget him.

"Monsieur seemed suffocating; he tore off his lace cravat, and scattered its fragments on the floor—still she clung to him. At last he flung her from him; he reproached her with the bread she had eaten, and heaped odium upon her mother's memory! But though Amelie's nature was tender and affectionate, the old spirit of the old race roused within her; the slight girl arose, and stood erect before the man of storms."

"'Did you think,' she said, 'because I bent to you, that I am feeble? because I bore with you, have I no thoughts? You gave food to this frame, but you fed not my heart; you gave me nor love, nor tenderness, nor sympathy; you showed me to your friends, as you would your horse. If you had by kindness sown the seeds of love within my bosom; if you had been a father to me in tenderness, I would have been to you—a child. I never knew the time when I did not tremble at your footstep; but I will do so no more. I would gladly have loved you, trusted you, cherished you; but I feared to let you know I had a heart, lest you

should tear and insult it.   Oh, sir, those who expect love
where they give none, and confidence where there is no
trust, blast the fair time of youth, and lay up for themselves
an unhonoured old age.'   The scene terminated by Monsieur's
falling down in a fit, and Amelie's being conveyed fainting
to her chamber.

   " That night the castle was enveloped by storms ; they
came from all points of the compass—thunder, lightning,
hail, and rain !   The master lay in his stately bed, and was
troubled ; he could hardly believe that Amelie spoke the
words he had heard : cold-hearted and selfish as he was, he
was also a clear-seeing man, and it was their truth that
struck him.   But still his heart was hardened ; he had commanded Amelie to be locked into her chamber, and her
lover seized and imprisoned when he came to his usual
tryst.   Monsieur, I have said, lay in his stately bed, the
lightning, at intervals, illumining his dark chamber.   I had
cast myself on the floor outside her door, but could not hear
her weep, though I knew that she was overcome of sorrow.
As I sat, my head resting against the lintel of the door, a form
passed through the solid oak from her chamber, without the
bolts being withdrawn.   I saw it, as plainly as I see your
faces now, under the influence of various emotions ; nothing
opened, but it passed through—a shadowy form, dark and
vapoury, but perfectly distinct.   I knew it was ' La Femme
Noir,' and I trembled, for she never came from caprice, but
always for a purpose.   I did not fear for Amelie, for ' La
Femme Noir ' never warred with the high-minded or
virtuous.   She passed slowly, more slowly than I am

speaking, along the corridor, growing taller and taller as she went on, until she entered Monsieur's chamber by the door, exactly opposite where I stood. She paused at the foot of the plumed bed, and the lightning, no longer fitful, by its broad flashes kept up a perpetual illumination. She stood for some time perfectly motionless, though in a loud tone the master demanded whence she came and what she wanted. At last, during a pause in the storm, she told him that all the power he possessed should not prevent the union of Amelie and Charles. I heard her voice myself; it sounded like the night wind among fir-trees—cold and shrill, chilling both ear and heart. I turned my eyes away while she spoke, and when I looked again, she was gone! The storm continued to increase in violence, and the master's rage kept pace with the war of elements. The servants were trembling with undefined terror; they feared they knew not what: the dogs added to their apprehension by howling fearfully, and then barking in the highest possible key: the master paced about his chamber, calling in vain on his domestics, stamping and swearing like a maniac. At last, amid flashes of lightning, he made his way to the head of the great staircase, and presently the clang of the alarum-bell mingled with the thunder and the roar of the mountain torrents: this hastened the servants to his presence, though they seemed hardly capable of understanding his words. He insisted on Charles being brought before him. We all trembled, for he was mad and livid with rage. The warden, in whose care the young man was, dared not enter the hall that echoed his loud words and heavy footsteps, for when he went to seek his prisoner, he found every bolt and bar withdrawn, and the iron door wide open;—he was gone! Monsieur seemed to find relief by his energies being called into action; he ordered instant pursuit, and mounted his favourite charger, despite the storm, despite the fury of the elements. Although the great gates rocked, and the castle shook like an aspen leaf, he set forth, his path illumined by the lightning. Bold and brave as was his horse, he found it almost impossible to get it forward: he dug his spurs deep into the flanks of the noble animal, until the red blood mingled with the rain. At last it rushed madly down the path to the ' bridge the young man must cross; and when they reached it, the master discerned the floating cloak of the pursued a few yards in advance. Again the horse rebelled against his will, the lightning flashed in his eyes, and the torrent seemed a mass of red fire: no sound could be heard but of its roaring waters: the attendants clung as they advanced to the hand-rail of the bridge. The youth, unconscious of the *pursuit*, proceeded rapidly; and again roused, the horse plunged forward. On the instant, the form of 'La Femme Noir' passed with the blast that rushed down the ravine; the torrent followed in her track, and more than half the bridge was swept away for ever. As the master reined back the horse he had so urged forward, he saw the youth kneeling with outstretched arms on the opposite bank— kneeling in gratitude for his deliverance from this double peril. All were struck with the piety of the youth, and earnestly rejoiced at his deliverance; though they did not presume to say so, or look as if they thought it. I never saw so changed a person as the master when he re-entered the castle gate : his cheek was blanched—his eye quelled—his fierce plume hung broken over his shoulder—his step was unequal ; and in the voice of a feeble girl, he said—' Bring me a cup of wine.'   I was his cupbearer, and for the first time in his life he thanked me graciously, and in the warmth of his gratitude tapped my shoulder : the caress nearly hurled me across the hall.   What passed in his retiring-room, I know not.   Some said, the 'Femme Noir' visited him again ; I cannot tell, I did not see her ; I speak of what I saw, not of what I heard.   The storm passed away with a clap of thunder, to which the former sounds were but as the rattling of pebbles beneath the swell of a summer wave.   The next morning Monsieur sent for the Pasteur.   The good man seemed terror-stricken as he entered the hall ; but Monsieur filled him a quart of gold coins out of a leathern bag, to repair his church, and that quickly ; and grasping his hand as he departed, looked him steadily in the face.   As he did so, large drops stood like beads upon his brow ; his stern, coarse features, were strangely moved, while he gazed upon the calm, pale minister of peace and love.   ' You,' he said, ' bid God bless the poorest peasant that passes you on the mountain ; have you no blessing to give the master of Rohean ?"

"' My son,' answered the good man, ' I give you the bless-ing I may give :—May God bless you, and may your heart be opened to give and to receive.'

"' I know I can give,' replied the proud man ; ' but what can I receive ?'

"'Love,' he replied. 'All your wealth has not brought you happiness, because you are unloving and unloved!'

"The demon returned to his brow, but it did not remain there.

"'You shall give me lessons in this thing,' he said; and so the good man went his way.

"Amelie continued a close prisoner; but a change came over Monsieur. At first he shut himself up in his chamber, and no one was suffered to enter his presence: he took his food with his own hand from the only attendant who ventured to approach his door. He was heard walking up and down the room, day and night. When we were going to sleep, we heard his heavy tramp; at daybreak, there it was again; and those of the household who awoke at intervals during the night, said it was unceasing.

"Monsieur could read. Ah, you may smile; but in those days, and in those mountains, such men as 'the master' did not trouble themselves or others with knowledge: but the master of Rohean read both Latin and Greek, and commanded THE BOOK he had never opened since his childhood to be brought him. It was taken out of its velvet case, and carried in forthwith; and we saw his shadow from without, like the shadow of a giant, bending over THE BOOK; and he read in it for some days; and we greatly hoped it would soften and change his nature: and though I cannot say much for the softening, it certainly effected a great change; he no longer stalked moodily along the corridors, and banged the doors, and swore at the servants; he rather seemed possessed of a merry spirit, roaring out an old song—

> ' Aux bastions de Genéve, nos cannons,
>   Sont branquez ;
>   S'il y a quelques attaque nous les feront ronfler,
>   Viva! les cannoniers ! '

and then he would pause, and clang his hands together like a pair of cymbals, and laugh. And once, as I was passing along, he pounced out upon me, and whirled me round in a waltz, roaring at me when he let me down, to practise *that* and break my embroidery frame. He formed a band of horns and trumpets, and insisted on the goatherds and shepherds sounding reveillés in the mountains, and the village children beating drums ;—his only idea of joy and happiness was noise. He set all the canton to work to mend the bridge, paying the workmen double wages ; and he, who never entered a church before, would go to see how the labourers were getting on nearly every day. He talked and laughed a great deal to himself; and in his gaiety of heart would set the mastiffs fighting, and make excursions from home—we knowing not where he went. At last, Amelie was summoned to his presence, and he shook her and shouted, then kissed her ; and hoping she would be a good girl, told her he had provided a husband for her. Amelie wept and prayed ; and the master capered and sung. At last she fainted; and taking advantage of her unconsciousness, he conveyed her to the chapel; and there beside the altar stood the bridegroom—no other than Charles le Maitre!

"They lived many happy years together; and when Monsieur was in every respect a better, though still a strange man, the 'Femme Noir' appeared again to him—once. She did so with a placid air, on a summer night, with her arm extended towards the heavens.

"The next day the muffled bell told the valley that the stormy, proud old master of Rohean had ceased to live."

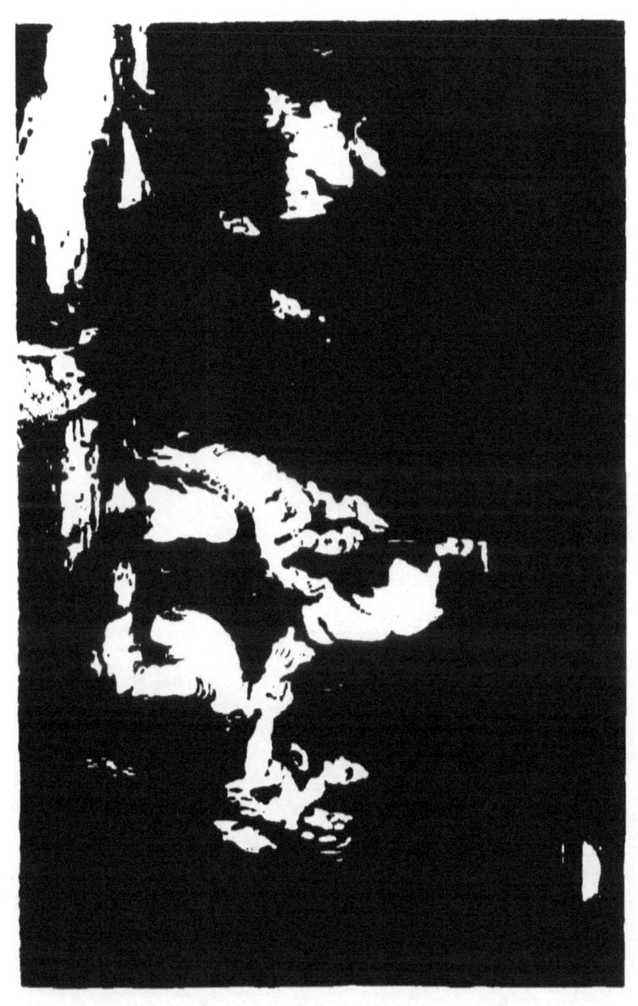

Cassandra.

"THEY hurried to the feast,
    The warrior, and the priest,
And the gay maiden with her jewelled brow:
    The minstrel's harp and voice
    Said, ' Triumph and rejoice ! ' "
One only mourned !—many are mourning now !

    " ' Peace ! startle not the light
    With the wild dreams of night :'—
So spake the princes in their pride and joy,
    When I in their dull ears
    Shrieked forth my tale of tears,
' Woe to the gorgeous city !—woe to Troy ! '

    " Ye watch the dun smoke rise
    Up to the lurid skies ;
Ye see the red light flickering on the stream ;
    Ye listen to the fall
    Of gate, and tower, and wall :
Sisters, the time is come !—alas, it is no dream !

" Through hall, and court, and porch,
Glides on the pitiless torch ;
The swift avengers faint not in their toil :
Vain now the matron's sighs ;
Vain now the infant's cries ;—
Look, sisters, look, who leads them to the spoil ?

" Not Pyrrhus, though his hand
Is on his father's brand ;
Not the fell framer of the accursed Steed ;
Not Nestor's hoary head ;
Nor Teucer's rapid tread ;
Nor the fierce wrath of impious Diomede.

" Visions of deeper fear
To-night are warring here ;—
I know them, sisters, the mysterious Three :
Minerva's lightning frown,
And Juno's golden crown,
And him, the mighty Ruler of the sounding sea.

" Through wailing and through woe,
Silent and stern, they go ;—
So have I ever seen them in my trance !—
Exultingly they guide
Destruction's fiery tide,
And lift the dazzling shield, and poise the deadly lance.

"Lo! where the old man stands,
Folding his palsied hands,
And muttering, with white lips, his querulous prayer:
'Where is my noble son,
My best, my bravest one,—
Troy's hope and Priam's,—where is Hector, where?'

"Why is thy falchion grasped?
Why is thy helmet clasped?
Fitter the fillet for such brow as thine!—
The altar reeks with gore;—
O sisters, look no more!
It is our father's blood upon the shrine!

"And ye, alas! must roam,
Far from your desolate home,
Far from lost Ilium, o'er the joyless wave:
Ye may not from those bowers
Gather the trampled flowers,
To wreathe sad garlands for your brethren's grave.

"Away, away! the gale
Stirs the white-bosomed sail;
Hence!—look not back to freedom or to fame:
Labour must be your doom,
Night-watchings, days of gloom,
The bitter bread of tears, the bridal couch of shame.

" Even now some Grecian dame
Beholds the signal flame,
And waits expectant the returning fleet :
' Why lingers yet my lord ?
Hath he not sheathed his sword—
Will he not bring my handmaid to my feet ?'

" Me too the dark Fates call ;
Their sway is over all,
Captor and captive, prison-house and throne ;—
I tell of others' lot ;
They hear me, heed me not !
Hide, angry Phœbus, hide from me mine own."

The Dream.

THE time of the occurrence of the little legend about to be narrated, was that of the commencement of the reign of Henry IV. of France, whose accession and conversion, while they brought peace to the kingdom whose throne he ascended, were inadequate to heal the deep wounds mutually inflicted by the inimical parties. Private feuds, and the memory of mortal injuries, existed between those now apparently united; and often did the hands that had clasped each other in seeming friendly greeting, involuntarily, as the grasp was released, clasp the dagger's hilt, as fitter spokesman to their passions than the words of courtesy that had just fallen from their lips. Many of the fiercer Catholics retreated to their distant provinces; and while they concealed in solitude their rankling discontent, not less keenly did they long for the day when they might show it openly.

In a large and fortified chateau built on a rugged steep overlooking the Loire, not far from the town of Nantes. dwelt the last of her race and the heiress of their fortunes, the young and beautiful Countess de Villeneuve. She had spent the preceding year in complete solitude in her secluded abode; and the mourning she wore for a father and two brothers, the victims of the civil wars, was a graceful and good reason why she did not appear at court, and mingle with its festivities. But the orphan Countess inherited a high name and broad lands; and it was soon signified to her that the King, her guardian, desired that she should bestow them, together with her hand, upon some noble whose birth and accomplishments should entitle him to the gift. Constance, in reply, expressed her intention of taking vows, and retiring to a convent. The King earnestly and resolutely forbade this act, believing such an idea to be the result of sensibility over-wrought by sorrow, and relying on the hope that, after a time, the genial spirit of youth would break through this cloud.

A year passed, and still the Countess persisted; and at last Henry, unwilling to exercise compulsion—desirous, too, of judging for himself of the motives that led one so beautiful, young, and gifted with fortune's favours, to desire to bury herself in a cloister—announced his intention, now that the period of her mourning was expired, of visiting her chateau; and if he brought not with him, the Monarch said, inducement sufficient to change her design, he would yield his consent to its fulfilment.

Many a sad hour had Constance passed—many a day of tears, and many a night of restless misery. She had closed her gates against every visitant; and, like the Lady Olivia in "Twelfth Night," vowed herself to loneliness and weeping. Mistress of herself, she easily silenced the entreaties and remonstrances of underlings, and nursed her grief as it had been the thing she loved. Yet it was too keen, too bitter, too burning, to be a favoured guest. In fact, Constance, young, ardent, and vivacious, battled with it, struggled, and longed to cast it off; but all that was joyful in itself, or fair in outward show, only served to renew it; and she could best support the burden of her sorrow with patience, when, yielding to it, it oppressed but did not torture her.

Constance had left the castle, to wander in the neighbouring grounds. Lofty and extensive as were the apartments of her abode, she felt pent up within their walls, beneath their fretted roofs. The clear sky, the spreading uplands, the shady wood, associated to her with every dear recollection of her past life, enticed her to spend hours and days beneath their leafy coverts. The motion and change perpetually working, as the wind stirred among the boughs, or the journeying sun rained its beams through them, soothed and called her out of that dull sorrow which clutched her heart with so unrelenting a pang beneath her castle roof.

There was one spot on the verge of the well-wooded park, one nook of ground, whence she could discern the country extended beyond, yet which was in itself thick set with tall umbrageous trees—a spot which she had forsworn, yet whither unconsciously her steps for ever tended, and where now again, for the twentieth time that day, she had unaware found herself. She sat upon a grassy mound, and looked wistfully on the flowers she had herself planted to adorn the verdurous recess—to her the temple of memory and love. She held the letter from the King which was the parent to her of so much despair. Dejection sat upon her features, and her gentle heart asked Fate why, so young, unprotected, and forsaken, she should have to struggle with this new form of wretchedness.

"I but ask," she thought, "to live in my father's halls—in the spot familiar to my infancy—to water with my frequent tears the graves of those I loved; and here in these woods, where such a mad dream of happiness was mine, to celebrate for ever the obsequies of Hope!"

A rustling among the boughs now met her ear—her heart beat quick—all again was still. "Foolish girl!" she half muttered: "dupe of thine own passionate fancy; because here we met; because seated here I have expected, and sounds like these have announced, his dear approach; so now every cony as it stirs, and every bird as it awakens silence, speaks of him. O Gaspar! mine once—never again will this beloved spot be made glad by thee—never more!"

Again the bushes were stirred, and footsteps were heard in the brake. She rose; her heart beat high: it must be that silly Manon, with her impertinent entreaties for her to return. But the steps were firmer and slower than would be those of her waiting-woman; and now emerging from the shade, she too plainly discerned the intruder. Her first impulse was to fly :—but once again to see him—to hear his voice :—once again, before she placed eternal vows between them, to stand together, and find the wide chasm filled which absence had made, could not injure the dead, and would soften the fatal sorrow that made her cheek so pale.

And now he was before her, the same beloved one with whom she had exchanged vows of constancy. He, like her, seemed sad, nor could she resist the imploring glance that entreated her for one moment to remain.

"I come, lady," said the young knight, "without a hope to bend your inflexible will. I come but once again to see you, and to bid you farewell before I depart for the Holy Land. I come to beseech you not to immure yourself in the dark cloister to avoid one so hateful as myself;—one you will never see more. Whether I die or live in Palestine, France and I are parted for ever!"

"Palestine!" said Constance, "that were fearful, were it true; but King Henry will never so lose his favourite cavalier. The throne you helped to build, you still will guard. Nay, as I ever had power over thought of thine, go not to Palestine."

"One word of yours could detain me—one smile—Constance—;" and the youthful lover knelt before her: but her harsher purpose was recalled by the image once so dear and familiar, now so strange and so forbidding.

"Linger no longer here!" she cried. "No smile, no word of mine will ever again be yours. Why are you here—here, where the spirits of the dead wander, and, claiming these shades as their own, curse the false girl who permits their murderer to disturb their sacred repose?"

"When love was young and you were kind," replied the knight, "you taught me to thread the intricacies of these woods—you welcomed me to this dear spot, where once you vowed to be my own—even beneath these ancient trees."

"A great sin it was," said Constance, "to unbar my father's doors to the son of his enemy; and dearly is it punished!"

The young knight gained courage as she spoke; yet he dared not move, lest she, who, every instant, appeared ready to take flight, should be startled from her momentary tranquillity; but he slowly replied:—"Those were happy days, Constance, full of terror and deep joy, when evening brought me to your feet; and while hate and vengeance were as its atmosphere to yonder frowning castle, this leafy, star-lit bower was the shrine of love."

"*Happy?*—miserable days!" echoed Constance; "when I imagined good could arise from failing in my duty, and that disobedience would be rewarded of God. Speak not of love, Gaspar! a sea of blood divides us for ever! Approach me not! The dead and the beloved stand even now between us; their pale shadows warn me of my fault, and menace me for listening to their murderer."

"That am not I!" exclaimed the youth. "Behold, Constance, we are each the last of our race. Death has dealt cruelly with us, and we are alone. It was not so when first we loved—when parent, kinsman, brother, nay, my own mother breathed curses on the house of Villeneuve; and in spite of all I blessed it. I saw thee, my lovely one, and blessed it. The God of peace planted love in our hearts, and with mystery and secrecy we met during many a summer night in the moon-lit dells; and when daylight was abroad, in this sweet recess we fled to avoid its scrutiny; and here, even here, where now I kneel in supplication, we both knelt and made our vows. Shall they be broken ?"

Constance wept as her lover recalled the images of happy hours. "Never!" she exclaimed, "O never! Thou knowest, or wilt soon know, Gaspar, the faith and resolves of one who dare not be yours. Was it for us to talk of love and happiness, when war, and hate, and blood were raging around ? The fleeting flowers our young hands strewed were trampled by the deadly encounter of mortal foes. By your father's hand mine died ; and little boots it to know whether, as my brother swore, and you deny, your hand did or did not deal the blow that destroyed him. You fought among those by whom he died. Say no more—no other word ; it is impiety towards the unreposing dead to hear you. Go, Gaspar ; forget me. Under the chivalrous and gallant Henry your career may be glorious ; and many a fair girl will listen, as once I did, to your vows, and be made happy by them. Farewell! May the Virgin bless you ! In my cell and cloister-home I will not forget the best Christian lesson—to pray for our enemies. Gaspar, farewell !"

She glided hastily from the bower ; with swift steps she threaded the glade and sought the castle. Once within the seclusion of her own apartment she gave way to the burst of grief that tore her gentle bosom like a tempest ; for hers was that worst sorrow which taints past joys, making remorse wait upon the memory of bliss, and linking love and fancied guilt in such fearful society as that of the tyrant when he bound a living body to a corpse. Suddenly a thought darted into her mind. At first she rejected it as puerile and super-stitious; but it would not be driven away. She called hastily for her attendant. "Manon," she said, "didst thou ever sleep on St. Catherine's couch?"

Manon crossed herself. "Heaven forefend! None ever did, since I was born, but two: one fell into the Loire and was drowned; the other only looked upon the narrow bed, and returned to her own home without a word. It is an awful place; and if the votary have not led a pious and good life, woe betide the hour when she rests her head on the holy stone!"

Constance crossed herself also. "As for our lives, it is only through our Lord and the blessed saints that we can any of us hope for righteousness. I will sleep on that couch to-morrow night!"

"Dear, my lady! and the King arrives to-morrow."

"The more need that I resolve. It cannot be that misery so intense should dwell in any heart, and no cure be found. I had hoped to be the bringer of peace to our houses; and is the good work to be for me a crown of thorns? Heaven shall direct me. I will rest to-morrow night on St. Catherine's bed; and if, as I have heard, the saint deigns to direct her votaries in dreams, I will be guided by her; and believing that I act according to the dictates of Heaven, I shall feel resigned even to the worst."

The King was on his way to Nantes from Paris, and he slept on this night at a castle but a few miles distant. Be-fore dawn a young cavalier was introduced into his chamber. The knight had a serious, nay, a sad aspect; and all beautiful as he was in feature and limb, looked way-worn and haggard. He stood silent in Henry's presence, who, alert and gay, turned his lively blue eyes upon his guest, saying gently, "So thou foundest her obdurate, Gaspar?"

"I found her resolved on our mutual misery. Alas! my liege, it is not, credit me, the least of my grief, that Constance sacrifices her own happiness when she destroys mine."

"And thou believest that she will say nay to the gaillard chevalier whom we ourselves present to her?"

"Oh! my liege, think not that thought; it cannot be. My heart deeply, most deeply, thanks you for your generous condescension. But she whom her lover's voice in solitude—whose entreaties, when memory and seclusion aided the spell—could not persuade, will resist even your majesty's commands. She is bent upon entering a cloister; and I, so please you, will now take my leave;—I am henceforth a soldier of the cross, and will die in Palestine."

"Gaspar," said the Monarch, "I know woman better than thou. It is not by submission nor tearful plaints she is to be won. The death of her relatives naturally sits heavy at the young Countess's heart; and nourishing in solitude her regret and her repentance, she fancies that Heaven itself forbids your union. Let the voice of the world reach her—the voice of earthly power and earthly kindness—the one commanding, the other pleading, and both finding response in her own heart—and by my fay and the Holy Cross, she will be yours. Let our plan still hold.

And now to horse: the morning wears, and the sun is risen."

The King arrived at the bishop's palace, and proceeded forthwith to mass in the cathedral. A sumptuous dinner succeeded, and it was afternoon before the Monarch proceeded through the town beside the Loire to where, a little above Nantes, the Chateau Villeneuve was situated. The young Countess received him at the gate. Henry looked in vain for the cheek blanched by misery, the aspect of downcast despair which he had been taught to expect. Her cheek was flushed, her manner animated, her voice scarce tremulous. "She loves him not," thought Henry, "or already her heart has consented."

A collation was prepared for the Monarch; and after some little hesitation, arising even from the cheerfulness of her mien, he mentioned the name of Gaspar. Constance blushed instead of turning pale, and replied very quickly, "To-morrow, my good liege; I ask for a respite but until to-morrow; all will then be decided;—to-morrow I am vowed to God—or—"

She looked confused, and the King, at once surprised and pleased, said, "Then you hate not young De Vaudemont; —you forgive him for the inimical blood that warms his veins."

"We are taught that we should forgive, that we should love our enemies," the Countess replied with some trepidation.

"Now by Saint Denis that is a right welcome answer for the novice," said the King, laughing. "What, ho! my faithful serving-man, Don Apollo in disguise! come forward, and thank your lady for her love."

In such disguise as had concealed him from all, the cavalier had hung behind, and viewed with infinite surprise the demeanour and calm countenance of the lady. He could not hear her words; but was this even she whom he had seen trembling and weeping the evening before?—this she whose very heart was torn by conflicting passions?—who saw the pale ghosts of parent and kinsman stand between her and the lover whom more than her life she adored? It was a riddle hard to solve. The King's call was in unison with his impatience, and he sprang forward. He was at her feet; while she, still passion-driven, over-wrought by the very calmness she had assumed, uttered one cry as she recognised him, and sank senseless on the floor.

All this was very unintelligible. Even when her attendants had brought her to life, another fit succeeded, and then passionate floods of tears; while the Monarch, waiting in the hall, eyeing the half-eaten collation, and humming some romance in commemoration of woman's waywardness, knew not how to reply to Vaudemont's look of bitter disappointment and anxiety. At length the Countess's chief attendant came with an apology: "her lady was ill, very ill. The next day she would throw herself at the King's feet, at once to solicit his excuse, and to disclose her purpose."

"To-morrow!—again to-morrow! Does to-morrow bear some charm, maiden?" said the King. "Can you read us the riddle, pretty one? What strange tale belongs to to-morrow, that all rests on its advent?"

Manon coloured, looked down, and hesitated. But Henry was no tyro in the art of enticing ladies' attendants to disclose their ladies' counsel. Manon was, besides, frightened by the Countess's scheme, on which she was still obstinately bent, so she was the more readily induced to betray it. To sleep in St. Catherine's bed, to rest on a narrow ledge overhanging the deep rapid Loire, and if, as was most probable, the luckless dreamer escaped from falling into it, to take the disturbed visions that such uneasy slumber might produce for the dictate of Heaven, was a madness of which even Henry himself could scarcely deem any woman capable. But could Constance, her whose beauty was so highly intellectual, and whom he had heard perpetually praised for her strength of mind and talents, could *she* be so strangely infatuated! And can passion play such freaks with us? —like death, levelling even the aristocracy of the soul, and bringing noble and peasant, the wise and foolish, under one thraldom? It was strange—yet she must have her way. That she hesitated in her decision was much; and it was to be hoped that St. Catherine would play no ill-natured part. Should it be otherwise, a purpose to be swayed by a dream might be influenced by other waking thoughts. To the more material kind of danger some safeguard should be brought.

There is no feeling more awful than that which invades a weak human heart bent upon gratifying its ungovernable impulses in contradiction to the dictates of conscience. Forbidden pleasures are said to be the most agreeable. It may be so to rude natures, to those who love to struggle, combat, and contend; who find happiness in a fray, and joy in the conflict of passion: but softer and sweeter was the gentle spirit of Constance; and love and duty contending crushed and tortured her poor heart. To commit her conduct to the inspirations of religion, or, if it was so to be named, of superstition, was a blessed relief. The very perils that threatened her undertaking gave a zest to it—to dare for his sake was happiness;—the very difficulty of the way that led to the completion of her wishes, at once gratified her love and distracted her thoughts from her despair. Or if it was decreed that she must sacrifice all, the risk of danger and of death was of trifling import in comparison with the anguish which would then be her portion for ever.

The night threatened to be stormy—the raging wind shook the casements—and the trees waved their huge shadowy arms, as giants might in fantastic dance and mortal broil. Constance and Manon, unattended, quitted the chateau by a postern, and began to descend the hill side. The moon had not yet risen; and though the way was familiar to both, Manon tottered and trembled; while the Countess, drawing her silken cloak round her, walked with a firm step down the steep. They came to the river's side, where a small boat was moored, and one man was in waiting. Constance stepped lightly in, and then aided her fearful companion. In a few moments they were in the middle of the stream. The warm, tempestuous, animating, equinoctial wind swept over them. For the first time since her mourning, a thrill of pleasure swelled the bosom of Constance. She hailed the emotion with double joy. It cannot be, she thought, that Heaven will forbid me to love one so brave, so generous, and so good as the noble Gaspar. Another I can never love; I shall die if divided from him; and this heart, these limbs, so alive with glowing sensation, are they already predestined to an early grave! Oh, no! life speaks aloud within them. I shall live to love. Do not all things love?—the winds as they whisper to the rushing waters? the waters as they kiss the flowery banks, and speed to mingle with the sea? Heaven and earth are sustained by, live through, love; and shall Constance alone, whose heart has ever been a deep, gushing, overflowing well of true affection, be compelled to set a stone upon the fount to lock it up for ever?

These thoughts bid fair for pleasant dreams; and perhaps the Countess, an adept in the blind god's lore, therefore indulged them the more readily. But as thus she was engrossed by soft emotions, Manon caught her arm:—"Lady, look!" she cried; "it comes—yet the oars have no sound! Now the Virgin shield us! Would we were at home!"

A dark boat glided by them. Four rowers, habited in black cloaks, pulled at oars which, as Manon said, gave no sound: another sat at the helm: like the rest, his person was veiled in a dark mantle, but he wore no cap; and though his face was turned from them, Constance recognised her lover! "Gaspar," she cried aloud, "dost thou live?"— but the figure in the boat neither turned its head nor replied, and quickly it was lost in the shadowy waters.

How changed now was the fair Countess's reverie! Already Heaven had begun its spell, and unearthly forms were around, as she strained her eyes through the gloom. Now she saw and now she lost view of the bark that occasioned her terror; and now it seemed that another was there, which held the spirits of the dead; and her father waved to her from shore, and her brothers frowned on her.

Meanwhile they neared the landing. Her bark was moored in a little cove, and Constance stood upon the bank. Now she trembled, and half yielded to Manon's entreaty to return; till the unwise *suivante* mentioned the King's and De Vaudemont's name, and spoke of the answer to be given to-morrow. What answer, if she turned back from her intent?

She now hurried forward up the broken ground of the bank, and then along its edge, till they came to a hill which abruptly hung over the tide. A small chapel stood near. With trembling fingers the Countess drew forth the key and unlocked the door. They entered. It was dark—save that a little lamp, flickering in the wind, showed an uncertain light from before the figure of Saint Catherine. The two women knelt; they prayed, and then rising, with a cheerful accent the Countess bade her attendant good night. She unlocked a little low iron door. It opened on a narrow cavern. The roar of waters was heard beyond. "Thou mayest not follow, my poor Manon," said Constance,— " nor dost thou much desire;—this adventure is for me alone."

It was hardly fair to leave the trembling servant in the chapel alone, who had neither hope nor fear, nor love nor grief, to beguile her; but, in those days, esquires and waiting-women often played the part of subalterns in the army, gaining knocks and no fame. Besides, Manon was safe on holy ground. The Countess meanwhile pursued her way, groping in the dark through the narrow, tortuous passage. At length what seemed light to her long-darkened sense gleamed on her. She reached an open cavern in the over-hanging hill's side, looking over the rushing tide beneath. She looked out upon the night. The waters of the Loire were speeding, as since that day have they ever sped—changeful, yet the same; the heavens were thickly veiled with clouds; and the wind in the trees was as mournful and ill-omened as if it rushed round a murderer's tomb. Constance shuddered a little, and looked upon her bed—a narrow ledge of earth and a moss-grown stone bordering on the very verge of the precipice! She doffed her mantle (such was one of the conditions of the spell)—she bowed her head, and loosened the tresses of her dark hair—she bared her feet—and thus, fully prepared for suffering to the utmost the chill influence of the cold night, she stretched herself on the narrow couch that scarce afforded room for her repose, and whence, if she moved in sleep, she must be precipitated into the cold waters below.

At first it seemed to her as if she never should sleep again. No great wonder that exposure to the blast and her perilous position should forbid her eyelids to close. At length she fell into a reverie so soft and soothing that she wished even to watch—and then by degrees her senses became confused —and now she was on St. Catherine's bed—the Loire rushing beneath, and the wild wind sweeping by—and now—O whither?—and what dreams did the saint send, to drive her to despair, or to bid her be blessed for ever?

Beneath the rugged hill, upon the dark tide, another watched, who feared a thousand things, and scarce dared hope. He had meant to precede the lady on her way, but when he found that he had outstayed his time, with muffled oars and breathless haste he had shot by the bark that contained his Constance, nor even turned at her voice, fearful to incur her blame, and her commands to return. He had seen her emerge from the passage, and shuddered as she leant over the cliff. He saw her step forth, clad as she was in white, and could mark her as she lay on the ledge beetling above. What a vigil did the lovers keep!—she given up to visionary thoughts: he knowing—and the consciousness thrilled his bosom with strange emotion—that love, and love for him, had led her to that perilous couch; and that while dangers surrounded her in every shape, she was alive only to the still small voice that whispered to her heart the dream which was to decide their destinies. She slept, perhaps —but he waked and watched; and night wore away, as, now praying, now entranced by alternating hope and fear, he sat in his boat, his eyes fixed on the white garb of the slumberer above.

Morning—was it morning that struggled in the clouds? Would morning ever come to waken her? And had she slept? and what dreams of weal or woe had peopled her sleep? Gaspar grew impatient. He commanded his boatmen still to wait, and he sprang forward, intent on clambering the precipice. In vain they urged the danger, nay, the impossibility of the attempt; he clung to the rugged face of the hill, and found footing where it would seem no footing was. The acclivity, indeed, was not high; the danger of St. Catherine's bed arising from the likelihood that any one who slept on so narrow a couch would be precipitated into the waters beneath. Up the steep ascent Gaspar continued to toil, and at last reached the roots of a tree that grew near the summit. Aided by its branches, he made good his stand at the very extremity of the ledge, near the pillow on which lay the uncovered head of his beloved. Her hands were folded on her bosom; her dark hair fell around her neck and pillowed her cheek; her face was serene, sleep was there in all its innocence and in all its helplessness; every wilder emotion was hushed, and her bosom heaved in regular breathing. He could see her heart beat as it lifted her fair hands crossed above. No statue hewn of marble in monumental effigy was ever half so fair; and within that surpassing form dwelt a soul true, tender, self-devoted, and affectionate as ever warmed a human breast.

With what deep passion did Gaspar gaze, gathering hope from the placidity of her angel countenance! A smile wreathed her lips; and he too involuntarily smiled, as he hailed the happy omen; when suddenly her cheek was flushed, her bosom heaved, a tear stole from her dark lashes, and then a whole shower fell, as starting up she cried, "No!—he shall not die!—I will unloose his chains!—I will save him!" Gaspar's hand was there. He caught her light form ready to fall from the perilous couch. She opened her eyes and beheld her lover, who had watched over her dream of fate, and who had saved her.

Manon also had slept well, dreaming or not, and was startled in the morning to find that she waked surrounded by a crowd. The little desolate chapel was hung with tapestry—the altar adorned with golden chalices—the priest was chanting mass to a goodly array of kneeling knights. Manon saw that King Henry was there; and she looked for another whom she found not, when the iron door of the cavern passage opened, and Gaspar de Vaudemont entered from it, leading the fair form of Constance; who, in her white robes and dark dishevelled hair, with a face in which smiles and blushes contended with deeper emotion, approached the altar, and kneeling with her lover, pronounced the vows that united them for ever.

It was long before the happy Gaspar could win from his lady the secret of her dream. In spite of the happiness she now enjoyed, she had suffered too much not to look back even with terror to those days when she thought love a crime, and every event connected with them wore an awful aspect. " Many a vision," she said, " she had that fearful night. She had seen the spirits of her father and brothers in Paradise; she had beheld Gaspar victoriously combating among the infidels; she had beheld him in King Henry's Court, favoured and beloved, and she herself—now pining in a cloister, now a bride—now grateful to Heaven for the full measure of bliss presented to her, now weeping away her sad days—till suddenly she thought herself in Paynim land; and the saint herself, Saint Catherine, guiding her unseen through the city of the infidels. She entered a palace and beheld the miscreants rejoicing in victory; and then descending to the dungeons beneath, they groped their way through damp vaults, and low, mildewed passages, to one cell, darker and more frightful than the rest. On the floor lay one with soiled and tattered garments, with unkempt locks and wild matted beard. His cheek was wan and thin; his eyes had lost their fire; his form was a mere skeleton; the chains hung loosely on the fleshless bones."

"And was it my appearance in that attractive state and winning costume that softened the hard heart of Constance?" asked Gaspar, smiling at this painting of what would never be.

"Even so," replied Constance; "for my heart whispered me that this was my doing: and who could recall the life that waned in your pulses—who restore, save the destroyer? My heart never warmed to my living happy knight as then it did to his wasted image, as it lay, in the visions of night, at my feet. A veil fell from my eyes; a darkness was dispelled from before me. Methought I then knew for the first time what life and what death were. I was bid believe that to make the living happy was not to injure the dead; and I felt how wicked and how vain was that false philosophy which placed virtue and good in hatred and unkindness. You should not die: I would loosen your chains and save you, and bid you live for love. I sprung forward, and the death I deprecated for you would, in my presumption, have been mine—then, when first I felt the real value of life—but that your arm was there to save me, your dear voice to bid me be blessed for evermore."

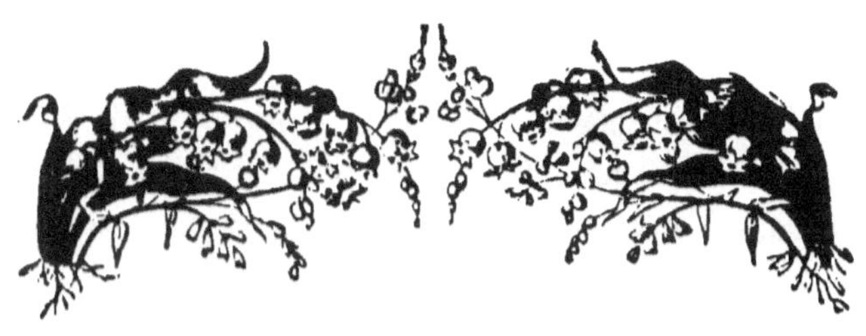

The Exile.

I was in the spring of the year 1660 that a well-mounted Cavalier was seen riding leisurely through a forest, or chase, in one of the northern counties of England. He was a tall, well-proportioned, and rather handsome man, of about eight and twenty; but an expression of thoughtfulness and care gave him the appearance of being somewhat older. His dress was that of a country gentleman of the first class, and as remote from the precision which distinguished the Puritan, as from the gaiety so generally affected by the Cavaliers of that period. The evening was one of uncommon loveliness, and the traveller seemed lost in the contemplation of the beauty which reviving nature had flung over the rich landscape before him. His attention was diverted by the appearance of a horseman, issuing from one of the bridle roads by which the forest was intersected, and continuing his journey about a hundred yards in advance. He was younger, by some two or three years, than the other; and his attire, although travel-soiled, was of a more fashionable and courtly character. His horse, however, was much inferior, and from its jaded step and frequent stumbling, appeared to have borne its rider many a mile since the morning.

The elder horseman, after observing his precursor for some seconds with great earnestness, put spurs to his steed, with the intention, it would seem, of overtaking him. At that moment the report of a gun was heard from an adjoining thicket. The horse of the younger Cavalier started at the sound, and in plunging, missed its footing and fell, flinging its rider some paces before it into the road. The prostrate horseman, imagining that the shot had been aimed at him, and concluding that either himself or his horse was wounded, drew a pistol from his belt, and fired it, fortunately without effect, at the elder traveller, who was riding up to his assistance.

"Why, Harry Pierrepoint," exclaimed the latter, quoting from his favourite poet, "'What a fall was there, my countryman!' Thou hast bitten the dust, man."

"I don't know what you call a bite, Winterton, but I happen to have a mouthful of it," rejoined the other, sputtering; "however, we are well met, in times when friends are somewhat scarce with me."

"Ay, and if your hand were as sure as it is ready, you had made them one the fewer. Nevertheless, Harry, I am glad to see you, although I would that I had encountered you in better plight; 'twere hard to say which of the twain is the sorrier spectacle, you or your horse. That piece of carrion will scarce bear you a league further."

"It will be well if he carry me another mile," was Pierre-point's reply.

"And far enough, too," continued the other, "since within that distance stands the house of my fathers, which, fallen as are our fortunes, can still shelter an old friend. But whence come you?"

"From Brussels," was the answer.

"And the news?" rejoined Winterton.

"Oh! bad as may be. Charles's cause is desperate, and his person, for aught I know, scarcely at liberty, though, if he have been permitted free egress from Brussels, he will be at Breda by this time. For myself, having lent and spent the little I had in his service, here I am, wasted in purse and person, in old England again."

"Which is certainly not the safest asylum you could have chosen under such circumstances."

"Perhaps not," pursued Pierrepoint, "but the Round-heads have got my estate, and old Noll is in his grave, while Master Dick, not being able to take up his father's cards and play out the game, has left the matter in the hands of the Parliament, who, just now, have something else to do than to look after one of whom they can get nothing but his blood; an article of which, methinks, they should be well-nigh surfeited by this time. Yet, let the worst come of it, I can but die, and death is preferable to herding among profligates and fools, to make up the mockery of a court at which the finger of scorn is pointed by every State in Europe."

"And when," inquired Winterton, "did you quit

this same court, of which you give so dolorous an account?"

"Two months since," answered his companion; "for, hearing that Cavaliers returning directly from Flanders were subjected to stricter scrutiny than it would suit either my temper or my purpose to endure, I took a circuitous route, which, with some impediments upon the road, has protracted my return."

"Then my news from the exiled court," said Winterton, "are of later date, and, it may be, of better complexion than yours. But see, we are at home: fling your rein to the only serving-man we can at present boast of; and he, by the way, is but half a one, seeing that he is drunk the greater portion of his time."

"What! my old friend Hubert turned drunkard?" exclaimed the young Cavalier; "I remember him the steadiest fellow alive, and one who always kept himself sober upon principle."

"And now," said Winterton, "he gets drunk upon principle."

"It must be one of very questionable orthodoxy."

"Perhaps so," continued the other; "but assuming that it would be derogatory from the dignity of the family that a less quantity of ale should be brewed than when there were more throats to swallow it, he does his utmost that so much good liquor may not be wasted: secondly, as he professes to discharge the aggregate duties of those of his late fellows whom our altered fortunes have compelled us to dispense with, he makes it a point of conscience not to omit their performances at the ale flagon."

"By the way, Winterton," said Pierrepoint, "if he perform but one half of what he professes, his duties are somewhat of the heaviest."

"So it would appear," was the rejoinder, "for he frequently lies down under them."

What little the reader may have failed to glean, from this dialogue, of the respective characters I have introduced to him, will be supplied by a slight sketch of their histories.

The elder Cavalier, having been detected in a correspondence with the exiled Monarch, with a view to his restoration to the throne of his ancestors, had been permitted to retain his estate only upon the payment of an oppressive pecuniary penalty, termed a composition, which reduced him to the necessity of curtailing his establishment, and retaining, of a once magnificent stud, but a single horse, and of a numerous retinue, the solitary male servant already mentioned, who, with a female domestic or two, formed the whole of his household.

The younger Cavalier was also born to high expectations, but had lost his patrimonial estate in consequence of his father's attachment to the cause of the unfortunate Monarch, who paid the price of what some have termed firmness, and others obstinacy, with his blood. Harry Pierrepoint, whose father died in exile, followed the fortunes of the second Charles in all his vicissitudes, until, having spent his last shilling in the service of that prince (who had little delicacy in drawing on the purses of his friends), he returned to his native country at the crisis at which I have presented him to the reader.

After the younger Cavalier had partaken of a substantial supper, to which his host was not slow in introducing him, he was quite an altered man. His spirits, naturally elastic, rose in proportion as he recovered from his fatigue, and he began to see the world and his own condition in a much ameliorated point of view, through the medium of a flask of excellent Rhenish produced upon the occasion.

His host, perceiving the improvement in his guest, began to rally him, by saying,—

"Pierrepoint, you do not mean to say, that an abstract love of England, the pure *amor patriæ*, has brought you back hither at the hazard of your personal liberty, to rate at the lowest the danger you have incurred? Confess now, is not a certain damsel, of whom I wot, the object of attraction?"

"Supposing your conjecture correct," said the other, "what then?"

"Nay, I know not that I have any right to question you on the subject; but I would fain know your motive for seeking her under your present circumstances," said Winterton.

"You will laugh at me," rejoined Pierrepoint, "when I tell you, it is to ascertain if the hopes I have dared to encourage have any better foundation than my own conceit."

"And if it should prove that they have not?" inquired the elder.

"I shall then," answered his friend, "have travelled some hundred miles, or so, on a fool's errand, and shall bid adieu to merry England for ever, and take such chance as the fortune of war, in some foreign service, shall send me."

"And your first step," continued Winterton, "towards the execution of your hopeful project is—"

"To find out the lady," interrupted Pierrepoint, ' and throw myself at her feet."

"You must first throw yourself over a thirty feet wall, then," said the other, "taking care to clear the spikes on the top of it."

"Winterton, you alarm me!" exclaimed the younger Cavalier.

"Nay, never fear, man; your lady love is safe enough, I promise you. Your friend Noll, as you are wont to designate him, placed her and her sister, the Lady Blanche, in the guardianship of the present possessor of your estates, doubtless with a view to your convenience, in order that, if affairs should take a turn, you might regain possession of your property and the lady at once."

"But do they never walk out?" inquired Pierrepoint.

"Never, by any chance," said the other : "their respectable guardian wisely deems the grounds within the castle walls sufficiently spacious for every purpose of air and exercise."

"But you surely magnify the difficulties of gaining access to them?" rejoined Pierrepoint.

"*Tout au contraire*," said Winterton ; "I have been for

the last six months doing all in my power to diminish them."

" True," pursued the other ; " now I bethink me, you had a penchant for the Lady Blanche, who, I recollect, regarded your suit with more favour than her sister Elinor extended to mine."

" Nay," replied his companion, " there you do her wrong. I have it from a sure hand, that she is not altogether so indifferent to your pretensions as your modesty would lead you to imagine."

" I would, then," exclaimed Pierrepoint, " she had admitted me to some portion of her confidence upon a subject in which she can scarcely be more interested than myself."

" And when do you propose to attempt this notable achievement, and win your way to the presence of the damsel, in spite of stone walls, six stout serving-men, and their Argus-eyed master?" inquired Winterton.

" On the very first opportunity," was the reply.

" Nay," said the other, " to wait for opportunity is beneath the chivalry of so redoutable a knight."

" Well, then," rejoined Pierrepoint, " to-morrow morning perhaps."

" And in your present plight, doubtless," said his host, " in order that if you fail in exciting her love, you may, at least, be certain of moving her pity; passions, by the way, not so closely allied as some wiseacres have opined. Credit me, there is nothing like making love with a joyous countenance; therefore, wait, I pray you, until those lank cheeks have done honour to my hospitality ; or, at any rate, until your mail chests have arrived, lest, by exhibiting yourself to the lady in your present travel-soiled habiliments, you may appear desirous of securing another suit before you are compelled to part with the one you have. Come now, if I certify you that your interest with the Lady Elinor is not at so low an ebb as you estimate it, will you consent to defer this hopeful attempt for a few days, when, as I trust to show you, circumstances will be more propitious to its execution ?"

"Ay," said the other ; " make that appear, and you shall e'en guide me as you please."

"Well, then," continued Winterton, "thus much I promise you ; and, in the meantime, I would inquire after certain of our friends in Flanders. How is Frank Sackville ? The King promised to take care of his fortune."

"And has kept his word most royally, to the last stiver of it," was the answer.

"And where is poor Frank now ?"

"In a garret at Brussels," said Pierrepoint, "of such circumscribed dimensions, that he cannot stretch himself without flinging open the window for elbow-room."

"And does he flaunt it as bravely as ever ?" pursued the querist.

"Alas, no !" was the reply. "Poverty is now his only tailor, and has slashed his doublet sadly. He told me, with tears in his eyes, that the last of his shirts he had six different ways of getting into, until, on undressing himself one night, he missed it altogether, and at last found its melancholy remains coffined in his boot."

" Has he recourse to the wine-flask as frequently as was his wont, drowning his cares after the manner of Clarence?" said Winterton.

" Oh, no !" rejoined the other; " he has descended to the alcohol, which he obtains as he can; begs, borrows, or perhaps steals it, as did Prometheus fire of another sort; and, like him, suffers for it in his liver."

" And how fares it with old Sir John—absent Jack as we used to style him? Is he still subject to those fits of abstraction, under the influence of which he was accustomed to forget his meals?"

" Fortunately for him, as much so as ever," replied Pierrepoint; " a circumstance that administers marvellously to his convenience, seeing that his dinner is frequently as absent as himself."

" He had a turn for poetry, had he not?" said Winterton.

" Call it a *twist*," replied the incorrigible Pierrepoint; " for nothing could be more foreign to his nature. He had a fancy for bell-ringing, you will remember; and when he gave that up, he took to jingling of another sort, and nick-named it poetry."

" Gliding, by a natural transition, from poetry to music, I would inquire how goes the world with music and Dick Crotchet; is he as indefatigable a scraper as ever?

" Confound him ! yes," said Pierrepoint; " he lodged in the next room to me, where he fiddled from morning till night, and taught me, by sad experience, that the punishment of the bow-string is not confined to Turkey."

Although Winterton acquitted himself of his promise by convincing Pierrepoint that the Lady Elinor was favourable to his pretensions, he had much difficulty to restrain his impatience in seeking an interview. After the lapse of a few days, however, Winterton, with some reluctance, sanctioned the undertaking ; and on being consulted by his friend as to the best mode of insuring success, replied,—

"Old Hubert is, of all others, the most likely man to aid you ; but, in the ordinary routine of his business, you can scarcely reckon upon his services after noon, when he begins his devotions to the jolly god, and he usually carries his worship to prostration in his temple, the beer-cellar ;—in more scientific language, abandoning the perpendicular for the horizontal. You must therefore request of him, as a particular favour, that he will be so obliging as to get drunk betimes in the morning, so that he may be sober and fit for your purpose in the afternoon."

"For my part," said Pierrepoint, "I know of no other method than fording the moat at the most accessible point."

"I would counsel you," said the other, "not to attempt it; for, setting aside its impracticability, you will lose, what I hold to be essential to your success, the co-operation of Hubert, who happens to be afflicted with hydrophobia, and will, on no consideration, allow water to approach his lips."

Hubert was accordingly summoned to council, being fortunately sober at the time. In whatever other respect he might have been disqualified for a privy councillor, he was, in an essential particular, admirably adapted for one : his secrecy, whether drunk or sober, might be implicitly depended upon; for naturally taciturn, the ale flagon, possibly from the glutinous properties of the beverage, sealed his lips hermetically.

When questioned as to the practicability of gaining admission to the castle, he answered, that he knew of but one thing more difficult, namely, to get out again. After musing some time, however, upon the problem, he placed his finger upon his forehead, and then on one side of his nose, and, with a look of peculiar significance and intellectuality, informed the Cavaliers that he had hit upon a plan of compassing the object. He occasionally, he said, condescended to a cup of single ale with the porter of the castle; and here he uttered an anathema, which it is not necessary, nor would it be very edifying to give verbatim, upon the churl who, for the sake of a few paltry bushels of malt, condemned his household to such thin potations. He added, that his friend the janitor, not daring to admit him by the gate, was wont to fling him a key, which procured him an entrance by a postern, without subjecting him to the notice of the proprietor, who was accustomed to look as black as Tophet at any stranger who approached his hold. He concluded by proposing that Pierrepoint should repair to the postern, and conceal himself in some underwood, while Hubert should obtain the key in the manner described, and deliver it to the Cavalier, who was to take his chance for the rest.

It previously happened, that, in an accidental rencontre with the waiting-maid of Lady Elinor, Pierrepoint had ascertained the precise situation of the apartments assigned to the sisters, which, being in a quarter of the building little frequented by the servants, he would be likely to gain without attracting observation, while Haslerigge, the possessor of the castle, either from respect to his captives or their cool reception of him, rarely troubled them with his company.

• Fortune appeared to favour Pierrepoint's enterprise; for he succeeded in obtaining the key of the postern, and, by means of it, admission to the castle; and although it required some address, combined with an intimate knowledge of the interior, he was also successful in gaining the apartments of the Ladies Elinor and Blanche.

He entered in the most romantic and approved manner, namely, by the window; and was, of course, greeted with a scream from the damsels in concert. The Lady Blanche was the first to speak.

"Master Pierrepoint," she exclaimed, "by all that's wonderful!"

"Even so," said Pierrepoint; "here I am, pitched into the enemy's very citadel, like a bomb."

"Ay; and like it," rejoined the lady, "threatening destruction to all in the apartment into which it has pleased you to descend."

The Lady Elinor, having recovered from her first surprise,

resumed her seat with an air of something like offended dignity, and it was not until the gallant had dropped upon one knee, and finished a flourishing oration upon the subject of his love and loyalty to his mistress—fifty per cent. of which, to do him justice, was true—that the lady condescended to address him, which she did, by inquiring where his loyalty was, when he kissed Dorcas, her waiting-maid, the preceding evening in the wood.

"I plead guilty of kissing, fair lady," replied Pierrepoint, "but not with intent to defraud. It is very true, I did bestow upon the aforesaid Abigail the kiss named in the indictment, but it was upon trust for your ladyship's behoof; and that she hath feloniously embezzled it, to her own base purposes, is more your fault than mine, seeing that your exemplary prudence was my sufficient warrant for your having none but honest and trustworthy persons in your service."

"Matchless assurance!" was the lady's exclamation.

"Matchless indeed!" echoed the Cavalier, purposely diverting the application of the expression; "and to demonstrate that my abhorrence of such unpardonable malversation is as strong as your ladyship's, I will avail myself of the first opportunity of taking back the kiss from the base purloiner, and appropriating it according to the intention of the donor. In the meantime I have one consolation at least under the miscarriage."

"And what, in the name of impudence, may that be?" inquired the lady.

"The regret which your ladyship expresses for the loss of

the kiss, as proving the value you would have placed upon the possession."

The Lady Elinor, perceiving that to lecture so incorrigible an offender would be a very profitless labour, indulged her better nature by laughing at him instead; but soon resuming her gravity, she inquired, "What could induce you, Pierrepoint, thus to peril your safety by putting yourself in the power of a man who has such urgent motives for seeking your destruction? He naturally regards you as the only person who can ever dispute his claim to the property he has usurped, and you well know him to be one whose conscience never yet stood in the way of his interest."

"My excuse," rejoined the Cavalier, bowing, "is before me, and none will dispute that it is a fair one."

"And a weak one, nevertheless," responded the lady; "but, admitting your right to sport with your own safety, what apology can you offer for hazarding mine?"

"My good sword, dear lady," replied the gallant, "and a strong arm, which I trust will prove a sufficient barrier between you and any evil which is likely to threaten you at present."

The words had scarcely passed his lips, when the Lady Blanche, who, from a reluctance to overhear the conversation of the lovers, blended with her anxiety to warn them of any danger which might approach, was looking from the casement, exclaimed, "Fly, Harry Pierrepoint, and save yourself! Master Haslerigge is in the garden beneath the window, and is hastening this way."

"By what path comes he?" inquired the Cavalier.

"By the ivy tower and the fountain," replied Blanche.

"Then, in attempting to escape, I must infallibly encounter him," said Pierrepoint.

"Oh, Pierrepoint!" exclaimed the Lady Elinor, bitterly, and wringing her hands, "why did you court this danger? Haslerigge may not be a match for you in courage or strength, but he is blood-thirsty and cruel, and there are those in this castle who, at his slightest bidding, would fling you from the battlements into the moat with as little compunction as they would a dog. Oh, Harry Pierrepoint! Harry Pierrepoint! you are lost, lost!—concealment is impossible!" ·

"And unnecessary," said the Cavalier. "I will brave the foul usurper and his myrmidons here in my own castle. In the meantime, dearest lady, calm your apprehensions, and, on the word of a gentleman, no harm shall come of it. I pray you resume your seat; this exhibition of your interest in my safety is not likely to diminish the anger you would deprecate. Oh, Elinor! in the day of my adversity, when its cloud was upon my fortunes and its blight upon my spirit, how had this blessed assurance of your solicitude for my welfare sustained me through the troubles that have well-nigh overborne me!"

The Lady Elinor, putting a strong guard upon her feelings, sat down, and drew her veil partially over her face, while Pierrepoint remained upon his knee before her, when Haslerigge entered the apartment.

He started on perceiving the Cavalier, but immediately

recovering himself, exclaimed, "Whom have we here?—the traitor, Harry Pierrepoint?"

The latter rose, and with much dignity of manner replied, "A traitor and Harry Pierrepoint both are here, but in different persons."

"He who comes in secret, and in arms," rejoined the other, "comes with no honest purpose. Have you stolen hither to assassinate me in my own castle?"

"Villain, it is mine!" replied Pierrepoint, "and therefore you are safe."

"You are forward, Sir Malapert," said Haslerigge, with a sneer, "in proffering a protection which I need not, and you have not to give. You will excuse me, if I cannot resign to you the castle which you so modestly claim; but I will accommodate you with an apartment in it, where you will have leisure, an it please you, to indulge your passion for those profane fancies which you call poetry."

"I thank you for your courtesy, Master Haslerigge," said the Cavalier; "but I would first claim your attention to a little composition in prose, in which, it may be, you will feel more interested."

As Pierrepoint spoke, he drew from his vest, and put into Haslerigge's hand, a copy of the manifesto which was the result of General Monk's negotiation between the Parliament and Charles for the restoration of the latter, and which had been transmitted by express to Winterton, who had long been in the confidence of the exiled Monarch, and was in constant, though secret, communication with his court, regardless of the penalty to which he was exposed.

Haslerigge's hand trembled exceedingly as he perused the proclamation, which he suddenly dropped, and made towards the door. Pierrepoint, anticipating his design, seized him by the arm, saying, " Stop, Master Haslerigge ; you are in great haste to quit one with whom, but a minute ago, you expressed so flattering a reluctance to part. I would a word with you. You have read in that document of certain exceptions to the proposed amnesty, and, if I mistake not, your services to the old Government have been of a nature not very likely to be forgotten by the new one."

" But I will defend the castle," said the other. " What, ho, there ! Humphrey !—Giles !—"

" Another word above your breath," said Pierrepoint, " and I will wind my bugle, and ere the hills can give back its echo, the castle will be beleaguered by my friends, in such numbers, and with such means, that resistance would be idle, and escape, though you had the ring of Gyges or the wings of Icarus, impossible. Wicked regicide and base usurper as you are, and well as you would become, and richly as your crimes deserve, the scaffold, I would not that the hall of my fathers were made a passage to it even for an enemy; else had I not incurred the personal risk of coming alone and in secret, when I might have come openly with a host in my train. Fly, then, while the path is open to you : wait the issue, and you are lost beyond a hope."

Either awakened to a sense of his danger, or unwilling to put the other's assertions to the proof, Haslerigge made a movement indicative of his desire to follow the advice he had received.

"One word more," said Pierrepoint, detaining him. "The blood of a martyr is upon your soul : remember there is One whose blood can wash out the stain, deep though it be. May it not have been shed in vain for you! Go now ; you are free : take the northern road, and you are safe."

The Ladies Elinor and Blanche were, as will be imagined, most interested witnesses of this exciting scene. They had heard that Pierrepoint was brave, and they knew him to be honourable, but they had to gather from the occurrences of that morning, that beneath a playful fancy, an exuberance of animal spirits, and much of what savoured of levity, there was an energy of mind which rose with the occasion, and stamped on his character a value that they had not previously assigned to it.

If the Lady Elinor had at any time wavered in her sentiments in regard to Pierrepoint, the dignity of his manner, and the manly generosity of his conduct upon this occasion, as well as the deep and solemn tone of feeling in which he pronounced his valedictory admonition to Haslerigge, were calculated to decide her choice. They did so : she gave him her hand, alleging, however, that she had but an election of evils—between the inconvenience of removing from the castle with all her goods and chattels, and encumbering herself with a husband.

The Lady Blanche, out of pure love for her sister, and a consequent desire of living near to her, took up her residence at Winterton Hall, under the style and title of Lady Blanche Winterton.

The fortunes of the two ladies enabled their liege lords to live upon their estates in a manner suited to their rank.

Upon our friend Hubert the restoration of his master's establishment wrought the happiest change; for being relieved of much of his duty at the ale flagon, he resumed his former habits of sobriety, although it was reported that he was troubled with hydrophobia till the day of his death.

Lady Alice.

N days far back, the sides of the deep and narrow glen in which Neidpath Castle stands were covered with wood, which gave a stern and gloomy appearance to the scene, and seemed to shut it out from the world beyond, where hill and valley looked bright, and where fountain and field seemed to smile in the sunbeams.

Even in our own days, when the raven no longer flaps his wings in the briered dell—when the hill-fox is driven from his haunts; even now, when fields of corn wave in the breeze like seas of emerald, and when the sheep pasture in safety, there yet lingers round the scene an air of sternness, as if, indeed, the dark scowl had been chased away, but had not given place to a smile.

Well, well; times change : fields grow to towns, towns return to the labours of the agriculturist—forests are cleared, others spring up—marshes are drained, fresh ones form. But no matter—we speak of the past.

Somewhere about two centuries ago this castle was in

possession of the Earl of March, who, being proud and rapacious—ever striving to enrich his family, no matter by what means—was very much disliked. Knowing this, the haughty mind of the Earl took fire. He rarely visited his mansion in the adjoining town of Peebles, —in fact he became a recluse in his Castle of Neidpath, having no other society than that of his two daughters.

Beautiful as Nature's models were the daughters of the Earl of March: but their dispositions were very opposite; the elder seemed to inherit all her mother's softness ; the younger, all her father's fire.

The elder was, however, the favourite of her father; and the declining state of her health served to make his affection grow deeper.

The disease under which the Lady Alice laboured was one of the mind. By a few it was called consumption, which in silence and secrecy destroys the life, and at the same time puts forth a semblance of health. The roses had, indeed, fled from her cheek, but the paleness which their absence left was that of the lily, and of so exquisite a hue was it, that her countenance seemed to be more beautiful than when painted with the flush of health. But her sister, with deeper penetration, pronounced it to be love-melancholy. Tears would frequently start to the poor girl's eyes when a word bordering on unkindness was uttered; while a sudden step or an abrupt question would bring the blood in an instant to her cheek.

The age of the Lady Alice was the romantic one of eighteen, when the bud of youth is just opening into womanhood; but the flower seemed withering on the stalk, in place of unfolding a richer bloom.

Love, however, it was, which was the cause of the poor girl's illness,—a deep, calm love, which preyed upon her heart. She never acknowledged it, but let concealment, "like a worm in the bud," devour her strength and consume her beauty.

The maternal ancestors of the Lady Alice were not natives of the vale of Tweed. She had come of an old Border race who still kept footing on the shore of the Teviot; and, until weakened by illness, she had been accustomed to go several times a year to visit the relations of her deceased parent.

Whenever her arrival was expected, she found her path beset by young Scott, the son of the Laird of Tushielaw and the descendant of the Border King. The same blood flowed in the veins of both, and, while yet children, Scott seemed to have fixed upon Alice for his future wife.

But years soon pass away: Scott grew to manhood, Alice approached womanhood; yet with freeness and frankness they met each other.

They were not lovers of the drawing-room, or the library, or the lawn. They were children of the hardy Scott, to whom the heavens seemed the fittest roof, and the greensward the fittest carpet. They galloped side by side over glen, and heath, and mountain, their cheeks fanned by

the fragrant breezes, and their bright eyes lit up by the
morning beams.

The eighteenth summer's sun which had shone upon the
Lady Alice was making all nature beautiful, when she paid
her last visit to the "wild and willowed shore of the
Teviot." But Scott of Tushielaw seemed not to welcome
her approach in his usual way—the gay light-hearted-
ness of his spirit had vanished, and a deep thoughtfulness
clouded his lofty brow. Still, as if the solemn mountains
and the tangled bushy glens were their proper home,
they rode side by side, down rocky steeps and through
gloomy ravines, where nature presents all wildness, and
majesty, and wonder.

It was on one of these occasions that the heart of
young Scott seemed more than usually heavy—though
all around was exquisitely beautiful. In vain the lovely
Alice strove to discover the cause of this strange
transformation. He declared repeatedly that nothing
pained or ailed him; and a smile—faint and flickering, indeed, but still a smile—dimpled his cheek and
lit up his eye. Though so feeble, Alice rejoiced at
the sight, and she laughed and talked away, and patted
her favourite pony's beautifully-arched neck, who, seeming
to share his mistress's pleasure, cantered along with greater
speed.

The appearance of the youthful pair at this time is dwelt
upon with delight by those who record the tale. The tall
and robust form, together with the proud bearing, the
lustrous eye, the noble and open brow of Scott, contrasted

finely with the fragile form and gentle manners of Alice. Her eye was bright too—bright with the brightness of love. Her smooth and snowy brow—her cheeks, tinted with the flush of health, like a kiss from the rose— her coral lips and pearly teeth,' served to make her the *beau ideal* of female perfection, as much as the strength and symmetry of his limbs, and the expression of his countenance told that he was "indeed a man." They both, in some sense, carried the peculiarities of sex to a degree of extravagance; he being stronger in manly pride than became a man, she softer in woman's weakness than became a woman.

The sun was at its meridian height when Scott and Alice reined up their steeds, and seated themselves beside the crystal waters of a fountain which ran murmuring and meandering through the grass and fern, and seemed sighing to the sweet harebells that grew upon its margin, which, when the breeze passed by, rang a merry peal in answer.

Many sombre fir-trees grew around, and stretched their roots far out, to draw in moisture from its sweet waters. It was under the shade of a clump of these trees that Scott and Alice sat; but the young laird was silent, and Alice vainly strove to enter into conversation. To all her questions he answered very briefly. She was looking upon the dancing waters which went rippling onwards beneath her feet in gentle wavelets, whose tops were sparkling like diamonds where the sunbeams fell upon them, when suddenly

Scott broke the silence with the expression, " Oh, Alice !"

" What would you, Tushielaw? why that word uttered in so mournful a strain? is Alice the cause of your melancholy?" exclaimed the maiden. "Tell me what I have done to bring such sorrow."

Scott, however, continued silent, but his eyes rested on his companion, with a steady yet mild look, and his heart beat so loudly that its throbbings could be heard.

"Is my crime then so enormous that it cannot be forgiven? speak—tell me—you set my heart upon the rack by your silence."

"I have nothing to forgive," replied young Scott: then, as if ashamed of his words, he continued, "Oh; would I had!—would that you had injured me deeply, that I might have much to forgive! But it is I who have to entreat pardon, for having dared to love. Alice, will you be mine?" He took her hand and pressed it respectfully to his lips.

Alice answered only by blushes. Her lips moved as if to articulate, but words would not come from them.

"My happiness, my glory," replied Scott impatiently, "nay even my life, depends upon you. Oh! say but yes, and here I vow to renounce all that the world holds precious. Wealth and ambition are but as feathers in the balance, when weighed with your love."

But still Alice remained silent. She looked up to the sky which like an azure zone belted in the earth, and then down on the waters of the fountain which were rippled by the gentle breeze, as if to find a thought from them, but in vain.

The eyes of Scott had followed those of Alice. He eagerly exclaimed, "Give me that which is symboled by these sunny skies and dancing wavelets. Make what request you will in exchange, and if mortal power can procure it, I will lay it at your feet. Only grant my boon!"

"What is that?" replied Alice.

"Look upon that azure arch without a speck, without a cloud,—everywhere deeply, beautifully blue, and these dancing wavelets as they flow on and on so gently: the one is the emblem of love; the other, of constancy. Give me but these, and I am blessed beyond the whims and caprices of fortune. Alice! Alice! you are very, very dear to me; all my hopes are centred in your love. Will you be mine?"

The heart of Alice beat "yes," but her thoughts wandered to her home, and she thought of her father; she knew his stern mould—she knew his pride, his ambition, and she feared to answer.

The young laird grasped the hand of the hesitating maiden and pressed it to his lips. "Speak, Alice! dear Alice, say but yes or no, but remain not silent."

Tears fell from the eyes of Alice in a copious stream, and she muttered a few broken sentences, but the only words she uttered distinctly were, "My father! my father!"

"Your father loves you too well to refuse anything that would make his daughter happy," replied Scott.

"Alas," exclaimed Alice, "I know his nature too well. But he may frown upon me, spurn me as he would a dog, heap curses upon my head, drive me from under his roof, still love I must—I am thine!" Overcome with her contending feelings, she fell senseless upon the grassy bank.

A deep cry, as if a voice were uttering "Woe! woe!" rose from the trees beneath whose shade they were seated, and immediately a raven of enormous size flew out, and, with a loud flapping of his wings, circled round and round above the heads of the lovers.

Young Scott, however, was too busily occupied in restoring the unconscious maiden, to notice the omen, which portended many and great disasters; but, after her death, he remembered the strange cry and the unusual flight of the bird.

The happiness of Tushielaw now seemed perfect: he had heard the wished-for sentence pronounced by the lovely Alice. He raised her from the ground, and let her head recline against his shoulder, and kissed her pale cheek a hundred times. Her blue eyes soon unclosed themselves, and colour came once more to her cheeks. Her father's anger seemed forgotten, and she thought only of her lover, whose arm was encircling her waist.

As they thus gazed upon one another, they seemed to forget that they were mortals: they seemed transported to a happier clime, and invisible spirits appeared to hallow the scene with their presence.

Such an event happens but once in a person's lifetime — there is something so pure and heaven-like in the heart's first love, before sorrow and worldly care have seared and hardened it. While the fervour and warmth of youth fan its fires, there is something, we say, holy and pure in such a love: it is the love of souls, burning, spiritual—such a love as perhaps angels enjoy in the abodes of celestial bliss. Such a love as this cannot possibly fade, cannot wane away. Like the flames of genius, it can only burn out by the intensity of its own fires. It is not like other loves—not such as the miser has for his gold, or the ambitious for the laurel crown, or the man of pleasure for the sparkling rosy wine: these are " of the earth, earthy;" but the love of young hearts—this is a flower fairer, more beautiful than any other which has root in this world

In vain, gray-headed philosophers, do ye assure us that the raptures of such a season are unreal and visionary—mere illusions of an over-heated imagination—mere freaks of fancy—as unsolid as the morning dew, and as soon dried up. In vain, sage men, do ye tell us that a love like this has no true pleasure—that it passes away like an unreal though beautiful dream, and, like a dream, is as soon forgotten. It may be a magic spell, a cabalistic ring which encircles young lovers, and the world's frown may break the enchantment, but the charm shall hold on till the end of life; and in old age they shall remember with pleasure that such a thing once was. It may be the delusions of imagination or the aspirings of hope; but hope gives man eagle's wings, by which he may leave this dull and care-consuming earth far behind; while imagination gives bright and fairy-like realms, where there are lovelier suns, and balmier breezes, and more glorious landscapes, than ever were given to earth. Happy are those who have this blissful period yet before them ! Happy, thrice happy, are those who, when it arrives, have a soul worthy of its enjoyment ! for it is a balm in saddest hours; and, though forsaken and desolate, there is a pleasure so great as almost to make misery happiness, in the thought of having once been an object of fervent love.

With hand clasped in hand the lovers sat trance-bound, seeming to think that earth had no sorrow, the heavens no clouds, and that life would be always the thing it then appeared. They pictured the happy times which were still in store for them—they talked of their future prospects, their sunny and enchanting hopes, and thus time imperceptibly stole on, and it was not until the shadows were thrown to the east that the lovers thought of returning home.

But the bright days which they had pictured to themselves were soon ended. The Earl of March, the father of Alice, was, as we have said before, proud and grasping; and he at once rose in arms to prevent the marriage of his daughter with the young Laird of Tushielaw. His proud soul rose indignantly at the thought that the son of a laird should think to wed the daughter of the Lord of Queensberry. "Do eagles mate with crows?" said the Earl, in the bitterness of his spirit, when first he heard that Scott and Alice were lovers. " I will let the young laird know that Alice has blood in her veins which would never mingle with his—no, not though poured into the same basin and stirred together. I would rather see her a corpse at my feet, than know that she had degraded my name by such a marriage. I could look upon her cold, still, dead, without a tear being drawn from my eye. I could see her nailed down into the narrow coffin, where there is neither sight, nor sound, nor motion, and yet not weep. I could follow her to the silent grave—ay, and think that corruption had dimmed the eye which had looked so fondly upon me, and that worms were feasting on those cheeks to which my lips had been pressed. All this, and more than this, I could do ; but I could not see her degrade my name—I could not see her wed a laird, without my heart boiling at the sight, and my lips uttering curses on the head of my child, —which God grant may never be breathed."

If the pride of the Earl of March was wounded, so were his hopes of further aggrandizement baffled. He knew well how lovely his daughter was; and he also knew well that the sons of the proudest nobles who dwelt in Scotland were captivated by the charms of her beauty. His aspiring mind had already pictured her as matched with one of the first families in the realm, and he almost raved at the thought of her giving her hand to the young Laird of Tushielaw. What was it to him that he claimed descent from the Border Kings! They had all been exterminated by James V. Young Scott inherited none of their power, none of their wealth ; and the thought, how fallen, and consequently how poor he was, was madness to the Earl.

" It must be broken off !" mused the Earl one day when alone. " She must see young Scott no more !—absence will dispel the girlish dream. It cannot be a very deep root her love has taken—the chain of affection is not very strong, the cord of love not very thick. To see Scott again, would only be to add another link to the chain which is drawing her to Teviot. She must see him no more!"

But though the Earl was bent upon limiting the rambles of Alice to the garden of Neidpath; though he was determined to sever the cord which bound her to Scott, even if in so doing he broke the poor girl's heart; yet he was not generally a cruel man, or a harsh father: his pride and ambition prompted him to the action, though his love for his daughter almost amounted to idolatry.

When her father communicated his determination to her, she listened without a murmur, and obeyed without an attempt to thwart her parent's will. There were no prayers, no entreaties, no shrieks, no hysterics, and a casual observer would have thought her perfectly indifferent.

But when she withdrew to silence and solitude, she threw off her seeming apathy, and the tears flowed freely from her eyes. Still she loved to be alone, that she might have him present in her memory—call to mind all his kind looks, all his fond words, all his noble actions.

It was with a bursting heart that Scott heard of the Earl's resolution. He cursed the proud and avaricious man, who, for the sake of honour or gold, could thus cleave hearts in twain. His own country became hateful to him; every scene, every spot, reminded him of her he had lost, and with bitter anguish he buckled on his sword and went forth to other lands.

From the day of her captivity the lily of the vale of

Tweed began to wither: life seemed to have no enjoyment. She read, or painted, or embroidered with her sister; but these occupations soon grew monotonous: her sole delight was to wander in her garden, trimming her plants and watering her flowers—and there, from morn till eve, she lingered, alone, companionless. Her form had lost its roundness; her cheek was as pale as the lily she tended; and the bones of her taper fingers might be seen beneath the smooth white skin which covered them. Her eye however, was, still bright and beaming, as if the heavens she loved to gaze upon had tinted it with their own bright blue.

She looked more like a spirit than a creature of earth; and as she moved along, her light feet seemed to pity the grass they pressed down, and the flowers appeared to rejoice in her presence, and to unfold their lovely colours wherever she came.

She was ever performing the actions of love, and if the flowers had been her children they could not have been watched with greater assiduity. She lifted the drooping with her gentle hands; sprinkled refreshing water on those which the sun had withered; and supported the weak with rods and bands.

She seemed the very emblem of gentleness, and, allured by her fond looks and fragile form, the wild things of the air grew enamoured of her presence. The glittering insects, as they floated in the breeze, displayed their glorious hues of purple and crimson, and, seeming like golden boats in a sea of ether, would buzz playfully above her head; and the honey-bee, ere it flew to its hive, would hum around her, as if to speak its thanks for the rich profusion of flowers her hands had nurtured; whilst the glorious butterflies, whose food is the nectar of the flower-cup, would alight on her arms and head, instead of passing to and fro from flower to flower; and those little blue ones, the tamest of their species, flitted round her feet, like attending spirits gamboling round their fairy queen. And the wild squirrel, which starts when the leaf rustles in the brake, would take its food from her harmless hands; and the turtle-dove, too, would come, and, after having partaken of her bounty, would coo its thanks, and fly to its wild woods again.

"Thou hast a mate, beautiful bird," poor Alice would exclaim, as her favourite returned to his native wilds. "Thou wingest thy flight to thy home, fond bird, where thy sweet mate will welcome thy return with eyes reflecting thine own pure love. She will welcome thy return with her affectionate voice, and will press her gentle head against thine, and fondly kiss thy bill. Thou mayest freely roam through the tangled woods, or skim the light and ambient air. And what, O what am I, that I should linger here? I have a voice sweeter and more melodious than thine; a spirit nobler than thine, outstripping thy most rapid flight; a face and form more beautiful; a heart more formed for love—I have affections, feelings, sympathies which thou knowest not: and here am I wasting these surpassing powers within these gloomy walls. There is no sound to answer when I speak, save the echo of my own voice, and it comes mockingly to my ears. I wander on alone, an isolated being, without a kindred spirit

to whom to breathe my thoughts, my hopes, my affections;
whilst thou mayest freely range wherever thou wilt, until
the sea and the heavens join to form thy utmost boundary."
This thought would often bring a pang to her heart, a quiver
to her lip, and a tear to her eye.

But when her father, as sometimes was his wont, came
to visit her beautiful flowers, she would run to welcome
him: a colour would come to her cheek, her eye would beam
more brightly, and a smile, faint, feeble, and flickering as a
taper's last gleam—but still a smile— would play upon her
countenance.

The smile was a balm to the Earl's heart, for he could
not but regard· his action as cruel. "It was as I thought,"
mused he; "her affections were not so firmly fixed—she
begins to smile again."

But, for all this, Alice grew worse and worse: walking
became a fatigue—her steps were slow and languid—her
cheeks grew hollow—her voice began to lose its musical
cadence, and she seemed wasting slowly. away.

The Earl grew alarmed—the sternness of the worldly-
minded *man* was giving away, and the tenderness of the
father returning. "What do you think of her?" asked he,
of his younger daughter, in alarm.

"The same as I did at the commencement, father," replied she: "that she has not forgotten him, and never will,
till death blot out all things from her remembrance."

"Death!" exclaimed the Earl, and in such a tone that his
daughter started at the sound. "Am I the murderer of my
daughter!—my gentle and affectionate child, who never gave

me a moment's pain, or thwarted my slightest wish? I said, indeed, that I would rather see her die than wed young Scott, but I cannot be her murderer. Fetch her hither, that I may see her—may tell her that my mind is altered, and that I will not oppose their union."

While his daughter was absent, the Earl thus reasoned with himself:—"It is very hard," said he, "very hard, that she must wed that young laird or die. I have tried all but one thing; if that fail, then will I give my sanction to this hateful union. Yes, I have heard of potions which cure the power of love; and of learned women, who, by weaving spells and making charms, drive it away from the hearts of their patients. I will try one of those sage women. What matters it whether she be a witch or not, so long as she effects a cure? But I will only try for a month—not a day, not an hour beyond, were a kingdom to be won by the delay."

Alice entered the room leaning upon the arm of her sister —but so thin, and wan, and wasted, that the Earl could hardly believe the evidence of his eyes, when he saw her advance with so slow, noiseless, and spectre-like a step. The momentary flush which suffused her cheek whenever he approached, the light elastic step with which she always advanced to meet him, had deceived her father, and he did not think, until this moment, that she really was so ill.

"Alice," said the Earl, in a broken and husky voice. She instantly left her sister's arm and went up to him. He took both her hands in his, and looked long and wildly in her face, scanning very carefully the pallid forehead—the sunken eye—the hollow check—the bloodless lip. "Alice," said he again, in a voice more husky, "you are ill, very ill; I knew it not till now, and I—I—." He could say no more, but pressing her close to his bosom, he sobbed aloud.

"My father!" said Alice, "do not weep; I am not ill—not so very ill—I feel no pain."

"'Tis of the heart, my Alice," said the Earl, as soon as he could speak, "and no medicine can remove its troubled thoughts—no physician can heal its wounds."

Alice fixed a wild, strange stare upon her father's face, as if she did not quite comprehend his words; the blood instantly rose to her cheeks, her eyes looked bright, and for a few moments she looked better in health and more beautiful than ever—but it was transient and evanescent, as the glowing tints a fitful sunbeam paints upon the snow-wreath, which returns at once to its native whiteness when the bright light is withdrawn. The blood retreated instantly, the light and loveliness fled, and nothing remained upon those features but a beauty resembling that of the sculptured marble.

The Earl, however, persisted in the resolution he had formed, and a few days afterwards the Castle of Neidpath received another inmate, in the person of Dame Esther MacAlpine. If age might be reckoned by years, she was old; but if by strength, she could hardly be said to have passed the prime of life. Though she had numbered sixty summers, she was still hale and hearty, and would have matched in strength and activity many whose years had not reached hers in number by nearly a score. She was well skilled in charms, and amulets, and spells ; and by all that knew her she was reputed a wise woman, though many hesitated not to affirm that she was leagued with dark and fiendish powers, and that if justice had its course the stake, would have another victim.

But, happily for Dame Esther, the rage against witches had subsided ; and though, when anything went wrong, many scrupled not to affirm that it was through the conjurations of this old woman, still she followed her occupation of weaving destinies, telling fortunes, and curing diseases by charms and spells, without the least interruption.

Her great power, however, lay in her love-charms, and she had at one time or other been an inmate of. most of the castles of the nobility near Pœbles. Many were the marriages which had been brought about by her means ; and many more had been broken off, when young and artless girls dared form an attachment which their parents disapproved.

Such was the woman whom the Earl of March appointed as the physician to his daughter, in the hopes that it would happen to him as it had to many other fathers, and that his child would be cured of her romantic love.

Dame Esther was, in reality, a wise woman ; she knew the secrets of the female heart ; she could follow passion and feeling in all their ramifications and windings—and she brought other powers to bear than the charmed stone or the bitter draught made out of herbs gathered at the dark hour of midnight. These were her ostensible means of cure; but the powers of oratory—the persuasion, the hint, the secret whisper, the half-supressed laugh at the folly, the raising of jealous thoughts, mention of the silent sneer with which the world would regard the action,—these had a more powerful effect than all her arts of magic; for the distillation of jealousy was more powerful than the henbane, and half-raised doubts, and well-timed suspicions, these warded off more love than ever did the charmed amulet or the most famed spell.

She was well prepared to encounter scorn and opposition —she knew that she should have to face them, and came well armed for the conquest; and there was not a spirit, however high or haughty, she had not brought down and subdued. And now in the Lady Alice she expected to meet with the same opposition she had always seen in the damsels she had cured. But in this she was mistaken. Alice was informed by her father that Esther had come to attempt her cure, and she was as passive as a child in the old woman's hands. Charm and spell had no effect upon her, potion and magic draught equally failed. No remonstrance, no insinuation or secret hint which the old woman threw out, had any power. The poison of jealousy failed to work, and Alice still remained as deeply and firmly in love as ever.

But still her health visibly declined: walking became so fatiguing that she seldom left her chamber; and even then, it was only to enter an adjoining room which was used as the work-room, the library, the—no matter what, to which the sisters retired, when either sought complete solitude, to sigh or weep, to hope or fear, to joy or grieve, as life and the things of life troubled or pleased them.

In furtherance of her object, Dame Esther had well versed herself in legendary lore. She could tell tales of disastrous loves—loves which had been consummated against the wish and will of parents. She could tell of omens which had been granted, sights which had been witnessed, evils which had been predicted to discourage lovers: but all had been unheeded!—all granted, witnessed, predicted to no purpose, save to imbitter after-life by the knowledge that they might all have been avoided, had a due regard been paid to the warning.

Such were the tales that Esther poured into the ears of the hapless Alice. The old woman would follow her into the library, and seating herself by her side, would take the hand of the love-sick girl within her own, and then recount the history of some unhappy maiden, whose heart had been gained by a romantic lover such as had won the heart of Alice.

The room was well chosen for such a subject. The sun's rays penetrated with a sombre glow threw the lattice, which was partly hidden by thick ivy. The hangings and furniture all wore. an antiquated and worm-eaten appearance; and grim and gaunt suits of mail hung against the wall, interspersed with swords, and lances, and battle-axes of ponderous size, giving a stern and somewhat sad appearance to the place. In the midst of these memorials of bygone years and of battle-scenes Dame Esther told her tales of blighted affections and unhappy loves.

At first Alice listened to the old woman's tales with pleasure: she felt interested in the fate of maidens who, like herself, had been struck down by the keen shafts of love. But when Esther sought to infuse jealous thoughts and doubts into her mind, she commanded her at once to be silent. Her very soul seemed to take fire, and she repelled the thought with scorn.

Here the old woman's skill was completely baffled. Charms and insidious speeches were equally unsuccessful: the arts which had proved efficacious on other occasions were of no avail; and, after trying all the means in her power, Esther was compelled to give up the task as hopeless.

The tales, however, when told without the biting inferences which Esther generally contrived to draw from them, somewhat raised the spirits of Alice. She loved to listen to stories of fairies—to deeds of gallant knights and high-born dames—to the love-songs of the Troubadours, and to accounts of wounded affection; but when the old woman turned upon her, then Alice became all ice and apathy, and she listened to the words as though she heard them not, or did not understand.

The month thus wore away, but Alice was no better. All that time she had been gradually wasting, and her face now wore the hue of death. Her eyes were intensely bright; but her cheeks were sallow and sunken, and the bloodless lip was now exchanged for livid purple.

The Earl could endure it no longer. "Alice," he exclaimed one day, "you are dying! I know you are

dying for the love of the young Laird of Tushielaw. I will
no longer oppose your union. Only live, promise me that
you will try to recover, and I will try to make life no hard-
ship. Oh! promise me that, or my brain will go distracted.
I shall be haunted everywhere by the spectral form of my
murdered daughter. The very winds as they rush through
the world will be burdened with the tale. Oh! promise me
to live, and I will set out for your lover this day—this hour."

"My father! my father!" said Alice, "life and death are
in God's hands. I will pray, and he will hear me: I feel—I
know—I am sure that I shall live."

The Earl folded his daughter in his arms, and kissed her
pallid forehead, and then rushing wildly from the room, before his daughter could arrange her fluttered thoughts he
was far up the glen on his way to the Teviot.

From that hour—from that moment, the Lady Alice did
really amend in health; she became more cheerful—her step
was more buoyant, and her face and features began to assume a more healthy appearance. Her father was overwhelmed with joy at the change, and he trusted that now,
when hope and fear had given place to certainty, the
presence of him she loved would save her life, and
snatch her, the young, the beautiful, the innocent, from the
dark and silent grave.

At length the day came which was to witness the return
of her lover. On the morning of that day Scott was expected to pass through the town of Peebles on his way to
Neidpath, to meet the object of his love—from whom he
had long thought himself separated for ever.

On that day Alice was up with the dawn. She had spent the night in dreaming of her lover, instead of enjoying calm and refreshing slumber; and this gave so wild and unnatural a look to her marble-like face, that her sister dreaded lest the approaching interview should prove too much for her strength.

Alice herself had no fear but that her lover would not come; or that, having arrived, he would be shocked by the traces of sickness, and would no more see in her pallid and sallow look the Alice of his love.

She would now braid her hair before a mirror—then arrange and re-arrange her dress—then, struck by a sudden thought, she would pause in consternation, and let the flowers and jewels fall from her hands.

Her sister did all in her power to calm and cheer the love-sick maid, conscious that her happiness—nay, even her life, depended upon this interesting day. But Alice could not remain idle for a moment: she flitted about from place to place, like a spirit that had been driven from its home. Her mind never seemed to rest, and her hand grew weary before the task she attempted to perform was half finished. She would take her lute and commence a lively air; then, changing her mind suddenly, would alter it to a mournful strain, as solemn as a death-dirge.

Her restlessness increased as the day wore on, and she at length declared that she would go to Peebles, and meet her lover there; and her sister, catching with eagerness at the girlish whim, in the hopes that the drive might amuse the mind of the invalid, ordered the carriage at once.

When at length they arrived at the castellated mansion of the Earl of March, in the town of Peebles, the two sisters took their stand on the balcony, which commanded a considerable extent of view.

Fatigued with her short drive, Alice leaned upon the balustrade, and gazed intently into the distance, though no one was visible. On a sudden her eyes kindled—they seemed to emit flashes of fire—she threw back her hair from her ears, and listened attentively.

"He comes! he comes!" she cried, at length, to her sister. "Hush! hark! Do you not hear the ring of his horse's hoofs, as they strike fire from the ground?"

"It is nothing, Alice," said her sister; nothing but the sound of the wind as it sweeps through the trees. You are fevered—you had better retire to the room."

"No, no," replied Alice; "it is his gallop—I would know it from an army of horses. Hush! hark!—there! Do you not hear?—and do you call that the sound of the wind?"

And now, indeed, the tramp of horses was audible. "I do certainly hear it at last, Alice," said her sister.

"I knew it!" said Alice; "he comes on—on very fast. 'Tis he himself! He comes! he comes! But, oh! if he should despise this wasted form!" Tears gushed from her eyes, and her whole frame trembled with emotion.

Young Scott pressed steadily forward. His heart—his whole soul was in Neidpath Castle, and his eye only rested casually upon the elder of the two ladies, as he passed the balcony.

Perhaps some secret sympathy, some shade of likeness, some recollection, made him bestow a more earnest glance than was due to a stranger. His thoughts, his longings, his hopes were all in Neidpath Castle; and in the wan and wasted countenance which he looked upon he recognised not the object of his love. He did not, could not know that she had come to Peebles to meet him. He turned away his head, without having slackened his pace. He passed on!

The effect upon Alice was as might have been expected. She neither shrieked nor swooned; she looked upon the retiring horseman a long, fixed, burning look, and then sunk down insensible. The single thread which bound her to life had been snapped—the sole tie which bound soul and body together was broken. The young girl was dead!

The Cat's-Paw.

I HAVE a deep respect for that dear sex,
　　Gallantly named, *par excellence*, the tender;
Though some are tough, and beaux and husbands vex
　　By their extreme reluctance to surrender.
　　I knew a damsel, on the prudent side
　　Of thirty, whose refined fastidious fancy
Was hard to please, and hence the dame defiéd
　　Ten years' assault;—'twas called the siege of Nancy:
Disdaining of her heart to yield possession,
　　She was as obstinate as Harry Tudor;
So, rather than surrender at discretion,
　　She married her tall footman John: *proh pudor!*

I crave the reader's pardon, though: confessing
I'm shamefully addicted to transgressing,—
And lamentably wanting in that ease
With which some plunge, *pêle mêle, in medias res.*
Yet to my subject: in my introduction
　　My deep devotion to the sex I cited;

And thus, for their particular instruction,
　　The apologue which follows have indited.

In some rich nabob's house, among a number
　　Of useless creatures, which the Scots call *flunkies*,
Was kept, to swell th' amount of living lumber,
　　An individual of the race of monkeys.
He was an ugly brute, as you'll suppose,
　　But not the less a coxcomb for all that;
　　For, with a visage as a pancake flat,
He piqued himself upon his Grecian nose!
He was a finished master in the art
Of flattery withal; and had a heart
　　As hard as was his native rock, Gibraltar.
His paws for ever were to mischief turned,
And, being a huge thief, he daily earned
　　An undisputed title to a halter.

Co-servitor with Jacko was a Pussy,—
　　A sly sleek-coated mouser—as demure
　　In look as though her velvet paws were pure
From midnight murders and stolen cream, the hussy!
But that, you'll say, was all in her vocation.
　　Most true, Sir Sage, but Rumour has divulged
　　That, 'spite of her demureness, she indulged
With Jacko in most scandalous flirtation.
'Twas matter, sir, of public notoriety ;—
　　They walked about together paw in paw,

As most *pas pas* it was, and 'gainst all law
Of animal decorum and propriety.

But what was most surprising, and, of course,
Made Pussy's indiscretions ten times worse,
  (Such conduct was of folly the quintessence)
She had three sons grown up to cat's estate,
Four marriageable daughters, besides eight
  In various states of feline juvenescence.
The cat loved flattery, and she had enough,
For Jacko crammed her with all sorts of stuff ;—
  Declared he never heard one sing so sweetly,
Alluded to her beauty with much tact,
Extolled her slender shape, her air,—in fact,
  Bamboozled Mistress Pussy most completely.

In Jacko's metaphysical formation,
  The aptitude for theft was most predominant ;
In truth, the organ of appropriation
  Rose on his cranium singularly prominent.
In one of his marauding expeditions,
Some chesnuts were among his acquisitions,
  Which, raw, are not so easy of digestion.
It chanced, too, that our monkey was dyspeptic,
And in the Abernethian code no sceptic,
  So how to cook them next became the question.
Not having near at hand a fork to toast them,
He placed them on the laundry stove to roast them.

This method answered just as he desired,
  While Jacko on his roast exulting looked ;
And, before twenty minutes had expired,
  No dish could possibly be better cooked.
He found them to the touch, though, far too warm,
  For one of his refined organization,
So cast about for one who could perform
  The task, as merchants sign, *per procuration.*
Now Jacko, never in expedients sterile
When his own precious person was in peril,
  Thought of his feline friend in his distress :
And straight the old sure game of flattery plied,
To coax our flirting Pussy to his side,
  And, sad to say, with most complete success.

Our monkey then began t' enact the lover,
  And squeezed her paw with fervour while he
    pressed—
  The cunning rogue !—her head into his chest,
The better from her eyes his aim to cover ;
Then gently stretched her paw towards the stove :—
" He used to prate about the warmth of love,
But this," said Pussy to herself, " beats all"
Next moment, though, a most emphatic squall
  Spoke her alive to Jacko's vile invention.
Stung by the monkey's baseness and the pain,
Puss turned on her betrayer, and the twain
  Came tumbling on the floor in fierce contention !

Our monkey battled stoutly—kicking, biting ;
　　While Puss with right good-will returned the loan :
I have remarked, though, when it comes to fighting,
　　That most of the dear sex can hold their own.
Puss knew his face was his most tender part,
And, plying her keen talons with much art,
Made sundry memoranda in red ink
On Jacko's visage, who was glad to slink
Back to his kennel, roaring mad with pain,
And never ventured to the *scratch* again ;
While Puss retired triumphant from the strife,
　　Though not without her portion of vexation :
She made a vow to lead a single life,
　　And—broke it on the very next temptation.

The Convent of St. Ursula.

T was near the close of a brilliant autumn day, that a solitary horseman, descending a mountain road seldom visited by travellers, and rough in proportion to its disuse, stopped at the door of a wretched posada, that seemed to possess few attractions for a guest of his apparent quality. But though the tenement itself was mean almost to repulsion, the rich province of Granada could boast few more lovely or romantic valleys than that where he had chosen to make his halt. The deep masses of forest trees, just tinted with the golden glow of the waning year, threw their broad shadows around the margin of a lake, where ever-flowing rills, that leaped fantastically from rock to rock, glided gracefully into repose beneath the slanting rays of the sunset. The luxuriant hills, scarcely yet denuded of the purple wealth that soared even to their summits; and the long line of shadowy mountains beyond, reflecting with diminished lustre rather than loveliness the bright radiance of evening; might well have atoned, to a less susceptible heart, for any lack of accommodation, in a country more celebrated for its scenery than its hospitality.   Yet the pause of the traveller, though his eye wandered eagerly through the valley, seemed actuated by some deeper feeling than mere enthusiasm. It was the glance of one whose soul was in his gaze.   In the absorbing interest of the moment he saw that object alone on which his eye was fixed, and he withdrew his attention only to pass into the house, whither the hostess, in some amazement, and even consternation, at so uulooked-for an arrival, hastened to attend him.   The trepidation of the poor woman was not diminished by a nearer view of her guest, whose dress, though travel-soiled, was rich in material, and whose form and manner were in a high degree commanding and dignified.   He was tall and eminently handsome; but though his years could not have numbered thirty, care or toil had already left traces on his cheek and brow even more indelible than those of time.   His first inquiries, in a voice of melancholy sweetness, were of a neighbouring convent.

"You might have seen the spires above the forest, señor," replied the hostess: "it lies but a short way behind those old cork-trees, and few there are that visit it now-a-days, except on some grand ceremony, like that of to-morrow."

"To-morrow!" repeated the stranger, in faltering accents —"What ceremony is this of which you speak?"

"One seldom witnessed at the Convent of St. Ursula, señor," replied the good woman; "though in my mind it is a sad sacrifice of a beautiful young lady: for if all be true that I have heard, God's light never shone on a fairer creature than that novice who is to take the black veil to-morrow."

"To-morrow!—and the black veil!" said the stranger, shuddering.

"It is even so," cried the hostess. "Her great wealth, no less than her loveliness, will bring the country from far and near to look on one who, in the flower of youth, can cast from her the golden gifts of fortune! But there is One who reads the heart, and hers, poor lady, may have been wrung."

"Know you her name?" demanded the stranger, hastily.

"Juana de Guidova."

He groaned, and struck his clenched hands on his fore-head with a violence that affrighted the poor hostess.

"Alas! I fear me these are bitter tidings for you, señor!"

"They are, indeed! but, brief as is the space, Juana, I will tear thee from thy bondage, ay, though it be even at the foot of the altar!"

"Saints and angels protect us, señor!—if you are come for aught but to witness the ceremony, you had better have been in your grave! The Abbess is a stern, proud woman, who will rather die than loose her grasp of a prize like the Lady Juana—one that can bring riches and fame to a poor, decayed convent; and, alas! were it not impious to wish—"

"I cannot reason it with you, hostess," returned the stranger, with a bitter smile; "I must see this Abbess, and that quickly. Expect me back to sleep—if indeed it be my fate ever to sleep again;—and let my good steed, I pray you, be cared for; he hath served me well at need, though something seems to whisper that I shall never mount steed more!" He waved his hand impatiently, as if to forbid reply, and walked rapidly forth in the direction of the convent. The hostess looked anxiously after him: "Poor gentleman!" she exclaimed, "he will run himself into danger; and all in vain! A true lover, I'll warrant him! but what can true love do against the power of the Church? The Abbess has a heart of stone, and Father Miguel is watchful and wary. Come what will, I must warn him of his peril, even though a heavy penance should be my only reward."

The stranger meanwhile pursued his way to the convent, now scarcely distinguishable, amid the closing shades of evening, from the dark foliage by which it was encompassed. On knocking at the gate, and inquiring for the Abbess, he was conducted, after a pause, to the parlour of the superior, who with some difficulty consented to give audience to a guest that declined to announce his name.

"You will pardon me, señor," cried the Abbess, coldly, "if I request you to be brief: there are yet arrangements to be completed for our holy rites of to-morrow, which at this time demand my undivided attention."

"I have a boon to ask," replied the stranger, faltering. "It is, to speak—for one moment only—but alone—with the Lady Juana de Guidova."

"Holy St. Ursula!" exclaimed the Abbess, raising her hands, "what impiety is this!—to break in on the awful communings of one devoutly praying to become weaned and purified from all earthly feelings, and longing for her acceptance as a bride of Him—"

"It may not be!" interrupted the stranger: "Juana is bound by vows, which not even the Church has power to unloose, to me, her betrothed husband! Her own breath alone can dissolve our solemn contract."

"What profane mocker art thou," cried the indignant superior, with flashing eyes, "who darest to impugn the power of the Church, and vainly seekest to withdraw from her saintly purpose one whose heart is irrevocably fixed on divine love? But it recks not who or what thou art—thy boon is rejected; and as thou wouldst escape the vengeance due to a scoffer at holy rites, begone, ere the hour of mercy be past!"

"Of mercy!' repeated the stranger scornfully; "say rather of cruelty unexampled, of treachery unparalleled; but not, I trust in Heaven, of craft or force to consummate thy unholy will. Know me, proud Abbess, for one fearless of thy power, and resolute to defeat thy purpose. Ere the command of our Emperor claimed my devoted service on the distant plains of war, Juana was affianced to me, in the presence of her deceased father, by the hand of a venerable priest, who yet lives to avouch our hallowed contract. My long absence and reported fall may have aided a belief that her vows were absolved by death; but when she knows that I live, live to demand the fulfilment of her promise—"

"It is too late!" cried the Abbess, with vehemence: "the Church has power to bind and to loose! and potent as you may deem yourself, Alphonso de Mondemar—for I know you now—you have yet to learn, that the weak woman who stands before you is stronger in the delegated service of Heaven, than you, the favoured servant, it may be, of the mighty Charles! Be wise, therefore, in time, lest I denounce your impiety to the Grand Inquisitor, whose will not our righteous Emperor himself dares dispute. Were he in presence—"

"Behold his signet!" cried Mondemar; "his mandate requiring you to deliver up Juana, on pain of forfeiture!"

"It is an imposture!—he has been deceived!" interrupted the superior, with increasing vehemence: "our gracious Monarch is too fast a friend of holy Church to dispute her decrees. But were he now before me, I would tell him, that, sovereign as he is, there is a power superior to that even of God's Vicegerent upon earth—a power derived from Heaven alone, whose vengeance, Mondemar, you would do well to avoid."

"Say rather that I will brave; ay, at the foot even of the altar, whence Mondemar will rend thy devoted victim, or perish in the attempt."

The Abbess involuntarily trembled as she listened to the denunciations of one inflexible as herself, and potent in the favour of a mighty Monarch; yet her eye blanched not, her brow relaxed not; and Mondemar, perceiving the hopelessness of expostulation with a being wholly devoted to the interests of her order, looked his defiance, and departed.

The indignation that had excited and sustained him during his interview with the Abbess faded into doubt and dread as he slowly retraced his steps towards the posada. He knew too well the power of the Church, more especially in a remote valley, to hold the threats of the superior lightly. Aid was distant and uncertain; the danger pressing and imminent. Foreign as it was to the high-souled impulses of his nature, he now regretted that he had not endeavoured to oppose art to art; to have gained by gold or daring some means of at least apprising Juana that he yet lived and loved. He trembled to meditate on the effect that the surprise even of joy might produce on so sensitive a frame; yet to hope that now, when the suspicions of the Abbess were roused, and her vigilance alarmed, he could succeed in gaining access to Juana, was beyond even the sanguine expectation or enterprise of a lover. Yet still he lingered in faltering irresolution, lingered till a deep and heavy step warned him of the danger of discovery. Silently and stealthily he then sought a neighbouring thicket, whence the thick enshrouding darkness only enabled him to perceive the dim outline of a shadowy figure that passed hastily onward. "Some homeward-bound peasant, probably," he exclaimed. "O that I could change destinies with one who, if he hath not wealth, power, or nobility, is far richer in contentment, lowliness, and love, that precious balm and solace of existence! O Juana! that with thee I might retire to some humble cottage, some peaceful vineyard, far from the reach of worldly cares or riches! Through the shelter of this night even might I have borne thee, but for my fatal rashness, swiftly and securely. Why not now? Yet no; 't were hopeless to expose myself, or that sweet deluded one, to the vindictive rage of the Abbess. In the face of day only must I confront our foes, and trust in Heaven to uphold the right."

It was with difficulty that he retraced his route to the posada; the darkness of the hour, increased by an impending storm (the distant thunders of which were heard to tremble along the mountains) preventing all recognition of the path by means of external objects. Large heavy rain-drops began now also to patter among the leaves; and he had probably been overtaken by the tempest, but for the care of his good-natured hostess, who placed a lamp at her door, which served as a beacon to his uncertain steps. She met him on the threshold. "There is one within awaiting you, señor," she said, in a low voice; "the confessor of the convent, Father Miguel. He pretends much good-will towards you; I pray Heaven he may be sincere! but trust him not too far."

Mondemar, murmuring his thanks, yet musing on so singular a warning, passed on to the inner apartment, where he was saluted by an aged ecclesiastic, with an air of humility too strongly contrasted with the haughty demeanour of the Abbess not to excite suspicion as to the sentiment which so unlooked-for a deportment might express. The monk was a thin, spare man, whose deeply-lined features seemed rather to speak of the austerities of his religious practice than of the ravages of time, though he was evidently declining into the vale of years. His looks were meek and lowly, and his hand was placed on his breast, as if to denote the sincerity of his vocation.

"Your blessing, father!" exclaimed Mondemar, with a sullen inclination of the head: "how may I have deserved this late visit from so holy a man?"

"By your misfortunes, my son, your unmerited misfortunes," replied the monk, with an air of sympathy. "I grieve to know that I am weak in power, though strong in will, to aid you."

"My misfortunes, father?" cried Mondemar.

"I have not to learn, my son," interrupted his companion; "in fact, I know the purport of your visit to our convent. I know also its unsuccessful termination. To me, as father confessor to the community, the Abbess has divulged all that passed; and I lament that you have been seduced into the utterance of threats as vain as irreverent."

"Father," replied Mondemar, "on this head I am impenetrable as adamant: if you know my wrongs, if you are apprised of the arts which would tear from me one bound by vows which Heaven alone can absolve, you must feel that I have now no choice but in the face of Heaven to claim from my deceived Juana a renunciation of oaths which it were impious even to administer."

"My son," interrupted the monk, "a cause may be just, but if rashly urged—"

"What other course remains?" said Mondemar, with vehemence. "Your Abbess has defied me—has denounced, as the most flagrant profanation, my request to see or communicate with the Lady Juana, who will be lost to me unless redeemed by that one bold act which you stigmatize as rash and irreverent."

"I would," said the old man, mildly, "that I had the power to join your hands; but I can only pray that right may prevail, and counsel you to a reliance on above as your best stay: for what, alas! is all mortal wisdom but weakness and folly?"

"We must use the means vouchsafed to us, father," returned Mondemar. "We must act by that light which Heaven hath permitted; and those means—that light—impel me—

"Yet, my son," interrupted the confessor, "the counsels of age not vainly temper the fervour of youth. I will own to you, our superior is firmly bent that the Lady Juana shall become a nun. The wealth, the distinction, I may confess, which our house will acquire by the intended rite, are too alluring to be easily abandoned; and the zeal of the Marquis D'Aranda—the guardian of our novice, and her near relation—in the same course, renders all opposition nearly hopeless. Yet, my son, if I have not power, save by those gentle, admonitory breathings, which, like the airs of heaven, steal softly and sweetly to the heart, these humble aids shall not be wanting to awaken a purer feeling."

"Father!" cried the drooping Mondemar, "my spirit sickens at such aids, which seem to me but unavailing fantasies."

"Fantasies call you them!" said the friar, reddening. "But you are wet and travel-worn, and the inward man requires to be sustained no less in strength than in spirit. Within there, hostess? Wine, wine and viands!—You are faint, my son, from exhaustion: take freely—your fare, though rude, is salutary. Come, my son!" he continued, seizing a drinking-cup; "follow the example of an old man, who, for your sake, will this once indulge in the generous juice of the grape. You have need of its exhilarating influence. "Why! how now, daughter?" he exclaimed, angrily;—"you have spilled, by your carelessness, a portion of the wine I had poured out for your guest."

"Your pardon, Father Miguel," said the hostess, submissively; "I will bring in another flask."

"How! would you waste the remainder?" demanded the monk, angrily: "thus disregarding the sin of misusing the gift of Heaven."

"I will not tempt her to rebel," said Mondemar, raising the cup, and hastily swallowing its contents. In the abstraction of the moment, he had not marked the changed and excited features of the monk—an excitement altogether disproportioned to the occasion; but he now regarded with no less astonishment the inflamed countenance of the self-subduing friar than the mournful and disappointed looks of the hostess. The monk, perceiving this effect, so contrary to his desires, hastened to reassume his meek and humble port; but, finding that other feelings than those which had marked their latter conference now possessed the bosom of Mondemar, he murmured something of the lateness of the hour, and rose at once to depart. "I must to my sacred calling, and chiefly to labour, not, I would fain hope, without success, in your cause. But, be that issue as it may, depend on me as your true friend and advocate; one who can at least prepare the Lady Juana for your unexpected appearance, should you still persevere in that public appeal, which, as a servant of the convent, no less than a minister of religion, I would yet deprecate, as tending to scandal and disgrace on our holy Order. Yet I pray that Heaven may order it otherwise, and that those who have dared to outrage the sanctity of holy vows may be fearfully punished."

"Father, if I am to depend on your words—"

"Say rather on my deeds!" cried the retreating monk; "for it is only on these that I rely." He lifted his hands above the bending form of Mondemar, and slowly retired with the hostess, with whom he remained some time in deep conference.

Exhausted alike in mind and body, the hapless lover sought a restless couch, where, sometimes in insensibility, but scarcely in sleep, the hours of night passed slowly on. If slumber at any time visited his over-wrought frame, the fearful visions of an excited and distempered imagination destroyed its balmy influence; wild creations of fancy, combining with real yet uncertain fears, awakened his sensitive spirit to transitory horrors, but too well aided by the convulsions of the elements. At one moment he beheld Juana in the power of an exasperated inquisitor, condemned to the tortures that await a relapsed nun; while he, spell-bound and powerless, was denied the use of speech and motion. At another, he seemed to be flying with her from the pursuit of her persecutors, whose steps he distinctly heard gaining rapidly on them. Again, he stood with her on the brink of a precipice, from which she was hurled by an unseen hand, shrieking for help, while he remained in impotent despair.

Now they were abandoned to the fury of wild beasts; and now were hurried to the flames kindled to avenge their delinquency to the mandates of the Church. It was from a dream of hopeless imprisonment within walls never again to unclose, with the cry of the fainting, dying Juana still ringing in his ear, that he suddenly awoke to a consciousness of life and liberty. It was morning, and a morning of great beauty. Hill and dale, field and forest, glistened alike in tearful loveliness, as each slowly kindled into light and animation beneath the smiling sunbeam and the freshening breeze. Mondemar only arose pale, languid, and dispirited. He looked from the lattice with an anxious eye on the crowds already assembling to witness the gorgeous spectacle which the profession of a noble and wealthy novice offered to their curiosity.

"Yes!" he exclaimed, with a bitter smile, "it is time that I also should nerve myself to that effort which must terminate in rapture or despair! It is time that I should throw off this torpid feeling that presses on my heart, and gird up my limbs and my spirit, to abide the issue of my fate!—Why look you so strangely on me?" he cried, as the hostess clasped her hands in seeming terror on meeting his morning salutation.

"Holy Mother!" she replied, "you are ill, señor, and, I fear—"

"What, my good hostess?" said Mondemar, faintly smiling.

"That which it were vain even to speak," answered the trembling dame, "even if I dared. Yet go not to the convent, señor;—it will be vain; it is but rushing into danger."

"Nay, but I have a friend there in the holy confessor."

"A friend!" repeated the hostess, crossing herself. "One moment only, señor : if you will go, trust not in aught but your own true heart; and may He who upholds the virtuous give you good deliverance."

Mondemar looked, as if to demand an explanation of her warning, but the hostess had already retired within her own dwelling, and he passed languidly onward among the smiling groups, who gazed with wonder on one unmoved by the general festivity. It was not that his resolution was less firm, his hope less vivid;—his frame alone, that frame which had defied the fatigues, the perils of war, now shrunk from the impending crisis on which his future destiny depended. Yet, feeling the necessity of exertion, he rallied his fainting strength, and, mingling with the throng, entered the chapel of the convent where the ceremony was to take place, seemingly unrecognised, and certainly unmolested. Seeking the shelter of a massive pillar, where unseen he could thence command a full view of the altar, he looked anxiously around for the father confessor; but, though he once thought that he perceived the monk looking warily on the assembled multitude, he was either deceived, or the monk eluded discovery by immediately retiring. In the meantime the throng gradually increased, till the chapel was entirely filled, excepting the space kept apart for the performance of the ceremony. At length the pealing organ woke on the listening ear, the voices of the nuns arose in one triumphant strain, and the novice, preceded by the Archbishop, who was to receive her vows, and the superior, decorated with the insignia of her office, advanced towards the altar. Her guardian, the Marquis D'Aranda, and a train of attendant nobles, slowly followed.

With intense, with almost overpowering interest, did Mondemar gaze on the mistress of his affections, his betrothed, his chosen bride;—on one who believed him to be no more, who was to listen to his voice as to a voice from the dead;—on one who was to seal his bliss, or confirm his despair. Now, now was the hour for effort; and now he felt his strength, his resolution, yield to a torpor unknown till this fatal moment. He gazed on her as in a bewildered dream, from which he vainly endeavoured to awake. Juana looked pale, yet calm; her eye was tranquil, but it was the tranquillity of extinguished hope:—she smiled, but her smile was beamless. Her obedience seemed the yielding of an unresisting or uninterested victim, rather than the eagerness of an aspirant for divine love. The impassioned, the elevating principle, that, soaring from earth to heaven, rapturously embraces the self-interdiction that bars a return to an abjured world, Juana knew not. Hers was the meek submission of one who delegates to others the exercise of that will which seeks only to hide a blighted heart in silence and seclusion. . Yet, pale, passionless as she looked, never had Juana appeared so lovely in the eyes of Mondemar as at the moment when he beheld her, as it were, snatched from his powerless grasp. His eyes grew dim;—he scarcely saw the severing of those lovely locks which at their parting he had adorned with a chaplet of pearls, the last offering of his love ;—he scarcely beheld her cast aside the rich jewels, those vain symbols of her former state, which she was about to resign for ever;—he heard not the inaugural discourse of the Archbishop, nor marked the glance of hatred and alarm which the haughty Abbess threw around the chapel as the fatal ceremony commenced. But when the vow, the irrevocable vow, fell tremblingly on his ear, and the faint response of Juana faltered on her lip, life, power, and energy seemed rushing through his veins like the vivid blaze of an expiring flame. "Juaná! Juana!" he exclaimed, in a voice that thrilled to every heart, "forbear!— thy vows are mine—mine, thy betrothed husband's—the living, the faithful Mondemar's !"

"Mondemar!" repeated the shrieking Juana; "am I awake !—do I look on thee !—or is it but a fantasy of the Deceiver to wean me from my holy purpose ?"

"No, no ! thy purpose is unholy—is impious !—thou art mine—mine only!" continued the frantic Mondemar, rushing forward, regardless of the stern denunciations, or the impeding multitude that would have barred his progress. It was a noble but an expiring effort. Even as he reached the fainting Juana he met the glance of the confessor, a glance of almost demoniacal rage; and, as he fell in the agonies of death, of horrid triumph. It revealed to his awakening sense the source of those pangs which were consuming his vitals. The crafty friar had mingled poison with his wine ; poison so deadly, that, but for the well-intentioned but vain stratagem of the hostess, it had numbered him with the dead ere the morning rose.   "Juana! we meet but to part," cried Mondemar faintly, as the last agony dimmed his sight and speech; "yet to hold thee once more in these arms—to impress this last kiss on thy cold lips—to die in thy dear embrace!—yes, there is bliss even in death! Look on me, sweet!—speak but one word to the expiring Mondemar—tell him that he was still loved, and that treachery alone—but I grow faint—"

"Mondemar!—my love!—my husband!" cried the heart-stricken Juana, "you must not.die; these lips shall yet breathe life. Oh, had I but known! Cruel, cruel that ye were," she exclaimed, turning to D'Aranda and the Abbess, to deceive me thus! Has Heaven no thunderbolts—has earth no justice?"

"Yes!" cried the Emperor, suddenly entering the chapel, while the terrified superior and her guilty instrument quailed before his frown, "you shall have such justice, Mondemar, as no less befits my regal oath than my gratitude to a brave and worthy servant."

"It is too late," murmured the dying Mondemar; "but for this sweet innocent—let her not be compelled to utter vows—"

"My vows are thine, Mondemar, thine only!" cried the frantic Juana, clasping her expiring lover to her bosom; "in life or death we will not part."

He pressed his lips to hers by a convulsive effort; looked one moment upward, and expired! They hastened to unclasp the living Juana from his grasp. She waved them off, and gazing wildly at those distorted features which had only beamed on her with love and tenderness, turned to the Monarch, as if to demand vengeance on his destroyers. The Emperor seemed to understand her silent appeal, and at a glance the trembling Abbess and the conscience-stricken confessor were led away guarded. A smile of exultation lightened for an instant the brow of Juana; she clasped her hands, sunk on the silent corse, and in one wild sob her spirit fled for ever!

The Frosty Reception.

RANK FURROWFIELD was one of the six sons of a substantial yeoman in Kent. He was a genius, and, happily, the only one in his family. He soon began to furnish evidence of a superior mind, by the original manner in which he acquitted himself of the duties that he appeared to have been brought into the world to perform. His father requiring his services at the farm, he was taken early from school, where, to do him justice, he made the most of his time, seeing that, before he was twelve years old, he had read Robinson Crusoe, the Seven Champions, and the Farmer's Boy; and had Chevy Chase, Robin Hood, and other interminable ballads, by heart.

His first employment was to tend a herd of cattle, and take care that they did not break bounds ;—a task which he executed in such a way that his father had frequent demands upon his pocket, for their release from a certain narrow enclosure to which some good-natured neighbour or other had consigned them.

In due course he was promoted to the handles, or, as our northern countrymen designate them, the stilts of the plough. Here he contrived to achieve that combination of the *utile et dulce* of which he sagely imagined rural life to be peculiarly susceptible, by constructing a sort of reading-desk in the wood-work of the implement, and thus making the culture of the earth and that of his mind concurrent operations!

The system was admirable, but, like every other of human origin, it had its defects : in illustration of which it may be mentioned, that he was one day so absorbed by his literary, as entirely to forget his agricultural pursuits ; while the urchin who drove the horses, taking advantage of the mental absence of his young master, absconded in search of birds' nests ; and Frank, unconsciously following the plough through a gap in the hedge, contrived, before he discovered the mistake, to convert into fallow half an acre of growing corn belonging to a neighbour ; who acknowledged the obligation through the medium of his attorney on the following morning.

Old Furrowfield bore these indications of genius in his son with exemplary patience, till at length Frank suffered himself to be shot through the heart by a dairy-fed Cupid, and fell in love with the milkmaid.

The votary of Apollo has no business at the altar of Hymen, and so probably thought the farmer, who, determined to remove his son from the farm at all hazards, encouraged a design which Frank had for some time entertained of proceeding to London, and making his fortune at once by a poem, the composition of which had cost him six months' labour and his father three actions of trespass.

It happened that Frank had a maternal uncle, living in London, where he had acquired a large fortune in trade. Now, as our hero would at any time have been happy to see his relative, he naturally concluded that his relative would be equally overjoyed to see him. Frank accordingly obtained an elaborate letter of introduction from his mother, set out for London, and presented himself at his uncle's door in high spirits.

Mr. Doublepenny, (such was the worthy trader's name,) had been very successful in the pursuit of civic honours, and ate his way to the gout and a common-councilman's gown before he had attained his fortieth year. He was remarkable for his dislike of French wines, and his affection for everything English, but small beer and the pure element. Indeed, it is said that the aversion of the citizens generally to the crystal spring is absolutely hydrophobic, and that, if it were their lot to walk on four legs instead of two, not one of them would escape hanging in the dog-days. This, however, is a gross exaggeration, for I have it upon excellent authority that on one of their grandest festivals they take water every year at Blackfriars.

"Is Mr. Doublepenny at home?" inquired Frank of the servant who opened the door.

"The *Deputy*," answered the woman, laying a reproving emphasis on the word, " is at home, but he can't see nobody."

"Poor gentleman!" exclaimed our hero, much shocked, " is he so ill then?"

"Ill? no," replied the other, "he is quite well now; but I tell you again you can't see him, for he is at dinner."

"Does he dine in the dark then?" asked Frank with great simplicity.

"Dine in the dark? no!" responded the damsel; "but master don't like to be interrupted at meal-times, and won't see nobody."

"None are so blind as those who won't see," exclaimed the applicant; "but tell him that his nephew Frank Furrowfield is just arrived from the country, and would be glad to speak with him."

The maiden returned to her master, closely followed by Frank, who had misunderstood her direction to take a chair in the hall till she should come back, and thus enjoyed the satisfaction of hearing his message duly delivered. The sudden retreat of his conductress, on perceiving the mistake which he had committed, rather damped his expectations of a welcome from the worthy Deputy, with whom he now found himself face to face.

Mr. Doublepenny, be it observed, had been laid up with the gout for six weeks, during which his heels had been as much upon the pillow as his head. Having at last been permitted to abandon the antiphlogistic system, he was, as Frank knocked at the door, sitting down to one of his favourite dishes, and had just raised the first morsel upon his fork, when the entrance of his visitor arrested it *in transitu.*

The most lordly and magnanimous of brutes has an objection to being disturbed at his dinner, and our Deputy was less patient of intrusion on such occasions than any brute of them all. Had a ghost or his physician suddenly appeared and commanded him to abstain from the untasted banquet, he would scarcely have met with a more "frosty reception" than our hero encountered.

The Deputy eyed the intruder for some time with an expression of countenance in which astonishment and displeasure were blended. At length recovering the power of utterance, he inquired: "And what, pray, may be the urgent nature of your business with me, young gentleman, that it could not keep until to-morrow morning?

Frank briefly explained the purport of his visit to London, when his relative exclaimed, "And is that all! why I thought nothing less than that the farm-house, barn, stack, and stable, had been burnt to the ground, or swept off by a hurricane. Do, pray, young man, allow me to eat the only dinner I have seen for these six weeks in peace; and, as you perceive it is getting cold, just write down your address in the next room, and I will let you know when it will be convenient for me to see you. Good day, sir."

Frank, who, in the confusion of the moment, had forgotten his mother's letter of introduction, took it from his pocket, and, having placed it on the table, hastily withdrew.

Before, however, he quitted the house, he was, by the direction of the Deputy, sumptuously regaled on bread and cheese and small beer; which latter luxury may be compared to advice, inasmuch as it is often very liberally dispensed to others by those who will, on no account, be prevailed on to take it themselves.

Frank, having finished his repast, quitted the house, notwithstanding the thinness of his potations, with an internal conviction of being "the worse for liquor." But, like the writer of this article, he was a moderate man, and never drank a tumbler of table-beer without feeling that he had taken a glass too much.

. On the following morning, our hero, whose experience of London relationship, it must be acknowledged, had not been the most encouraging, determined to fling himself upon the mercy of the booksellers, and accordingly, MS. in hand, he made the grand tour; in the course of which he received every possible civility, for publishers are the most obliging creatures upon earth, particularly in the way of refusals. As, however, it is difficult to meet with one disposed to purchase an article without some slight prospect of being able to sell it, poor Frank returned to the Smithfield Hotel with his poem on his hands, and a strong suspicion on his mind, that, like another man of genius, who marched to Moscow and found the element hotter than he expected, he had " made a mistake."

While he was ruminating on his disappointment, a note was brought to him from his uncle, requesting to see him at a certain hour that afternoon. Although he felt little gratitude for the Deputy's reception on the preceding day, Frank could not afford to throw away the chance of assistance, and therefore obeyed the summons.

On entering the house, his nostrils were saluted by a very tantalizing odour of roast beef. He was shown up to the Deputy, whom he found seated by the fire, while his afflicted toes, having been divested of some dozen folds of flannel, had insinuated themselves into a slipper not more than twice the size of his shoe. Matters were evidently upon an improved *footing*, for Mr. Doublepenny, with the assistance of his crutch, regained his legs, and, shaking his nephew by the hand, complimented him on his punctuality, and added, that he had a few words to say to him, which, as dinner was just coming to table, he would defer until they had discussed the beef.

When the cloth was removed, the Deputy gravely asked which fare he preferred ; the bread and cheese and small beer with which he had been regaled on the day before, or the roast beef and plum-pudding which had just graced the board.

Frank replied, that his choice certainly rather pointed to the roast beef.

"And now," said the Deputy, "let us see the—epic I think you call it;" and as his nephew was unfolding it, he continued, " Nay, you need not trouble yourself to open it, the first page will do. Ah ! a very fair running hand, I protest."

While our hero was speculating upon what the city dignitary would observe next, the latter resumed the conversation by saying :—

"Your mother, in her letter, I see, places some reliance upon my good offices for you ; and she has a right to do so, as, when I quitted home to seek my fortune, she doubled my capital by slipping half a crown into my hand, while her sisters would have sold me into slavery, if they could have gained a cast gown or a new ribbon by the bargain. Now, it happens that I have just lost my clerk, and, if you like to fill the vacancy, I think you will find the employment more profitable than writing epics."

Frank expressed his gratitude for the offer, but modestly hinted a doubt of his qualifications for the office.

"As to that," said Doublepenny, "I see you write a tolerably good hand, and your mother says you have some knowledge of figures, while, in anything else you may require to know, I can probably instruct you."

Observing Frank to glance at his somewhat rustic habiliments, the Deputy added, "I know what you would say : your coat is a little out of fashion, to be sure; but, if you determine on declining business as an author, I will purchase your stock in trade for fifty pounds, and I apprehend you will scarcely meet with a better bargain for your epic, either in 'the Row,' or at the 'West End :' so make up your mind, man, and choose between a crust in a garret and a hot joint with me in the parlour."

Alas! I record the sequel with a blush : Plutus prevailed over Apollo; the ignoble bard basely consented to sacrifice his literary first-born, which was accordingly bought, and burned by the Deputy; and thus, in the poet's eye, "in a fine frenzy rolling," the temple of Fame was eclipsed by a sirloin of beef!

The Deputy, I am informed, has since taken his nephew into partnership, and plumes himself on having made a trader and spoiled a poet.

The Sacrifice.

HE earliest beams of the rich sun of an eastern morning changed the crystal waters of the Nerbuddah into living gold, as the broad bright river caught the gorgeous ray on its clear, untroubled bosom. How lovely and how tranquil seemed the delightful valley, enriched by the ever-flowing springs of that fertilizing stream! and how beautiful a contrast did its verdant surface present with the dark and wild chain of the Goand Mountains which stretched almost around it! Not a trace was now visible of the desolating track of the fierce Pindarries, whose predatory incursions into that and the surrounding districts had till lately been made with the regularity of the harvests, which twice in the year the generous soil presented, almost spontaneously, to the inhabitants. Terror preceded and the most wanton devastation followed the march of these organized freebooters; for, not content with merely sweeping the flocks and herds of the defenceless people, they applied various species of torture to the young, the aged, and the feminine, in order to extort a discovery of the places where it was supposed they had, in anticipation of the inroad, concealed their more valuable and portable effects. The villages were destroyed by fire, after they had been ransacked even to nakedness; and the cool murder of children, with the violation of the females, were the usual concomitants of plunder and destruction. Such were the fruits of the wretched policy adopted by the Mahratta princes regarding the internal security of their dominions, and such the miserable situation of their deserted subjects, till the humane, wise, and energetic exertions of the Marquis of Hastings put an end to that singular system of lawless depredation, which had for so long a period of years devastated the fairest and the most fruitful tracts of India.

So complete had been the extirpation of the whole race, and so sudden the blessed effects of security, that in the beautiful valley connected with our tale not a trace was now discernible of the devastation caused by those fierce intruders; whose steps, but two years before, might have been too easily traced by the smouldering ruins which marked their ruthless progress from their own wild abodes, along the whole extent of the now fair and smiling valley. That dark and blood-stained host had for ever disappeared; and in the neighbouring topes or groves of thick-leaved mango trees, and under the shade of the widely-spreading and magnificent banian, which erected its green and curious colonnades near to a peaceful dwelling, that lay half-sequestered amid groups of the plantain, and partly shadowed by the lofty tufts of the stately palmyra, nought

was to be seen more wild or savage than the troops of
sacred monkeys, frolicking among the branches; and
flocks of beautiful paroquets, which delighted and dazzled
the eye as they flew from one part of the grove to
another, or plumed their variegated wings in the sunshine. The young Heena, advancing from the door of
her father's lowly dwelling, surveyed the peaceful scene
with a happy and a grateful heart. She had known
the grief of the late insecurity, and her father, an
old soldier in the service of the Rajah of Nagpore, had
been severely wounded in the defence of his native village
against the bands of the spoiler: but these sorrows had
ceased, and, young and sanguine, both hope and joy had
resumed their natural places in her breast; and she fondly
trusted that thenceforward the path of life would be as
brilliant, and strewed with as many flowers of pleasure, as
the sunlit and highly luxuriant vale around her. She contemplated with calm and thankful pleasure those flocks and
herds, which, preserved from the Pindarrie raids, now
promised to secure a future competency to the beloved
family so lately on the brink of irremediable destruction;
and she reposed with fearless confidence upon the security
afforded by the vigorous measures of the Company's government, and the vicinity of her present residence to Nagpore,
the capital of the kingdom, for the permanence of the tranquil state which had happily succeeded fearful periods of
alarm, havoc, and bloodshed. Still, the smile which
occasionally played around the rich, soft lip of the beautiful
and modest girl, and which illuminated her full, dark, and

tender eye, had in it a pensiveness which gave to it a character of needless melancholy;—at least so thought those who could not perceive the cause of uneasiness in a scene and a person of such sweet serenity. Her yet budding bosom, like the wave but newly lulled to rest, heaved at intervals with greater emotion than could easily be concealed by the folds of the graceful saree, the light and negligent, but not neglected drapery of which partially enveloped a figure light and elastic in its movements, and exquisite in its elegantly rounded proportions. With gentle, yet convulsive swells, the remembrance of former misfortunes would intrude, if not absolutely to darken, at least to cloud, the felicity of the present prosperous hour. She thought, and a tear glistened the while in the long black lashes of her drooping eyelids, of the idolized brothers and sisters, who one by one, by some awful and sudden calamity, had been swept away in the pride of their youth, or the innocence of their childhood; and many and bitter were the floods of sorrow she had wept over the pale corses of those gentle relatives, too early hastened to a violent dissolution. The fierce assault of the treacherous hyena, the more awful grip of the wary alligator, the quick-working poison of the cobra de capella, and the base dagger of the remorseless assassin, had at different, but shortly distant periods, been fatal to her nearest relatives; and two brothers, with herself, who was the eldest offspring, alone survived out of a fair and numerous family, who had gladdened the warm hearts of their anxious parents, and promised to excel in manly bravery and feminine loveliness.

Heena's grief was also renewed and perpetuated by the painful solicitude of her mother's watchful eye, which tearfully followed every movement of those beloved children who still remained, and for whose safety she suffered incessant and agonizing, but unexplained apprehensions. Yet the brightly variegated sky, the dancing, pearly waters, the glowing landscape, and, above all, the thoughts of one, the absent and the dear, whose dauntless and well-aimed javelin had saved her from a fate perhaps more terrible than the worst death that had visited her family, combined to chase away the memory of deeper griefs; and again Heena looked up, and smiled less pensively.

The peasants, happily relieved from the dangers that formerly attended their daily toils, speeded cheerfully to the labours of the field; and, with a view to a similar occupation, for which a healthy old age did not render him unfit, the mild and venerable Agundah blessed his daughter, as he passed forth from his cottage; and Jumba, the brother of Heena, and only one year her junior, embraced his young wife, and kissed his laughing infant, ere he sought the thriving plantation of sugar-cane, which, under his skilful management, promised to yield a crop of unusual abundance.

"Give me, Heena," cried Kyratee, a fine manly boy seven years of age, "give me the koorpa, that I may follow my father and my brother to the field."

"Alas, no!" exclaimed the too anxious mother, darting forward from the interior of the cottage, and clasping her boy with an eagerness for which there was no apparent reason;

"think, should some of the savage and lurking Goands still linger in the vicinity, they may tear thee away even before my eyes, mocking at my vain defence, and regardless of my agonized supplications. Ah! no, my son; till thou art able to defend thyself against a rude and warlike man, thou must not wander from the precincts of the cottage."

"Speak for me, Heena!" cried the bold but wayward boy. "I can throw the javelin well, I can draw the bow, and poise the difficult lance; for Muttaree taught me all, and his arm, thou knowest, never yet has failed. I have a dagger, too, at my belt; and I fear not the worthless and womanly people of the hills.   Nay, I feel ashamed to remain at home, sitting at ease, while I might be aiding my father to till the ground, or helping to plant the rice, or bringing down with my sling or my arrows the birds that come to disturb the grain in the furrows. You will persuade mother to let me go, kind Heena, I know you will; and the other boys of the village will not cry shame upon the indolent Kyratee."

Heena looked fondly on the coaxing, ingenuous urchin, and was about to plead in his behalf; but she caught at the instant her mother's imploring eye, saw the colour fade from her cheek, and compassionating the terror which she could not share, undertook to pacify the too adventurous boy, who now began to display the juvenile frowardness which follows disappointment. Offering to feather his arrows from the eagle's wing, and to bind his quiver like that of Muttaree, if he would remain contentedly by her side, Kyratee, pleased with the idea of the martial occupation, relinquished his project; and Heena's filial respect to her mother's slightest wish was rewarded by one of those tender, approving, but pensive smiles, which alone illumined the wan countenance of the care-worn parent. It was those gentle tokens of deep affection which repaid Heena for the assiduity with which she studied the happiness of those around her, and which she considered to be lightly earned by the greatest efforts she could make to obtain them. Bending with patient and inexhaustible sweetness over her self-imposed employment, while amusing her young and highly-interested companion, she solaced her own heart with sweet thoughts of her approaching felicity. Hitherto, though she had been sought by many in marriage, she had chosen to remain in virgin solitude, anxious only to lighten the domestic cares of her mother, to gladden with her light step and melodious voice the home of which she was the invaluable blessing, and to soothe the sorrows which, with little cessation, had, from her earliest remembrance, oppressed the hearts of those she loved. But now that her parents had removed from the exposed village, wherein all the disasters they so deeply mourned had befallen them, to a more secure locality; and that a young family, the offspring of her brother, were springing up, to bind new ties around those she was at last about to leave, she had unreluctantly consented to shorten the probation of her lover, and, the betrothed bride of the enraptured Muttaree, a very few days only were to elapse ere she should become his wife. Soon a well-known step bounded over the verdant sod—soon a well-known voice shed its music on her ear, and the shadow of a beloved form fell upon the spot where she sat—when Kyratee uttered a shout of joy.   Heena flew to the embrace of the cherished guest, and the fond mother, as she surveyed the meeting, in silence clasped her hands and raised her eyes, in which might be read the invocation of a blessing, to the bright and joy-inspiring heaven above her.   Eda, the young and lovely sister-in-law of Heena, sat toying with her prattling child, under the shade of a superb tamarind tree, which spread its light, green, delicate leaves in full luxuriance above her; and seldom, in south, has the monarch's palace presented so sweet a scene of love and peace as that which blessed the straw-roofed cottage of the venerable Soobrattee.   At this moment the calmness of the clear blue air was destroyed by a wild and piercing shriek:—"It is the death-cry of my son!" screamed the frenzied and prophetic mother, as desperately she darted forward; and in another instant an enormous tiger was observed bounding rapidly towards the neighbouring jungle, and bearing his victim in his enormous jaws with the same ease that Eda dandled her reposing infant.   While the females stood stupefied by terror and grief, the young Kyratee seized, with impotent courage, his tiny javelin; but the collected Muttaree took up his bow, from which the well-directed arrow flew to the heart of the animal, with at once the lightning's celerity and the lightning's fatal power.   The tiger dropped his prey, but the mangled and bleeding body lay motionless—as utterly devoid of life as that of the monster that stretched his huge bulk beside it.   The almost petrified Eda, uttering long, heart-piercing, and unearthly shrieks, flung her infant franticly into the arms of Kyratee, and, rushing towards the place, gazed upon the dismal spectacle till, unable to bear longer the ghastly sight, feeling and sense forsook her, and she sank on the gory grass and partly on the body of her dilacerated husband. Paralyzed by the fatal event which had so suddenly passed before her, Heena remained for a moment motionless, and almost apathetic, but the distracted state of her mother soon roused her to exertion. Until that dreadful day the unhappy woman had borne all the misfortunes which had unremittingly pursued her devoted offspring with a calm, enduring sorrow. That she felt them deeply was manifested by her fading, grief-worn form, her pallid cheek, and her ever-tearful eye. She wept abundantly, but it was in patient silence; and the keenness of the sufferings which wrung the core of her heart could only be discovered by the heavy sighs and the smothered groans, which all her efforts could not wholly suppress. But now she gave way to a burst of grief which threatened to end (and happy for her if it had ended) in insanity; and vainly, though earnestly, did Heena endeavour, by soothing words and affectionate caresses, to allay the storm of wildly bursting passion. It would not be controlled; and breaking, with unwonted strength, from the gentle bondage of her daughter's twining arms, she flew towards a distant thicket with a speed which distanced all pursuit, and Heena could only track her wretched parent's footsteps by the cries which burst from her overcharged heart, with all the shrillness of oriental grief; and she beheld her at last, half-kneeling, half-lying on the ground, beneath a tall pepul-tree, where, exhausted by the violence of her emotion, she had sunk in utter helplessness. Fearful of approaching too closely, as it was evident her mother had sought to indulge her sorrow in solitude, the weeping and anguished girl stood a little distance off, concealed by the intervening shrubbery of the jungle, watching with the greatest solicitude the actions of one who seemed to meditate some desperate deed, and listening with the tenderest compassion to her wild shrieks and passionate exclamations.

"My son! my son!" she cried; "brave as a lion in the field, mild and gentle as a dove beneath the plam-leaved roof of thy father's cot; beautiful as the young Camdeo, and wise as the favourite friend of Vishnoo; the parched and thirsty earth drinks thy heart's blood, the vulture's red eye already marks thee for its prey. No more shall thy fleet steps follow the deer, and thy sure matchlock carry death to the panther! No more shalt thou bring home the shaggy skin of the lion in triumph to those who rejoiced in thy valour! Oh! too revengeful goddess! will nothing avail, neither prayers nor offerings, to move thee to be merciful? Must all I prize beneath yon glorious orb be doomed to a miserable death to satisfy thy vengeance? Will not a mother's cries be heard? Will not the red hand be stayed—the insatiable sword be arrested, by those just powers who see that the measure of my grief is full, and that this torn and burdened heart can endure its agony no longer? The penalty of my disobedience has been paid

with the lives of six, for that one which my trembling
hands refused to sacrifice; and will nought appease thee,
thou too vindictive deity! nothing suffice to atone for the
maternal weakness, the fond and strong affection, which
could not immolate at thy tremendous altar the loved one,
the first born, the welcome guest, who gave the sweet
assurance that the curse of barrenness had been removed?
Could *my* hand snap the tender thread of my smiling, my
first, my only babe's existence? Could *my* lip devote the
innocent to instant and most awful destruction?—No! no!
—and on me then let the punishment be inflicted. Let my
life pay the forfeit of my crime—but spare the guiltless!—
let me not behold the few remaining and fragile branches of
a decaying tree lopped off successively by the ruthless fiat
of an unmerciful judge!—and let not for my offence my husband suffer in the loss of his children!"

"Mother! mother!—dearest mother!" said Heena, coming
forward, "thy words pierce my soul. Tell me, I beseech
thee—I, who am thine eldest born—am I, and in what
manner, the miserable cause of the calamities which have
pursued thee from my birth? Let not the dark and fatal
secret prey longer on thy lacerated heart; and perchance
some means may still, though late, be found to avert the
dreadful evils which threaten annihilation to all our race."

"Alas, my child!" returned the sorrowing parent, "how
wilt thou listen to the tale of thy mother's frailty? Bright
was the morning of my life. No bird in the glad valley
ever sang more cheerily, no flower ever bloomed more freshly,
than she who was the pride and delight of a tribe, all of

whom were lavishly endowed with the choicest of Nature's gifts. I loved, and was loved by, a youth of my own high caste, worthy of my virgin heart; and joyously sounded the guitar, the timbrel, and the conch-shell at our nuptials, and golden were the flowers that decked the festal ceremony. I was the cherished treasure of one whose heart was tender and faithful as the turtle-dove's; and I—but vain are words to paint the excess of my idolatry. Months fled away— brief and blissful months—but the flower-treading time brought no sweet hope that a mother's joys would be added to the bliss of a most happy wife. Years at length went over; and although no reproach escaped from lips which could not utter a chiding expression, there was a silent sorrow in the eye which had been wont to beam with un- alloyed gladness; the listless languor of hopelessness stole over a frame so lately lithe and active as that of the ante- lope. I looked around my childless home; I saw the scornful glances of my more fortunate companions—I heard their deriding words, and strove, long and sorely strove, to bear my shame and my grief in silence: but when a fourth year had winged its flight—and my miserable ex- pectation made it fly as rapidly as felicity would have urged it—and still no gentle voice greeted me with the fond and glorious name of mother; when the involuntary cloud deepened on the brow of my ever affectionate husband; and when his relatives crowded round him with cruelly com- miserating sorrow, I became miserable and desperate. Often in the silence and the darkness of the night I had pondered on the means of procuring the blessing I so earnestly desired, till at length, goaded to distraction by the failure of every plan, every drug, and every prayer, I flew to the temple of the stern goddess Bhowanee, and there registered a solemn vow, that if she blessed me with the wished-for fruit, which a frowning destiny had so long denied, I would devote the first-born—the pledge that the curse of barrenness had been removed—to the bestower of the coveted boon. Alas, my Heena! when thine infant eyes opened to the light, sparkling and lustrous as the gem from which we named thee; when thy coral lips parted in a cherub smile, such as I had never till then beheld, for I could not endure to look upon another's offspring, and thy tiny and helpless fingers clasped mine in a soft and innocent embrace—could I part with a gift so precious? Could I see those dark beaming eyes quenched in a death of my own infliction—thy tender limbs stained with blood—thy fair and clinging form mangled and distorted? I could not, would not, fulfil my rash, inhuman vow; and, striving, by frequent sacrifices of less precious things, to propitiate the deity I dreaded to offend, I lived for some time in the fond expectation that I should escape the punishment to which I had rendered myself obnoxious. Every year that now glided away brought with it a new and welcome claimant upon my affection; but still to thee, the loved, the treasured object of my heart's warmest feelings, I clung with fond and prophetic tenacity. Every new grace, every fresh virtue, that developed itself in thy expanding mind and person, rendered thee still more dear, more cherished, and more prized; and though I saw my other darlings torn away, I nursed a hope, in spite of my conviction of its utter fallacy, that each victim seized by the wrathful goddess would be the last, and that yet I might descend to the grave, having my eyes closed, and my pile lighted up, by the offspring I had purchased at so terrible a price. But now that weak prop is removed—now I see too plainly that I shall be doomed to live a bleeding witness of the cruel destruction of the only remaining blessings of my existence."

Heena listened with a sinking heart to this fearful narrative. She had long felt assured that a mysterious fate hung over her devoted family, and, though not most distantly imagining how deeply she was involved in the direful cause of the. calamity which she mourned, she too had wreathed garlands upon the altars of the gods, and poured out honey, and milk, and oil, and grain, before each hallowed shrine, in the hope of suspending or averting the infliction. Now, shuddering with cold horror, she felt the conviction that a higher, a more dreadful oblation was required from her; and she saw the fearful path she was destined to tread plainly revealed before her. Though she trembled, and wept tears even of blood, as she contemplated the terrible duty she thought herself called on to perform, her heart did not for a moment waver, but, locking within it the awful secret of her resolution, she prepared to execute the purpose which she fondly and piously believed to be holy. Her tender voice and her unremitting endearments succeeded at length in partially tranquillizing the violent emotions of her parent's breast, and they returned to their forlorn and dismal home together, bearing with meek patience the evils of their destiny. But the mother's tears streamed forth anew as she surveyed the melancholy arrangements which were already in preparation for the obsequies of her gallant son; and had Heena's purpose been less steadfast than it was, she could not have withstood the imperious necessity which demanded the sacrifice she secretly meditated. Eda, the lovely and gentle Eda, but too happy in being permitted to share her husband's repose, was calmly and, as she believed, virtuously preparing to ascend his funeral pile. Decked in her bridal ornaments, and wreathed in the fairest flowers, she wept only when she turned her eyes upon her unconscious infant, who uttered at intervals low, wailing cries, strangely according with the awfulness of the proceedings. This babe, thought Heena, and thou, too, my only remaining brother, must perish as miserably as he did who lies before me, if I fail to perform the appalling conditions of my mother's vow. Oh, Muttaree! beloved and lost for ever! should I be spared the agony of witnessing thy grief, I feel that I could unshrinkingly perform the sacrifice.

The sequestered spot of the valley was now a scene of lamentable activity; for the heart-stricken parents of the deceased saw their sympathizing neighbours preparing to perform the ceremonies of the suttee to the widow of him who had so long been the solace of their lives; and though tenderly anxious to prevent her purpose, they feared to oppose the selfish wish to a choice which was uncompulsorily made. Heena busied herself amongst the mourners. The lofty project which engrossed her whole soul gave to her eye a majesty almost divine; her pale, interesting countenance assumed a sublime expression, which did not, however, derogate from its natural softness; and her movements, always graceful, were marked with a dignity not in accordance with her hitherto characteristic meekness and modesty. Every pulse throbbed wildly as she beheld Eda, with a smiling countenance, ascend the funereal pyre, and, amidst the choral hymns of the attendant Brahmins, the deafening sound of numerous instruments, and the cordial prayers of the admiring spectators, take the head of her beloved husband on her lap, and consign herself to the destructive element. Turning her eyes from the appalling spectacle, they encountered the fond and commiserating glance of Muttaree; and it was then that the contrast between her fate and that of the fast consuming suttee smote her inmost soul with an almost overpowering agony. Eda was going to be reunited, and for ever, to the object of her fondest affection; while *she* must leave the worshipped idol of *her* heart to despair and misery. Was there no spot beneath the face of heaven to which they might fly—no refuge from the fury of that inextinguishable enmity which had already achieved such deep and deadly revenge? Or if there were, could she selfishly consult her own solitary happiness, and leave her parents to suffer the continuing wrath of the unappeased Bhowanee? It was impossible! And, as fresh visions arose in her mind, she saw her young brother and her orphan nephew springing up into blooming manhood only to be cut down in the prime of their strength and beauty, by the same relentless hand which had nearly exterminated her unoffending family. Again were her nerves restrung, and again she firmly resolved to execute her original design, which, however horrible, presented the only certain means of preserving the lives of those who were far dearer to her than her own.

Aware that the hapless family who were plunged into mourning by the late tragical event attributed their misfortunes to the pursuit of an evil destiny, Muttaree was not surprised when Heena, taking him aside, besought him to journey as far as the temple of Booddha, near the town of Azimgurh, and there perform certain religious ceremonies before the high altar. Only too happy to obey the slightest wish of her whom he loved to distraction, he lost no time in departing on his mission; but, on his arrival there, he found the temple shut, and the place deserted, in consequence of a dreadful contagion which had spread death and desolation throughout the adjacent country. Depressed by so ill an omen, he bent his way homewards again, but determined to visit a far-famed temple of Mahadeo, which was wildly situated in the midst of the Goand Hills, and at a small distance from Puchmurree, the principal hold of the savage inhabitants. As he drew near to the spot he heard the loud sounds of sacrificial instruments, and observed a numerous company winding up the adjacent defile towards the summit of a rock which was sacred to Bhowanee, the wife of Mahadeo. The scenery was wild and gloomy. Deep ravines, which might have been deemed bottomless but for the hoarse roar of the invisible waters which rushed beneath; rugged steeps, and masses of jungle-covered hills, the abode of unmolested beasts of prey of every hideous kind, formed the character of that dreadful locality. At the foot of the stupendous rock adverted to before was a cavern, hollowed by Nature's hand out of a huge but lower rock; and within this dark recess, and beyond a fountain which the ever-dripping roof supplied, was the altar of the goddess; and it was to the foot of this cave, from the fearful summit of the rock of sacrifice, that infatuated mothers were wont to hurl their first-born children, in return for the curse of barrenness being taken away by the power of Bhowanee. A strange sensation, a fearful presentiment, agitated the bosom of Muttaree as he approached the frightful precipice, which, rising perpendicularly and ruggedly to the height of one hundred and seventy feet, was associated with awful tales of the inexorable goddess, to whose horrid and revolting rites it had been dedicated for ages. A light female form, whose white garments fluttered in the breeze, was seen gliding to the summit. Muttaree darted forward; but ere he reached the spot, the officiating Brahmin had humanely drawn the intended victim back, and, by his actions, seemed to expostulate with anxious earnestness against the desperate enterprise. Muttaree rushed forward, and beheld the soul-harrowing sight of which his prescient heart had warned him.

"Strike, strike the gong and the cymbal!" exclaimed Heena, "to drown the voices of those who would dissuade me. But for this delay I had been spared the agonizing looks of one who may not melt my resolution, though his presence calls my soul too strongly back to earth from the heaven it was approaching. In pity, Muttaree, tear away those sad, those beseeching eyes—I *must* complete the sacrifice!—Ha! wouldst thou grasp me?" she exclaimed, as, dashing away his outstretched arms, and crying, " Thou art saved, oh, my mother !" she, with one wild and desperate bound, leaped from the topmost point of the rock, and sank, whirling like a stricken eagle, into the awful gulfs beneath.

Uncle Antony's Blunder.

IT would be no exaggeration of the fact to state, that on the morning of the 9th of May, 1828, nine-tenths of the young ladies in the populous neighbourhood of Sonnington were discoursing, or thinking at least, on one and the same subject—that subject a masquerade, which had been given on the preceding evening by a lady of rank. The entertainment had been planned to celebrate the twenty-first birthday of her eldest son, and executed with a splendour and good taste totally unprecedented in that quarter of England.

Availing myself of Asmodeus's privilege, I looked in for a few moments on two ladies, who were enjoying the luxury of lounging over a late breakfast-table. The parlour was small, but elegantly furnished; and one or two old family pictures gave it that peculiar air of respectability which no other ornament can impart. Through two large casement windows, flung open, the scents and sounds of spring came pleasantly in; and the eye wandered out over a fair, old-fashioned garden, decked with clipt trees, vases, and statues.

Here sat the mistress of the mansion and her niece; the former an elderly lady, with fine open features, upright figure, and perfectly white hair; and, opposite to her, in a huge easy chair, covered with brown damask, a damsel of twenty, not unlike her aunt, but far more beautiful than she ever could have been. She took my fancy so entirely, that I feel myself unable to give a distinct account of her loveliness: for the benefit of the curious, however, I may say that she had black hair; large, soft, blue eyes, with dark eyebrows and eyelashes; a small, delicate figure; a fairy foot; and a hand that had already twice served as a model to a Parisian sculptor. The two talked together as unreservedly as if they had been of the same age; and the elder lady's ready and good-humoured laugh was a clear evidence that, though unmarried and past the meridian of life, she had not survived a sympathy in the pleasures and the fantasies of the young.

"Go on, Georgina," said Miss Granville, "and I shall feel no regret that my head-ache kept me at home; and now tell me how you fared among all those strangers."

"Why, it was as easy an introduction to a new circle as any bashful young lady could possibly desire. Nobody knew me, and I knew nobody; and still every one seemed to take it for granted that I must be somebody he or she knew. The consequence was, that I was persecuted for the entire evening by hordes of cavaliers, each thinking that he had discovered some acquaintance. Twice I was addressed as *une fiancée;* a score of times as an heiress; and I am sure that once at least I was the innocent instrument of keeping some young lady waiting for her devoted squire."

"And Mrs. Dynevor?"

"The most discreet chaperon in the world; she kept my secret *à merveille*. But the strangest thing is, that I have managed to capture and secure a lover. I flatter myself that the conquest is complete, as my swain allowed me no rest, and at length became so eager for supper time ——"

"Horrid *gourmand !*"

"Nay, dear aunt, do not judge so hastily; it was, I believe, not a longing for the ice and champagne, but to see me unmask, that he manifested so much impatience; but I resolved not to gratify the old gentleman."

"Old gentleman! pshaw!"

"You shall hear more anon. I resolved not to gratify his curiosity, and returned home before supper. He would insist, however, on escorting me to the carriage, and, I fancy, contrived to discover that I was your visitor."

"But an old gentleman! who could it be?"

"I was most curious to discover, for he followed me with the most comical homage imaginable: he held my fan when I danced; and when I spoke, bent close to me, to catch what he called my melodious tones; whence I conclude that my *inamorato* is deaf."

"And his dress?"

"He was dressed simply in a dark domino. He is nimble for his years, for I beguiled him into dancing a country-dance with me : and this, I suppose, was my crowning fascination ; for, when it was over, he came close to me,

and whispered softly in my ear, 'Ah, then, you *do* not despise these hearty and unsophisticated amusements! What a sweet wife you would make!'"

"Upon my word! Was this after supper?"

"Pray, do not insinuate. I told you that I came home before supper; and then he trusted to be allowed to cultivate my acquaintance. Some gentlemen who spoke to him called him Uncle Antony."

At this name the elder lady laughed long and heartily; and, to spare prolixity, it may be as well in a few words to explain the cause of her mirth.

Captain Antony Nesfield, called by common consent, "Uncle Antony," had been long an inhabitant of that neighbourhood. He had come hither, on the decease of a relation, to settle, as he said, for the remainder of his life; had bought an estate of a few score acres; and then, being a man of courtly manners, not uncomely presence, and tender heart, had bowed before every neighbouring beauty in succession, in the hope of inducing her to share his cottage; to fill the vacant seat in his gig; in short, to give to his well appointed establishment what alone it wanted—a mistress. 'Twas all in vain. There are some men who are tolerated, nay, even thought agreeable, in society, till they assume the lover's character, when they become at once objects of dislike and avoidance. And he, with his gentle and feeble voice, his placid smile, his ready and somewhat obsolete gallantries, who was the very man to be acceptable to a country circle, had nevertheless contrived to run the gauntlet of more disgust than a casual thinker could imagine to have appertained to the possession of so sweet a residence as Nesfield Nook, and so sufficient an income as seven hundred a year.

Years passed, but Uncle Antony was still a single man, bearing still in his soul the settled intention of matrimony, and every year waxing more and more distasteful to the virgins of Sonnington and its vicinity. It was whispered that his last suit had been of a more *suitable* character than some of his previous flirtations; that he had been paying desperate court to Miss Granville, and with his usual success—an implicit and somewhat contemptuous rejection. Hence it was that the young lady affected some wrath at this sudden transfer of his devotion; and, protesting that he was a poor frivolous creature, who did not care whom he married, so that he only got married at all, resolved to treat him in such a way as to warn him from the commission of the like follies in future. Her devices were heartily aided and enjoyed by Miss Granville.

A week after this the old beau might have been seen daintily wending his way to White Wells one fine evening. He was more carefully dressed than usual; his wig curled with the most scrupulous formality; his uniform quite new; and his shoes polished till they reflected the rays of the sinking sun. Since Miss Granville's refusal, he had become, if anything, more precise and courtier-like in his demeanour than before. He had fitted up his house entirely anew, and made many modernizations and improvements in his grounds; and, so far from appearing dejected, had put on the semblance of greater juvenility and gaiety than of old. He had been, as

Georgina Arnold surmised, greatly smitten with her at the masquerade; and, after one or two slight encouragements, insidiously administered by her aunt, was now marching hopefully on his way, to see and to conquer; for this time he had his own secret reasons of being sure of unqualified success; and he vented his soul's contentment somewhat after this fashion:—

"Well!—to have succeeded at last!—for this time I think I am not deceived. After so many years—and with so little apparent difficulty too! I hope—I hope she is worthy"—and he stood still and sighed. "How strange it is that the first time—but here is the gate, and yonder is the angel herself walking in the garden. I feel in no particular humour to encounter Miss Granville's raillery, and will go to her at once and explain myself."

With that Uncle Antony opened the gate, with a trembling hand, and, crossing a small grass-plot, approached the young lady, who seemed rapt in a reverie. Apparently she was somewhat startled by his approach; for, on hearing a step, she let down in some haste a long thick muslin veil.

"Bashful!" said he, half aloud; "ahem! Good evening, Miss Arnold; I do not wonder to find you abroad enjoying so splendid a sunset."

Miss Arnold courtesied, and murmured some inarticulate reply. "To a mind like yours," pursued Uncle Antony, "the contemplation of the beauties of nature must be a favourite pursuit. Ah! I shall not soon forget your artless eloquence the other evening, when you made that uneffaceable impression--"

Another very slight murmur under the veil.

"Dear Miss Arnold," continued the old gentleman, "never, never before was I placed in so delicate, so embarrassing, a situation; never before did I feel the same anxiety. To plead the cause of one whom I flatter myself you have not forgotten is indeed an arduous task. Hear me but for one moment"—and he ventured to take her small gloved hand. It rested in his own, without any violent reluctance on her part. "Hear me but for one moment. I am an unfortunate, disappointed man. I have lived—no matter how long—the victim of—but I will not weary you by recounting my misfortunes. To you I must now look for consolation, to you for reparation, to you—pray answer me—the sound of my own voice without reply is fearful to me."

"You are very good—too good," replied the young lady in a low voice.

"Nay," cried he, rapturously, "not equal to your deserts. Let me place this gem on your finger, as a seal to the first step of so interesting a negotiation:" and he drew from his pocket-book a glittering ring; but the lady seemed unwilling to receive it, and gently repulsed his attempt to remove her glove. "Not yet," she said; "I am scarcely sure—"

"What! do you doubt the sincerity of my professions? Can you, for an instant, refuse to believe that I am in earnest—that this alliance is my dearest wish?"

"I *do* believe—I do trust you," replied she, fervently.

"Am I then at last successful?" cried Uncle Antony, in a transport of delight. "Nay, dearest Miss Arnold," continued he, as she sunk gracefully into a garden-seat, still allowing him to retain her hand, "let me hear those charming words of consent once more! Raise, raise, I entreat you, that envious screen which conceals your features, and let me not be tantalized by even the shadow of an uncertainty!" and, as he spoke, he advanced his right hand towards the veil.

"Stop," cried she, rather energetically, withdrawing to the corner of the chair, "none but myself—;" and, drawing her figure slightly up as she sat, so that his eyes might fall directly upon her upturned face, slowly she withdrew the muslin curtain.

For an instant Uncle Antony stood motionless, speechless, with dismay and disgust. He took a short and tremulous step backward, and his regular and well ordered queue coiled itself up in very horror at the fearful apparition revealed to him. Spirit of beauty! he met the dead eyes, he gazed on the flattened nose, and the thick lips, of a negress! and the sum of these features, the face, was animated by that composed and complacent expression, which, if translated into words, would have been—"You see, sir—I hope you are satisfied."

For an instant, I repeat, poor Uncle Antony stood motionless. The lady kept her seat with admirable presence of mind. At length he gasped out—"O worst of all! worst disappointment of all! my poor nephew! poor Frank!" and, turning on his heel, he fled precipitately, in his haste dropping the pocket-book from which he had drawn the *gage d'amour* destined for Miss Arnold's aceptance.

The sorely perturbed old gentleman was not, however,

allowed to make his escape without further molestation. Forth from a neighbouring labyrinth of evergreens sailed Miss Granville, with majestic step; and, confronting the discomfited suitor, "Surely, Captain Nesfield," said she, "you were not going to pass me without a greeting!"

"Good evening, then, madam," was his abrupt answer.

"Nay," replied she, detaining him, "that is a very dry reply, and something less than civil. Come, I shall make you my prisoner. Miss Arnold is already waiting for us at the tea-table, and—"

"Miss Arnold!—it is more than I can bear: to be rejected in my own person for these last six and twenty years is bad enough; but when, at last, I attempted to plead as my nephew's representative, to find myself so cheated, the victim of so hideous a mistake, is too much!"

"Your nephew's representative! I am amazed, sir! Pray do me the favour of accompanying me to the house; you seem much agitated."

"Madam, I say that it would provoke a saint. It was only a few months ago, when I was just recovering from certain vexations of which you may guess the cause, that I learned that I had a nephew—that my sister's son, born in Germany, still survived. The poor lad had been long and vainly endeavouring to trace out his relations; and, at last succeeding in his attempt, wrote to me, enclosing proofs that his tale was no fable. Wounded to the heart by repeated mortifications, I resolved to centre my hopes in him, and, should I find him worthy, to make him my heir. I wrote, therefore, in reply, requesting further particulars as

to his history, pursuits, &c. I found that the young man
had followed his uncle's profession, that he had conceived a
strong attachment to a young lady whom he had casually
met in Paris, but that he had felt himself bound in honour
not to declare his sentiments until he had earned himself a
name and a fortune. On this, I hastened up to London. I
found him, madam—no matter *now* what he is ! He will
be here to-morrow. I speedily learned, by a little cross-
examination, that the lady of his affections was a Miss
Arnold; and without much trouble succeeded in identifying
her with my fair friend of the masquerade."

"Sir, I am thunderstruck."

"Madam, I am dismayed beyond power of description at
my blunder. I thought that I was preparing an agreeable
surprise for my nephew. Judge, then, of my consternation!
Strangely precipitate as I have been, surely my folly has
scarcely merited such a *contretemps* as Fate has been pleased
to punish me with. And I fear that the—the—*dark* young
lady may have misunderstood me—that I had hardly time
to explain myself clearly. Pray, pray, good Miss Granville,
apologize for me as well as you can ! I have been abrupt ;
but you must feel what a blow this has been. I am
mortified—I am confused—I am ashamed—I can remain in
this neighbourhood no longer !"

"Stay, Captain Nesfield," replied his amazed auditor, who
had heard his whimsical and disjointed tale in great wonder ;
" stay, and I pledge myself that all may be right yet. Are
you not in a mistake ?—Is it possible that you can have
mistaken Miss Arnold's black maid, who accompanied her

from Jamaica, for her mistress?   Let us go in and inquire.
I saw the girl in the garden a quarter of an hour ago."

The old gentleman literally sprang from the ground in
ecstasy at so consoling a suggestion, and followed her willingly to the cottage.   They entered the parlour, where the
tea equipage was, and Georgina was not.   On seeking her,
Miss Granville found her in her dressing-room, in a deep
reverie, and holding a sealed letter in her hand.   " So, child,"
she said, "I hope you witnessed how beautifully Jella performed her part."

"Yes, but—"

"But what is the meaning of that letter, which you eye
with such an uneasy face?   I never saw any one whose
joke had succeeded so perfectly look so utterly woe-begone
as you do."

"Pray, aunt, spare me your raillery, I am really very
unhappy;" and out came the confidence, which, as may be
foreseen, was a confession of old acquaintance with a certain
Ensign Paulet, whom Georgina had met in Paris.   The
direction of the letter which had dropped from Uncle
Antony's pocket-book, and the broken words which she had
overheard from the evergreen thicket, where she had
stationed herself to enjoy his consternation, had perplexed
her with the shadow of an imagination that the old
gentleman might, for once in his life, be courting by proxy.
At all events the coincidence of names was enough to
agitate a young lady who was conscious of not being altogether indifferent to the delicate and respectful attentions
of the handsome young officer.

There sufficed but a few words from Miss Granville to finish the romance, as far as Georgina's perplexities were concerned; and the arrival of Ensign Paulet, *alias* Nesfield, Uncle Antony's acknowledged heir, completed the story, as all stories ought to be terminated, with a gay and promising wedding. The young couple resided with Uncle Antony, and made his home so pleasant as totally to extirpate any wandering ideas which he had formed of seeking a helpmate among the five Misses Sims, who took a house in the neighbourhood; all of whom, as he said, were " very accomplished women ; and, it would seem, hard to please, as the youngest owned to have rejected seven proposals of marriage before she was five and thirty."

The Child and the Flowers.

———

 HAST thou been in the woods with the honey-bee?
    Hast thou been with the lamb in the pastures
        free?
    With the hare through the copses and dingles
        wild?
With the butterfly over the heath, fair child?
Yes: the light fall of thy bounding feet
Hath not startled the wren from her mossy seat;
Yet hast thou ranged the green forest-dells,
And brought back a treasure of buds and bells.

Thou know'st not the sweetness, by antique song
Breathed o'er the names of that flowery throng;
The woodbine, the primrose, the violet dim,
The lily that gleams by the fountain's brim:
These are old words, that have made each grove
A dreary haunt for romance and love;
Each sunny bank, where faint odours lie
A place for the gushings of Poesy.

Thou know'st not the light wherewith fairy lore
Sprinkles the turf and the daisies o'er;
Enough for thee are the dews that sleep
Like hidden gems in the flower-urns deep;
Enough the rich crimson spots that dwell
'Midst the gold of the cowslip's perfumed cell;
And the scent by the blossoming sweet briar shed,
And the beauty that bows the wood-hyacinth's head.

Oh! happy child, in thy fawn-like glee!
What is remembrance or thought to thee?
Fill thy bright locks with those gifts of spring,
O'er thy green pathway their colours fling;
Bind them in chaplet and wild festoon—
What if to droop and to perish soon?
Nature hath mines of such wealth—and thou
Never wilt prize its delights as now!

For a day is coming to quell the tone
That rings in thy laughter, thou joyous one!
And to dim thy brow with a touch of care,
Under the gloss of its clustering hair;
And to tame the flash of thy cloudless eyes
Into the stillness of autumn skies;
And to teach thee that grief hath her needful part,
'Midst the hidden things of each human heart!

Yet shall we mourn, gentle child, for this?
Life hath enough of yet holier bliss!

Such be thy portion !—the bliss to look
With a reverent spirit through Nature's book ;
By fount, by forest, by river's line,
To track the paths of a love divine ;
To read its deep meanings—to see and hear
God in earth's garden—and not to fear !

Bessy Bell and Mary Gray.

IT was in the yet Doric days of Scotland (comparing the present with the past) that Kenneth Bell, one of the lairds of the green holms of Kinvaid, having lost his lady by a sudden dispensation of Providence, remained for a long time wrapt up in the reveries of grief, and utterly inconsolable. The tide of affliction was at length fortuitously stemmed by the nourice bringing before him his helpless infant daughter— the very miniature of her departed mother, after whom she had been named.

The looks of the innocent babe recalled the father's heart to a sense of the duties which life yet required of him; and little Bessy grew up in health and beauty, the apple of her father's eye. Nor was his fondness for her diminished, as year after year more fully developed those lineaments which at length ripened into a more matured likeness of her who was gone. She became, as it were, a part of the old man's being; she attended him in his garden walks; rode out with him on her palfrey on sunny mornings; and was as his

shadow by the evening hearth. She doted on him with
more than a daughter's fondness; and he at length seemed
bound to earth by no tie save her existence.

It was thus that Bessy Bell grew up to woman's stature;
and, in the quiet of her father's hall, she was now, in her
eighteenth year, a picture of feminine loveliness. All around
had heard of the beauty of the heiress of Kinvaid. The
cottager who experienced her bounty drank to her health in
his homely jug of nut-brown ale; and the squire, at wassail,
toasted her in the golden wine-cup.

The dreadful plague of 1666 now fell out, and rapidly
spread its devastations over Scotland. Man stood aghast;
the fountains of society were broken up; and day after day
brought into rural seclusion some additional proofs of its
fearful ravages. Nought was heard around but the wailings
of deprivation; and omens in the heavens and on the earth
heralded miseries yet to come.

Having been carried from Edinburgh (in whose ill-venti-
lated closes and wynds it had made terrible havoc) across
the Firth of Forth, the northern counties were now thrown
into alarm, and families broke up, forsaking the towns and
villages to disperse themselves under the freer atmosphere
of the country. Among others, the Laird of Kinvaid
trembled for the safety of his beloved child, and the arrival
of young Bruce, of Powfoulis Priory, afforded him an excellent opportunity of having his daughter escorted to
Lynedoch, the residence of a warmly attached friend and
relative.

Under the protection of this gallant young squire, Bessy

rode off on the following morning, and, the day being delightful, the young pair, happy in themselves, forgot, in the beauty of nature, the miseries that encompassed them.

Besides being a youth of handsome appearance and engaging manners, young Bruce had seen a good deal of the world, having for several years served as a member of the body guard of the French King. He had returned from Paris only a few months before, and yet wore the cap and plume peculiar to the distinguished corps to which he still belonged. The heart of poor Bessy Bell was as sensitive as it was innocent and unsophisticated; and, as her protector made his proud steed fret and curvet by her side, she thought to herself, as they rode along, that he was like one of the knights concerning whom she had read in romance; and, unknown to herself, there awoke in her bosom a feeling to which it had hitherto been a stranger.

Her reception at Lynedoch was most cordial; nor the less so, perhaps, on the part of the young lady of that mansion, because her attendant was Bruce, the secret but accepted suitor for the hand of Mary Gray. Ah! had this mystery been at once revealed to Bessy Bell, what a world of misery it would have saved her!

From the plague had our travellers been flying; but the demon of desolation was here before them, and the smoke was ceasing to ascend from many a cottage-hearth. It became necessary that the household of Lynedoch should be immediately dispersed. Bruce and Lynedoch remained in the vicinity of the dwelling-house, and a bower of turf and moss was reared for the young ladies on the pastoral banks of the Brauchie-burn, a tributary of the Almond.

It was there that Bessy Bell and Mary Gray lived for a while in rural seclusion, far from the bustle and parade of gay life, verifying in some measure what ancient poetry has feigned of the golden age. Bruce was a daily visitant at the bower by the Brauchie-burn: he wandered with them through the green solitudes; and, under the summer sun and a blue sky, they threaded ofttimes together the mazes of " many a bosky bourn and bushy dell." They chased the fantastic squirrel from bough to bough, and scared the thieving little weasel from the linnet's nest. Under a great tree they would seat themselves, as Bruce read aloud some story of chivalry, romance, or superstition, or soothed the listless hours of the afternoon with the delightful tones of the shepherd's pipe. More happy were they than the story-telling group, each in turn a queen, who, in like manner flying from the pestilence which afflicted Florence, shut themselves up in its delightful gardens, relating those hundred tales of love which have continued to delight posterity in the glowing pages of Boccaccio.

Under whatever circumstances it is placed, human nature will be human nature still. When the young and the beautiful meet together freely and unreservedly, the cold restraints of custom and formality must be thrown aside; friendship kindles into a warmer feeling, and love is generated. Could it be otherwise with our ramblers in their green solitude ?

Between Mary Gray and young Bruce a mutual and

understood attachment had long subsisted—indeed they only waited his coming of age to be united in the bonds of wedlock; but the circumstance, for particular reasons, was cautiously concealed within their own bosoms. Even to Bessy Bell, her dearest and most intimate companion, Mary had not revealed it. To disguise his real feelings, Bruce was outwardly less marked in his attention to his betrothed than to her friend; and, in her susceptibility and innocent confidence, Bessy Bell too readily mistook his kind assiduities for marks of affection and proofs of love. A new spirit began to pervade her whole being, almost unknown to herself; she looked on the scenes around her with other eyes; and life changed in the hues it had previously borne to the gaze of her imagination. In the absence of Bruce she became melancholy and abstracted. He seemed to her the being who had been born to render her blessed; and futurity appeared, without his presence, like the melancholy gloom of a November morning.

The physiological doctrine of temperaments we leave to its difficulties; although we confess that in Bessy Bell and Mary Gray something spoke in the way of illustration.

The countenance of Bessy was one of light and sunshine. Her eyes were blue, her hair flaxen, her complexion florid. She might have sat for a picture of Aurora. Everything about her spoke of "the innocent brightness of the new-born day." Mary Gray was in many things the reverse of this, although perhaps equally beautiful. Her features were more regular; she was taller, even more elegant in figure; and had in her almost colourless cheeks. lofty pale brow, and raven ringlets, a majesty which nature had denied to her unconscious rival. The one was all buoyancy and smiles; the other subdued passion, deep feeling, and quiet reflection.

Bruce was a person of the finest sense of honour; and, finding that he had unconsciously and unintentionally made an impression on the bosom-friend of his betrothed, became instantly aware that it behoved him to take some step to dispel the unfortunate illusion. Fortunately the time was speedily approaching which called him to return for a season to his military post in France; but the idea of parting from Mary Gray had become doubly painful to his feelings, from the consideration of the circumstances under which he was obliged to leave her. The ravages of death were extending instead of abating; and the general elements themselves seemed to have become tainted with the unwholesomeness. There was an unrefreshing languor in the air; the sky wore a coppery appearance; and over the face of the sun was drawn as it were a veil of blood. Imagination might no doubt magnify these things; but victims were falling around on every side, and no Aaron, as in the days of hoar antiquity, now stood between the living and the dead, to bid the plague be stayed.

With a noble resolution Bruce took his departure, and sorrow, like a cloud, brooded over the bower by the Brauchieburn. Mary sat in a quiet melancholy abstraction; but ever and anon the tears dropped down the cheeks of Bessy Bell, as her "softer soul in woe dissolved aloud." Love is lynx-eyed, and Mary saw too well what was passing in the mind, of her friend; but, with a kind consideration, she allowed the lapse of a few days to moderate the turbulence of her feelings ere she ventured to impart the cruel truth. So unlooked for, so unexpected was the disclosure, that for a while she harboured a spirit of unbelief; but conviction at once flashed over her, extinguishing every hope, when she was shown a beautiful necklace of precious stones, which Bruce had presented to his betrothed on the morning of his bidding adieu to the bower of the Brauchie-burn. As it were by magic, a change came over the spirit of Bessy Bell. She dried her tears, hung on the neck of her friend, endeavoured to console her in her separation from him who loved her, and bore up with a heroism seemingly almost incompatible with the gentle softness of her nature! She clasped the chain round the neck of Mary, and, kneeling, implored Heaven speedily to restore the giver to her arms!

Fatal had been that gift! It had been purchased by Bruce from a certain Adonijah Baber, a well-known Jewish merchant of Perth, who had amassed considerable riches by traffic. Taking advantage of the distracted state of the times, this man had allowed his thirst after lucre to overcome his better principles, and lead him into lawless dealings with the wretches who went about abstracting valuables from infected or deserted mansions. As a punishment for his rapacity, death was in a short time brought to his own household, and he himself perished amid the unavailing wealth which sin had accumulated.

Fatal had been that gift! In a very little while Mary sickened; and her symptoms were those of the fearful malady afflicting the nation. Bessy Bell was fully aware of the danger; but, with a heroic self-devotion, she became the nurse of her friend; and, when all others kept aloof, administered, though vainly, to her wants. Her noble and generous mind was impressed with the conviction that she owed some reparation for the unintentional wound which she might have inflicted on the feelings of Mary, in having appeared to become her rival in the affections of her betrothed.

As an almost necessary consequence, she was herself seized with the fatal malady. The evening heard them singing hymns together—midnight listened to the ravings of delirium—the morning sun shone into the bower of death, where all was still!

The tragedy was consummated ere yet Bruce had set sail for France; but the news did not reach him for a considerable time, the communication between the two countries being interrupted.   His immediate impulse was to volunteer into the service of the German Emperor, by whom he was attached to a squadron sent to assist Sobieski of Poland against the Turks. He never returned; and was supposed to have fallen shortly afterwards, in one of the many sanguinary encounters that ensued.

The old Laird of Kinvaid awoke from the paroxysm of his grief to a state of almost dotage, yet occasionally a glimpse of the past would shoot across his mind; for, in wandering vacantly about his dwelling, he would sometimes exclaim, in the spirit so beautifully expressed in the Arabian manuscript, "Where is my child?" and Echo answered, " Where ?"

The burial vaults of both the Kinvaid and Lynedoch families, who were related, were in the church of Methven; but, according to a wish said to have been expressed by the two young friends, "who were lovely in their lives, and in death were not divided," they were buried near a beautiful bank of the Almond. Several of the poets of Scotland have sung their hapless fate: Lednoch bank has become classic in story; and, during the last century and a half, many thousands of enthusiastic pilgrims have visited the spot, which has been enclosed with pious care.

Of the original ballad only a few lines remain: they are full of nature and simple pathos:—

> Bessy Bell and Mary Gray
>   They were twa bonny lasses;
> They biggit a bower on yon burn brae,
>   And theekit it owre wi' rashes.
>
> They wouldna lie in Methven kirk,
>   Beside their gentle kin;
> But they would lie on Lednoch braes,
>   To beek them in the sun.

The Great Balas Ruby.

WHILE the mind lingers with eager interest over many a page of our mediæval history, there is perhaps no one to which it more frequently turns, or on which it more delightedly dwells, than on that which records the splendid deeds of that brilliant reign which first saw the lilies of vanquished France quartered with the lions of England. In the earlier periods of our history, the interest excited by tales of lofty devotion, or wild and perilous enterprise, is marred by the rudeness or ferocity by which they were attended. The bold and danger-loving knight, "stern of heart and stout of limb," may indeed be found, but that singular and graceful combination of valour and gentleness, justice and courtesy, which characterized not merely the knight of romance but the knight of actual life at a later period, we seek for in vain.

In the splendid reign of Edward III., the lingering shadows of barbarism had well-nigh rolled away: Civilization was advancing with rapid steps, and the refinements of social life followed in her train; Romance, gorgeous Romance, with her thousand witcheries, had cast her spell of beauty over the whole land; and Chivalry, with her picturesque institutions and lofty doctrines of pure faith and unstained honour—not a mere creature of shows and tournaments, but a living, breathing, and influential spirit—had ascended her unquestioned throne of dominion, and swayed her graceful sceptre alike over monarch and people.

At the period when our tale commences, although the glories of Cressy and Poictiers as yet were not, these mingled influences of romance and chivalry pervaded every bosom. The spirit-stirring lay of the minstrel found an echo in every heart; the warlike tale of the *disour* had not been told in vain; and each knight, revelling in joyful anticipations of chivalrous enterprise, cast an eager glance toward the fair plains of Normandy and strong castles of Guienne, and awaited, impatiently as his falcon for her prey, as his war-steed for the battle-field, the summons that should bid him set lance in rest, and advance the red cross into the very heart of France. And now had the call been given, and a joyous response was returned by each valiant heart; for the high-minded Jane, Countess de Montfort, had sent Sir Amaury de Clisson to supplicate knightly aid of King Edward on behalf of herself and her small garrison at Hennebon, then straitly besieged by Charles of Blois. What knight could resist the call to do battle in the cause of a fair and noble lady, whose husband was captive in a far distant dungeon? a lady, too, whose chivalrous and "right valiant" bearing had rendered her the theme of admiration in every castle-hall throughout the land? King Edward gave instant assent; and, under the auspices of that bravest and gentlest of knights, that "flower and grace of all chivalry," Sir Walter Manny, a goodly array of knights and men-at-arms, with six thousand chosen archers, made ready.

On the evening preceding their departure, the streets of London were filled with a busy crowd; and, as the summer's sun sank brightly to rest, there might be seen armourers hurrying to and fro, with file and hammer, or brightly burnished armour; herald-painters with newly blazoned shield or pennon; esquires carefully bearing the long slender lance or richly gilded helmet; and young pages lightly bounding along with riband, scarf, or kind message, the parting gift of some " fayre damosel;" and many a man-at-arms, strong of limb and huge of size, and many a tall archer with sheaf of snowy-fledged arrows and coat of Lincoln green, pressed hastily on, carolling snatches of ancient ballads, and gazing with delighted wonder at the splendid show (even then) of the London shops, or stopping to admire the graceful beauty of the cross in West-cheap, at that period one of the "lions" of London. Amid these various but picturesque groups, a knight clad "in weeds of peace," the tight long hose, pointed shoe, short tunic, and flat cap, leading a lady of remarkable beauty, whose long and delicately pearl-braided hair and ample silken robe and mantle, which, but for the care of her attendant page, would have swept the ground, passed along, and at length entered a house where one of the foreign dealers in gems and in the superior kinds of armour had taken up his residence. They ascended the dark and narrow staircase, which seemed to lead but to some mean abode, (for the foreign merchant to whom the protection of the wealthy and powerful London guilds was denied found his safety in the apparent meanness of his dwelling,) and entered an apartment which, in its size, the richness of its furniture, and the splendour of the plate and armour scattered about, formed a strong and almost start-ling contrast with the rudeness of the entrance. There, at a table covered with a rich carpet, and surrounded by carved chests of various sizes, sat their owner, a Jew of advanced age and venerable appearance, who rose as the knight and lady entered, and, with more of dignity than might have been expected in one of that proscribed race, bade them welcome. Struck by the unexpected splendour of the apartment, and still more by the appearance of the master—for the Jews, although fifty years had elapsed since their expulsion, were still the objects of undefined and traditionary horror—the lady half drew back; while the knight, who seemed to be well known to the owner of these precious stores, advanced with a pleasant smile to the table. "Well, Eleazar of Bruges," said he, "I have come to put your boastful saying to the test, ere I cross the seas to-morrow; so unlock your caskets, bring forth your choicest jewels, and let me see if I can find a gem so beautiful that even I myself shall deem it a worthy gift to my lady."

Eleazar of Bruges returned the smile, and, taking a small casket, applied the key to the intricate lock. "Ay, most noble knight, jewels so costly and so richly set that Sir

Tristrem might have offered them to 'la belle Iseult,' or 'Morgain la fay' been won by them to release her long-slumbering King Arthur," cried the Jew, to whom the language of romance in the course of his various dealings among the fair and noble had become as familiar as his own.

"Nay, more costly, more beautiful, must they be," cried the knight, with a look of proud exultation, leading the lady toward the table, "since it is for one more lovely than 'la belle Iseult,' and more witching than "Morgain la fay.'"

"And fit lady-love for Sir Johan de Boteler, the Lord of Warrington, who made all Flanders ring with the praise of his valour," said the Jew.

"The Lord of Warrington's valour, if valour it might be called, was but owing to the remembrance of his lady-love," was the knight's modest and graceful answer; "nor can *his* deeds be thought of beside those of Sir Walter Manny, save as the faint light of the stars before the risen sun."

"The Lord of Warrington pleaseth to say so," replied the Jew, "but so will not thousands."

"Nay, peace, I pray you," said the knight; "time presses, bring forth your jewels."

"What say you to this, or this?" said the Jew, successively taking from the casket rings and brooches, enriched with gems of the finest water, and chains of the most delicate workmanship, while the lady looked on in silent admiration.

"Nay, none of these," said the knight. "Have you still

that carcanet of whose beauty ye so boasted at Bruges—the heart-shaped ruby, enclosed within a border of that knightly flower, the *fleur de souvenance ?*"

"We will see no more," said the lady, "for these are costly and beautiful enow, methinks, even for our sweet lady and Queen."

"They are so, fair lady," replied the Jew; "but choose not until you have seen the ruby, which I purchased not long since of a stranger at Bruges.   Father Abraham! 'tis without flaw or blemish, and gloweth like the carbuncle that lighted the hall of the Soldan of Babylon."   Thus saying, he arose, and from a trebly-locked iron chest drew forth another casket.

"Hasten, good Eleazar," said the knight, "name your price, and doubt not the depth of my purse."

"Shall Eleazar of Bruges take payment of the Lord of Warrington," cried the Jew, "when by his knightly prowess I was rescued with my treasures from the brutish populace at Lisle ?"

"Speak not of that," returned the knight, hastily; "a knight is ever bound to defend the defenceless—but bring it forth, and fear not for the price."

"I fear not," said the Jew, "for I would ye would but take it without payment."

"That may not be," said the knight peremptorily ; "the gift that a knight presents to his lady must either be won in fight or purchased with his purse—but hasten, I pray you."

The Jew took from the very bottom of the casket a small

box, and, opening it, displayed to the admiring gaze of the lady a carcanet, whose delicately enamelled border of forget-me-nots enclosed a ruby of such size and of such rich and dazzling brilliancy that the eye almost ached at beholding it.

"This doth indeed remind me of tales of the eastern land," cried the lady, as she took the splendid gem from the box by its delicate gold chain, and, holding it up, gazed with an intensity of admiration, which she in vain endeavoured to suppress.

"The price?" whispered the knight, beckoning to the page, who advanced with his purse—not the slender silk net of modern times, but a substantial leather pouch, embroidered and embellished with gold or silver studs, sometimes even with gems, which was at this period always either carried in the hand or suspended from the girdle.

"Say nought of payment," replied the Jew.

"It is for my lady, and I may not receive it as a gift," persisted the knight.

"Well then, thirty marks," replied the Jew.

Altogether unconscious of the value of gems, the knight, bidding the young page count out the specified sum, delightedly fastened the splendid gift around his lady's neck, and they both departed.

"Commend me to you of all jewellers," said the young page, laughing as he counted out the thirty marks; "the Lord of Warrington hath made a good bargain, even though he hath dealt with a Jew."

"How know ye that, my fair boy?" said Eleazar, looking at him with some surprise.

"I have not been under the roof of Sir Nicholas de Farendone, the King's jewel-master, so long not to know somewhat of the value of gems. St. Mary! thirty marks! methinks one hundred would scarce buy it."

" Ye would say more truly, my fair boy, did ye say it was worth *two*."

" Our sweet Lady be gracious! two hundred marks! and ye sold it for thirty! this passeth all knowledge. Saints! an Sir Nicholas de Farendone, my lady Edith's guardian, were not over seas, I would pray him to come hither and buy of you."

"Sir Nicholas, my fair boy, might not find such bargains," replied the Jew smiling; " but to the Lord of Warrington I am deeply bound, and I would right willingly have given him that carcanet, only he would not."

" No, truly, he is too knightly to offer to my lady what costs him nought. St. George and St. Michael send him good success in Brittany, and store of ransoms of captive knights ; and then, an he be able to purchase back his father's estates, Sir Nicholas de Farendone may be won perchance to give him my lady Edith."

" Alas, poor knight! then he hath no great store of wealth ?"

" But scant—though what of that ? What had Sir Walter Manny when he first set foot here ; and, when a knight gains fame and worship, wealth follows of course."

" It doth ; and Heaven grant it to yonder brave knight! for none, I have good reason to say, is more worthy."

" Would that Sir Nicholas de Farendone thought so!

But he holdeth with the rich knight, Sir Matthew Trelauny, and is most fierce against *him*. Well now, I will tell my lady in how noble and christian-like way ye have dealt with him; but I will say nought until after to-morrow, lest he should hear and be vexed at it."

"Do not, my fair boy. But be well assured that I have not in one tenth part repaid the Lord of Warrington for what he hath done for me."

The following day the fair armament destined for the relief of Hennebon departed, followed by the eager good wishes and prayers of the whole population. And now, as Froissart often so naïvely says, "why should I make a long story of it?" . Who acquainted with his delightful pages but remembers how the Countess, sorely besieged by the French, who had nearly beaten down the strong walls of Hennebon, day after day ascended her topmost tower, eagerly and anxiously looked over the sea, but in vain, for the coming succours—how, when her council, wise and valiant knights though they were, yielding up all hope, entreated, nay, demanded, that the town should be surrendered, she prayed for a respite of one more day—and how, when, hopeless of all relief, she cast her despairing eyes toward the treacherous sea, whereon she had so often looked in vain, ere one mast was visible to eyes less keen than hers, she exultingly cried, "The succours of England are coming!" —then, how the gallant armament, with broidered sails and blazoned pennons, bore proudly down, and the Countess, unmindful of feudal state, rushed from the castle, "and with joyful cheer greeted Sir Walter Manny and his company, like a right valiant dame." Nor need we delay the current of our story to tell how bravely the flower of English chivalry repulsed the French beneath the walls of Hennebon—how well the battle of Quimperlé was fought, when Don Louis of Spain, severely wounded, was forced to put to sea in a crazy boat, still followed by the victorious English. Alas! that brilliant victory was the beginning of misfortunes to the Lord of Warrington; for, after chasing Don Louis both by sea and land, on the third evening Sir Walter Manny and his gallant companions in arms, in the pride of victory, stood before the strongly fortified Castle of Roche Perion. Then said Sir Walter Manny, "Good gentlemen, I would that we might attack this strong castle, all weary as I am, had I but any one to aid me." Then said the knights, "Go on boldly, sir, for we will follow you even until death!" And, raising their battle-cry, "St. George for merry England!" and advancing the standard on which the lilies of France glittered beside the lions of Plantagenet, they rushed right valiantly to the assault. But Girard de Maulin was no mean enemy; he manned the walls with good cross-bowmen, who shot so unerringly from their high vantage-ground that many knights were slain, and some wounded, and among them the Lord of Warrington, and, by a singular fate, Sir Matthew Trelauny, his rival, also. Nor did his ill fortune end here: René, the brother of de Maulin, hearing news of the attack, armed forty men, and, coming suddenly on the knights and esquires who lay wounded in a field near at hand, took them all prisoners, and carried them to his tower of Favoet. Unable to reduce the castle, and grieving much for the loss of his slain and imprisoned companions, Sir Walter Manny returned to Hennebon, and prepared to give battle to Charles of Blois and Don Louis of Spain, who, having rallied their scattered forces, had now encamped within a short distance of the city.

One afternoon, while the archers were listlessly wandering up and down the town, eagerly awaiting the time that should again place them in battle-array against the host of France, and the knights were playing at chess, or pledging each other in Gascoigne wine to the success of the noble Countess, an instant message from their leader summoned them to the council, where with surprise and horror they learned that the two valiant knights, Sir Johan de Boteler and Sir Matthew Trelauny, had that morning been brought from Favoet to the French camp for instant execution, at the demand of Don Louis of Spain. Astonished beyond measure at this most unchivalrous and most unheard-of intention, the English knights looked at each other, wholly unable to determine what course should be pursued. Then Sir Walter Manny, ever prompt with wise counsel in the camp as with bold daring in the field, rose up, and thus said he: "Right gallant sirs, it would be great honour to us if we could deliver out of danger yonder two knights: and even if we should fail when we put it in adventure, yet will King Edward our master thank us, and so will all other noble men; for who would not put himself right gladly in peril to save the lives of two such valiant knights!" The proposal was joyfully received, and the chivalrous leader, having sent the greater part of his men out at the gate that fronted the French camp, in order to provoke an attack, he himself, with a hundred men-at-arms, and five hundred archers on horseback, sallied out at the postern, and, going round to the back of the camp, forced his way toward the tent, where, bound, and awaiting their almost immediate execution, the two knights lay. To loose them from their bonds, to place swords in their hands, and cause each to mount a steed which he had provided, was but the work of a moment; and, his generous plan thus accomplished, Sir Walter rode back swiftly as he came, to call off the main body of his forces from their feigned assault.

The first thought of the captives, so unexpectedly liberated, was to endeavour to enter Hennebon in the train of their valiant deliverer; but Sir Walter and his archer-band spurred so quickly, that they were soon left in the distance, and Sir Matthew Trelauny, who had been more severely wounded than his rival, with great difficulty urged his slower-paced steed onward.

" Good Sir Matthew," said the Lord of Warrington, suddenly turning, "your wounds are unhealed, and your horse less swift than mine—mount *my* steed, and make the best of your way to Hennebon, and St. George and St. Michael speed you !"

" I may not, my generous rival," replied the almost fainting knight. " St. George, patron of all good chivalry, forbid that I should accept an offer that might place your life in jeopardy !"

" Nay, deny me not," persisted the Lord of Warrington,

dismounting; "rivals though we be, we are brethren in misfortune; lose no time—look yonder."

Sir Matthew Trelauny turned his head, and clouds of dust in the distance too plainly showed that a company of the enemy were approaching.　He looked on the blood that was fast oozing from his unhealed wound, and on the sword which he was unable to wield—half an hour on a swift steed would place him safely within the walls of Hennebon—there was no time for either to lose in fruitless debate—the strong instinct of self-preservation prevailed, and he mounted the swifter steed.　"Farewell, my generous rival," said he; "no longer rival, but brother."

"That cannot be," said the Lord of Warrington mournfully; "ye are pledged to run three courses against me in the August tournament, and may I lose all favour of my lady if I meet you not there!　But, away! ride, ride for your life!"

The Lord of Warrington leaped on his rival's horse, and endeavoured to spur toward Hennebon.　Alas! ill fortune a second time pursued him: some of the scouts from the French army came up, and, after a brave but ineffectual struggle, he was led captive to Roche Perion.

It was in vain for our hapless knight that Charles of Blois was finally driven back, that a truce was completed, and that the victorious army, accompanied by the Countess, had sailed to England: closely confined, although no longer in danger of his life, in the topmost tower of Roche Perion, he sat disconsolately day by day, looking out upon the distant towers of Hennebon and the dark blue sea beyond.

One day, while thus mournfully sitting, almost questioning the justice of Heaven, which for a deed of knightly generosity seemed thus to have requited him with stern imprisonment, he heard the distant sounds of the heralds' trumpets, as they passed along the road leading from Hennebon, to proclaim in every town that owned the rule of the Earl of Montfort notice of the coming tournament. And nearer and nearer came the gay procession, until the proud blazonry of the banners, and the scarlet tabards glittering with gold broidery, were distinctly visible: he heard the peremptory flourish of the trumpets, and—harsh sound to a prisoned knight—almost the very words of the spirit-stirring proclamation, that summoned all the chivalry of France and England to assemble at the tournament in Smithfield, "on the morrow of the Assumption of our Lady."

"Saints! must my companions in arms, nay, my rival himself, take part in this gallant festival," cried the Lord of Warrington, leaning his head against the bars of his window, overcome with the feeling of his forlorn condition, "and must I remain here without chance of going forth, nay, without money to pay my ransom, and unable to fulfil my vow?"

Surely some one pronounced his name—he looked down, and Eleazar of Bruges was standing just below. "Alas, brave knight!" said he, "I have come over hither to seek thee—and now have I found thee thus! But be not cast down; I have money for thy ransom, and thou shalt go forth to the tournament."

"It may not be," replied the much-wondering Lord of Warrington. "Girard de Maulin will take no ransom, even though I might offer it, until Charles of Blois return. Would that he might but suffer me to cross the seas to fulfil my promise, and I would return right soon."

"It shall be so," said the Jew. "Girard de Maulin longeth for a right Damascus dagger greatly as ye do to ride forth to the tournament; I will seek him; leave all to me, and it shall be well."

The same evening the door of his dungeon opened, and the chatelain of Roche Perion stood before him. "Sir Johan de Boteler," said he, "I have heard of your great wish to be at the tournament, and, in return for your noble present, as Charles of Blois will not return until the end of August, I will grant you absence from hence for fourteen days, only taking your knightly word that ye will go straight thither, return straight hither, neither raising your visor nor declaring your name all the time of your sojourn in London."

"I accept your offer right gladly," cried the knight, "and pledge you my word that I will but proceed to the tournament, and then return hither and again yield myself prisoner."

The day of the tournament arrived, with all its gay devices, and gorgeous pageantry, and gallant show of mimic war, and all those festival sights and sounds which Chaucer, in his Knight's Tale, paints to the very life. And along the well-gravelled and tapestry-decked streets, from the Tower to the lists in Smithfield, fourscore esquires in gay apparel slowly passed by, each riding a noble steed, adorned with

plumed chanfrin, gilded martingal, and silken bases, rich
with armorial bearings; while, like a dream of fairy-land,
fourscore noble ladies, each mounted on a fair palfrey, led
by a chain of silver her favourite knight. These were the
English chivalry; but, on arriving at the lists, many French
and many Flemish knights, and among them the Earl of
Hainault, the Queen's brother, stood ready. But one there
was, who, in plain armour, and bearing a shield without any
device, and distinguished by a fetter-ring on his right ancle,
attracted much inquiry. Nought, however, could be learned,
save that he was a knight from Brittany, who had come
hither to fulfil his vow. Such vows were common in the
days of chivalry; and many a bright eye cast a look of more
eager interest upon the nameless knight than on him who
rode conspicuous in the richest Milan armour, or him whose
proud quarterings embossed his courser's bases to the very
ground. Nor did the nameless knight gainsay by his deeds
the interest thus excited: with the lance and with the
sword, in the lists as at the barriers, he was equally successful; and when the heralds, the King having thrown
down his warder, presented the victorious knights to the
Queen and the ladies, he received from the fair hand of
Philippa the second prize, an emerald ring of great value.

"Who is yonder Breton knight?" said the King; "bring
him before me, and tell him *now* he may well declare his
name;"—for it was frequently the custom with younger
knights to ride incognito to the tournament, and not to
make themselves known until they had achieved some
gallant deed of arms. It was, however, in vain that knight,

herald, fair lady, even the gentle Philippa herself, pressed him to unlace his helmet or declare his name: to their most urgent entreaties he replied that he was forbidden, by his vow;—and to the courteous and lofty feeling of chivalrous times that one word was sufficient.

The Queen and the ladies, accompanied by the knights, retired to the neighbouring pavilion, while the nameless knight leant against the barriers, absorbed in sorrowful reflection. He had crossed the seas to fulfil his vow, but his rival had not met him in the tournament. Lady Edith, too, on whose fair face he had hoped to gaze, was absent; he had been successful to the very height of his expectations—he had won praise from the Queen and honour from the Monarch; still, entangled, spell-bound, by his luckless vow, he must return to his harsh captivity, nor could even his lady-love know that the Breton stranger was indeed an Englishman and her own true knight. Turning, therefore, with a sick heart from the gay scene around him, and casting an anxious and sorrowful look toward the princely mansion of the King's jewel-master, into which he dared not trust himself to enter, he bent his steps toward the noble house of the Grey Friars, hoping that, since it was within "the soke and aldermanrie" of Sir Nicholas de Farendone, (whose father gave his name to the wards of Farringdon), he might obtain some little information at least from some prosing grey friar or garrulous lay-brother. But in vain did he pace the ample cloisters; neither grey friar nor lay-brother appeared; and, at the sound of the even-song bell, he reverently entered the splendid church; and, endeavour-

ing with strong effort to cast aside that burden of anxieties
and conflicting cares which well-nigh overwhelmed him, he
knelt at the altar, and earnestly addressed himself to his
devotions.

The psalms were duly sung; the prayers were said; the
grey friars, two and two, in goodly order, quitted the church;
the last note of the noble organ died away along the high-
arched aisles; and the scanty congregation had departed:
still the stranger knight arose not to go.   At length the slant
rays of the declining sun, streaming through the rainbow-
tinted panes, and shedding a gorgeous light, like the mingled
radiance of the ruby, and amethyst, and topaz, on every
clustered pillar and every fair-wrought shrine, warned him
it was time to depart, and seek some conveyance over seas,
alas! to his donjon, for the morrow.   He arose—but whence
was that low and sweetly-breathed voice? and who was that
beautiful damsel, who, not in holiday attire, but in simple
white robe, and unbraided, unjewelled, hair, knelt at the
neighbouring altar? Oh! who could it be—who, on an evening like this, when all were gay and joyous, would seek the
solitude of the church and the solace of prayer, save her who
mourned the sad captivity of her affianced knight—the fair
lady Edith !

Overjoyed at this unexpected meeting, scarcely conscious
of what he did, the unknown knight drew the ring, the
reward of his chivalrous feats, from his bosom, and laid it
before her. "Farewell, sweet Edith," said he; " my vow
compels me to return ere to-morrow; farewell !"

The lady arose hastily. " What say ye of returning ?—

and wherefore this disguise?—and wherefore this speed to depart, when Heaven hath thus sent you back?" cried she, immediately recognising him.

"Alas! sweet Edith, I must—I have pledged my knightly word, and it must not be broken.   Farewell! Heaven grant we may meet again!"

"O might ye not stay!" cried the lady; "but saints forefend that the daughter of a knight should urge her dearest friend to break his knightly vow!   Nay, take this token;" and, with trembling hand, she unclasped the rich ruby carcanet, her only ornament, from her neck.   "Refuse it not; ye know not its value, its great value," persisted she.   "O take it! who knows but it may defray your ransom!"

"It never shall," replied the knight.   "Sweet Edith, if I take it, it is but as a token from thee—farewell!" and, unable to repress his feelings, he rushed out of the church.

Unwilling to hazard the risk of recognition in the narrow streets of London, with a sorrowful heart the Lord of Warrington, again mounting his good steed, took the road outside the walls.   It was with a heavy sigh that his eye glanced over the fair scene before him: the barriers still graced with the pennons of the victorious knights, the pavilions with their rich blazonry shining amid the dark foliage, and the numberless groups of merry holiday-makers, lingering in pleasant converse by the road-side, or engaged at football in the fields beyond, while knights and esquires, their tilting armour laid aside, rode by in quaint and picturesque masquerade.   All was bright, all was joyous; the laugh, and the shout, and sounds of distant music, floated pleasantly on the light breeze, while from every tall and graceful spire rung out the witching music of the evening bells. And, as though inspired by the glad scene around them, a party of merry masquers, in coats of Lincoln green, with bugle slung about the neck, and quiver suspended from the baldric, rode blithely along, carolling the following song, with right pleasant melody :—

Seek thou not the royal hall,
Seek thou not the castle tall,
Nor the cloister arched fair,
Nor the Bourse where merchants are:
There are anger, strife, and pain;
There is readier loss than gain:
Wouldst thou joy and liberty,
Hither to the greenwood tree!

Envy not the monarch's crown,
Envy not the churchman's gown,
Nor noble's mantle gleaming bright,
Nor blazoned coat of gallant knight—
Each well lined with care I ween—
But the frock of forest green
Wraps a bosom light and free;
Then hither to the greenwood tree!

Hither, when the sun is high,
And the royal stag sweeps by,
And the brooklets sparkling run,
And each wild flower to the sun
Smileth her sweet welcoming,
And every bird is carolling—
And all is joyaunce, sport, and glee;
Then hither to the greenwood tree!

Ay, and when the sun is gone,
And the lady moon alone,
Abbess-like, in wimpled pride,
Riseth o'er the green hill's side—

"So, 'hither to the greenwood tree,' Sir Unknown Knight!" cried the leader of the troop of merry masquers, laying hold of his bridle, "for I am commanded by the queen of faërie to bring you to her presence."

It was in vain that the Lord of Warrington, fearful of delay, and yet more fearful of recognition, entreated, prayed, nay, half commanded, the masquer to relinquish his bridle-rein, and suffer him to pursue his melancholy way—the eve of the tournament was a gay carnival, in which it was the favourite pastime of the younger knights and ladies to enact as closely to the letter as possible the wild and brilliant incidents of chivalrous romance. "Nay, Sir Unknown," persisted the masquer, "the command of my sovereign lady, the faërie queen, must be obeyed at all hazards. What! a *Breton* knight, and think to gainsay her slightest wish! remember Lanval and Gruèlan"—for Brittany was the birth-place of all the bright and beautiful fictions of faërie.

Remonstrance was as vain as resistance; the luckless knight suffered them to lead him whither they would: and ere long he found himself in a richly decked pavilion, where, representative of the faërie queen, the gentle Philippa herself, fit presiding genius of so gay and romantic a scene, sat, surrounded by a company of the fairest damsels of her court, clad in the appropriate dress of her assumed character—the robe of grass green, the favourite colour of faëric, the "gridelin mantle," the narrow circlet of jewels on her open brow; while two beautiful white greyhounds, with golden collars, lay at her feet. And with graceful courtesy, and in language borrowed from the romaunt and the faëry tale, did the gentle Philippa greet the nameless knight, and urge him playfully to declare his name; while many an attendant noble cast looks of ill-suppressed rage at the so highly favoured stranger.

"And whence was that fair jewel ye wear round your neck?" said the Queen.

"Pardon me, my sweet lady and sovereign," interposed Sir Walter Manny, who, in the fancied dress of one of King Arthur's knights, stood near; "this knight hath come hither under vow of concealment; now to demand an answer wherefore he became possessed of that fair jewel might lead to some disclosure of whence he cometh, or who he is."

"Ye are right," said Philippa, smiling. "Sir Knight, we will ask ye nought—only let me one moment look at it, for, saints! I never saw ruby so bright!"

Fearing, though he scarcely knew why, that the carcanet so lucklessly brought to light as he bent before the Queen might cause him further mischance, the unhappy knight hesitated; and again Sir Walter Manny, with his characteristic courtesy, interfered. "My sweet lady," said he, "how do we know but that the jewel may have some device or motto, whereby the giver or the owner may be discovered? This nameless knight ye may well believe is captive to no light and fanciful vow, but to a stern and solemn oath—let him depart in peace, I pray you, that he may have no cause to complain of unknightly usage during his sojourn in this fair land."

"Be it so," said the gentle Philippa. "Farewell, then, right valiant knight, if indeed ye *must* go. But will not ye stay and disport yourself this evening? to-morrow and the following day ye will not miss of a conveyance over seas."

"Many thanks, fair Queen," said the unknown knight; "but I would pray you, let me depart this evening; the time allowed by my vow is nearly past."

"Sir Walter Manny," said the Queen, as the stranger knight with graceful obeisance departed, "bid one of our trusty watch and ward convoy yonder valiant knight safely to his destination. The commons love not the French, and they may chance to entreat him but rudely."

Willingly proceeded Sir Walter on his kind errand; and fearing little the chance of recognition, since even his friend and captain was unable to penetrate his disguise, the Lord of Warrington accepted the attendance of the billman without objection.

"And now, Sir Stranger, suffer me to offer you this purse," said Sir Walter Manny. "Your expenses may be greater than ye think, and, if ye will but accept the loan of it, ye will rejoice me, inasmuch as I shall be sure to see you again."

To receive money as a loan from richer knights was never considered degrading: the Lord of Warrington, well pleased at the fortunate chance which had thus easily supplied him with the means of paying part of his ransom, and of most probably obtaining his freedom to procure the rest, warmly thanked the chivalrous Fleming, and unrecognised by any, departed.

On the morrow, King Edward entered his council-chamber at Westminster, no longer the gay and chivalrous Monarch, the graceful president of the tournament, with a well-turned compliment for each victorious knight, and a word of gentle flattery for each fair lady, but moody and anxious, with stern brow and angry reply, even to his most cherished councillors.

" My lords," said he, " ye all know how fiercely France hath opposed our claim to her crown; and ye all know right well how in the council and on the battle-field we have no cause to fear her. But now, not content with a fair and open warfare, she hath sought other measures, and hath caused to be taken from our jewel-house a gem upon whose safe custody our success against her depends. Among our jewels is one, the Great Balas Ruby, which Cœur de Lion won from Philip Augustus, and which a wise man then declared, so long as it was in the keeping of England the fortunes of France should quail before her—this jewel is lost !"

An involuntary expression of alarm burst from the whole council; for the belief in the powerful and mysterious qualities of precious stones was during the Middle Ages an unquestioned article of the popular faith. " That this jewel should be missing," continued the King, "is no slight trouble; but the manner in which it hath I fear me been taken proves to my mind much treachery, nay, the existence even of some deeply-laid plot."

"Impossible, dear and most honoured master!" cried Sir Walter Manny; "I would gage my knightly faith for the honour of our chivalry."

"Ye judge others by yourself, my brave Sir Walter," replied the King; "your unblemished faith starts back from the thought of perfidy, like the ermine from the least touch of defilement—not so others. But our jewel-master hath returned this morning from Florence; we will forthwith bid him to our presence, for this matter shall be searched into to the utmost. St. Mary! an knight or noble have dared to take this precious ruby, Plantagenet though he were for three descents, he should hang on the gallows-tree; and should I find that the King of France possesses it, by my three patron saints, who never failed me, St. Edward, St. Michael, and St. George, I will prick forth to the very gates of Paris, and summon him to yield it on the lance point!" and, with flushed cheek and flashing eye, as though the King of France stood bodily before him, the chivalrous Monarch drew off his jewelled glove, and dashed it on the table.

Unconscious of the trouble that awaited him, Sir Nicholas de Farendone, worn and weary as one returned in eager haste, but with well-pleased look as one who bore glad tidings, entered the council-room, followed by several attendants bearing huge leather bags, carefully bound and sealed.

"Our sweet Lady hath been right favourable, my liege," said he, setting himself on his knee; "and I have brought with me ten thousand gold crowns from the Bardi, in part of the loan which I have raised." (This loan historical accuracy obliges us to say was never, alas! repaid, but caused the bankruptcy of that celebrated Florentine house two or three years afterward.)

"It is well," said the King carelessly, for to his excited mind the sight of the well filled money-bags, though his exchequer was almost empty, offered no solace; "but we would ask you respecting a jewel for which diligent search hath been made."

"Saints! what jewel?" cried the jewel-master; "every one was safe when I left England, and for those I took with me I found an excellent market—the great balas ruby alone sold for two hundred marks at Bruges."

"The great balas ruby! false traitor, daredst thou sell that jewel on which the success of my war depends?"

"There is some mistake, my liege," interposed the Chancellor, "for we have good and sufficient evidence that *that* ruby was carried away but yesterday. We further know that among the royal jewels are *two* great balas rubies, and that the second was placed there by your wise grand father (whom God assoil), to the end that, by their great likeness, the stealing of the fortunate one might be rendered more difficult."

"This is the list of jewels my liege commanded me to sell," said the jewel-master, producing a small piece of parchment;—for our earlier monarchs often found that selling a portion of the crown-jewels was a more speedy, if not more pleasant, way of raising supplies, than by extorting benevolences at the lance point, and gifts by threats of "donjon and gallows-tree."

"Yes, my lords," continued the Chancellor, "and that precious jewel, thus strangely lost, was undoubtedly in the possession of that stranger knight who yesterday won the second prize at the tournament. He was seen near the house of the Grey Friars hanging something cautiously about his neck: when brought to the Queen's pavilion this was discovered to be a heart-shaped ruby; and it was observed how fearfully he drew back when the Queen asked to look at it, and how earnestly, as though for his life, he prayed to depart. Moreover, Breton as he might pretend to be, he was an Englishman, and spoke—so saith the yeoman who conducted him to the Vintry—English as well as he,"—(the language of the higher classes at this period was Norman-French;) "while what places his perfidy beyond all doubt is, that he asked for passage not to Hennebon, but to Vannes, the very stronghold of Charles of Blois."

"'Tis plain as daylight!" said Edward, laying down the parchment. "You, Sir Jewel-master, are not to blame; you sold the *larger* ruby. The precious and charmed one, that enclosed in the wreath of *fleur de souvenance*, is smaller."

"St. Mary!" cried the jewel-master, "it was *that* I sold!"

"Sold *that*, false traitor?"

"My liege gave no description, save the 'largest'—that was the largest; I knew not the high value ye set on it, and I sold it to a Jew at Bruges full three months since."

"But a jewel just like it is said to have been seen not

long since in your very house," said the Chancellor, " where it was said to be kept secretly."

" I see it all!" said the King fiercely. " Ye pretended to mistake the jewel, and took it to your own house, and then, after having made your bargain with the King of France, fearing danger if it were in your own possession, ye sent a trusty messenger to convey it away. Hither, captain of the watch and ward! take this traitor, and keep him straitly in durance."

" My liege," said Sir Walter Manny, " be not so hasty; I would stake my knightly honour on that young stranger: I pray you send not yonder worthy knight to prison on such light evidence."

" Sir Walter Manny perchance knows somewhat more about the stranger knight, seeing that he interposed to save him from discovery, and caused him to be sent safely away," replied the Chancellor sternly.

" I did but what I would do again," replied Sir Walter proudly.

The council separated, and, lamenting the harsh doom of the jewel-master, and musing over the events of the preceding day, he bent his footsteps to the court-yard.

" Good Sir Walter Manny, what is this about a missing jewel and a stranger knight?" said a meanly dressed old man; " tell me, I pray you, for I may bring you aid."

" Alas! good man," replied the valiant knight, " it is beyond your skill."

" It must be difficult indeed then," returned the old man proudly. " Refuse not my aid, Sir Walter, though ye know me not—many a jewel, mean though I seem, hath passed through my hands, and perchance even this lost one."

There was somewhat in the manner of the aged man that commanded Sir Walter Manny's attention: he looked earnestly at him, and in the swarthy countenance and flashing eye recognised a Jew, whom, though he knew not his name, he had often met in Flanders. He hastily detailed the particulars, bade him use his utmost skill to discover the missing jewel, and promised him a fitting reward.

Again a smile, almost of scorn, passed over the old man's face. " Speak not of reward—*that* will be gained in restoring the jewel. I know where it is; I know who possesses it. Go to the King, Sir Walter; pray him to grant a respite of only ten days to the jewel-master, and all shall be well."

"But who hath taken it? and how may I tell that ye will not deceive me?"

The Jew drew nearer, and whispered two or three words in his ear.

" I will trust you to the utmost," cried the well pleased knight. "Farewell." He turned to depart; when, looking up to the palace windows, he observed the eyes of the King fixed upon him, with a mingled expression of anger and grief.

That evening there was high feasting at the palace; but even a deeper shade clouded King Edward's brow. Was it possible that his most favourite knight, his most cherished companion, was in league with his enemies against him?— and yet, it was Sir Walter Manny who had yesterday in terfered even thrice on behalf of that traitor knight; it was *he*, too, who had urged delay at the council; it was *he* who engaged in mysterious converse about the lost jewel with a stranger and a foreigner even under the palace windows; and, when charged with perfidy, had scarcely made a reply.

"A boon, King Edward!" cried Philippa, advancing with a gay smile to the recess where, involved in sad and conflicting thoughts, he moodily sat; "a boon for the queen of faërie!"

"It is granted, fairest," said the King, half unconsciously; "what would ye?"

"That ye take no further steps in the business of this lost jewel, until ten days are past."

"Madam!" said the King fiercely, starting up, "would that I might deny you! That perfidious knight, Sir Walter Manny, hath prayed you to ask this boon, that the leaders of the plot may escape. Alas! my word is pledged, and I cannot go back—but I here solemnly make mine avow, that never shall he advance my banner, never again see my face, until all and *every one* in whose hands that jewel hath been stand together before me."

While the rash vow of the King and the probable fate of the jewel-master occupied every mind, the vessel that bore the Lord of Warrington bounded swiftly along, and ere the close of the fourth day entered the harbour of Vannes. He proceeded to Roche Perion; but there new marvels awaited him. He was received with strange courtesy, complimented on his knightly honour, shown an order from Charles of Blois directing his instant liberation, and told that his ransom had been paid by a Jew, who had returned to England. Bidding a joyful farewell to his prison towers, the Lord of Warrington hastened away, and in little more than a week again stood upon Vintry quay, no longer the unknown knight, forbidden by his vow to disclose his name, but as the brave Sir Johan de Boteler, one of the valiant leaders of the army in Brittany, and the knight for whom Sir Walter Mauny had done so splendid a deed of chivalrous valour. Alas! short was his joy: from the busy groups that crowded the quay he soon learned the story of the lost jewel, the stranger knight, the disgrace of Sir Walter Manny, and the imminent peril of the luckless jewel-master, who, his ten days' respite having expired, was that very morning to be brought before the council. "It is through me and this luckless purchase," cried he bitterly; while the strangely generous conduct of the Jew, and his singular anxiety that he should purchase that jewel, assumed to his excited mind the guise of a deeply laid and malignant plot, to work not merely his ruin, but that of him from whom he had first received his gilt spur, and beneath whose auspices he had first unfurled his pennon. To make his instant way to Westminster, to acknowledge himself the stranger knight, and to exhibit the ruby carcanet, was his first impulse; and he wildly hastened to fulfil it.

Onward he went; but, as he drew near the King's palace, the busy gathering of the watch and ward, and the eager pressure of the crowd, as the hapless jewel-master was conducted along, caused him to turn aside, when an unseen hand grasped his collar, and an earnest voice exclaimed—

"Blessed be His name that hath sent you!" He looked round, and beheld Eleazar of Bruges.

"There is no time to lose," said he; "three messengers have I sent over seas for you—so hasten—give *me* the carcanet —all depends on it."

" And wherefore ?" said the knight, with a look of distrust.

" Peace !" said the Jew sternly; "thou wilt thank me ere long"—and, before he was aware, the delicate gold chain was broken, and the Jew had vanished with his prize.

" Ye must come hither with me, my fair sir," said one of the watch and ward, coming up. "Methinks I took you down to the Vintry a week agone: the next road that I shall lead you will be, through Our Lady's grace, to the gallows-tree."

King Edward and his assembled nobles sat in council; the hapless jewel-master was placed before them ; but, ere the proceedings commenced, another prisoner was brought in and placed beside him.

" Who is this ?" said the Chancellor.

" My right valiant companion in arms, and one who, to save my life, put his own in jeopardy," cried a young knight rushing forward. " My brave Sir Johan de Boteler, where- fore art thou *here ?* "

" Because I determined to fulfil my vow, Sir Matthew Trelauny," replied the Lord of Warrington; "and alas! that through it such unmerited disgrace should have befallen Sir Walter Manny."

" St. George is my witness I had kept my vow," returned Sir Matthew Trelauny, " had not the King sent me into Flanders, from whence I have but just returned."

"Then it was you, Sir Knight, who came to the tournament as a stranger from Brittany," said the Chancellor sternly.   "But what say ye of the jewel?"

"Alas! I purchased a ruby, heart-shaped, enclosed in enamel, for thirty marks, of a Jew, named Eleazar of Bruges; and it was *that* which I wore, and which was mistaken for one more precious."

"Produce it," said the Chancellor.

"Would that I could! but, even as I came hither, that accursed Jew—though, alas! I scarce should say so, since he hath ever seemed to have stood my friend—took it from me.   Would that Eleazar of Bruges were here!"

"He *is* here," said a hooded stranger beside him, "though no longer Eleazar of Bruges," throwing back his hood, and drawing himself up proudly, "but Matthias Ben Judah of Toledo.   King Edward, *thou* knowest me well?"

"I do, and most gladly do I welcome thee," said the King, instantly recognising the learned alchemist, whose fame had gone forth over the whole of Europe, and whose aid had been sought by many a Christian monarch, and by Edward himself, to replenish their exhausted treasuries by his fancied skill.

"And thou knowest this jewel," said the Jew, laying the ruby carcanet on the table.

"I do, right well — precious, priceless jewel!" cried Edward; "but how camest thou possessed of it?"

"By purchase from a stranger, but whom I find to be he who stands there; and I sold it to this knight."

"And for thirty marks *only?*" said the Chancellor.

"I did :—little do ye, little doth the Lord of Warrington, suspect the priceless service he rendered me, when my dwelling was beset by the brutal populace at Lisle. It was not for my gold that I trembled, not for my jewels, scarcely even for my safety, but for that precious vial of liquid, bequeathed to me by that learned adept, my father, by which I trust ere long to obtain the mighty secret. The brave arm of the Lord of Warrington drove back the craven churls; and I then vowed that, in whatever trouble he might be, or whatever gift he might wish to obtain, I would alway stand his friend. Good Sire, I have released you from your rash vow; the jewel and the purchasers are *all* before you: suffer me therefore to pray a guerdon, since it was for this purpose (as I know ye will scarcely refuse *me*) that I took from him this jewel—it is, that ye will restore to the Lord of Warrington the estates, which through poverty his father sold, and allow him to obtain the lady Edith."

"Grant it, good King," cried Sir Matthew Trelauny, sinking on his knee.

"Do *you* say thus, my generous rival?" exclaimed the Lord of Warrington, overwhelmed with joy and surprise.

"Not so generous as you, when ye gave me your steed," replied his fancied rival, smiling. "You suspected me your rival, and I did not undeceive you, since I had bound myself by a vow to watch over the orphan fortunes of my half-sister, the lady Edith, until I might see her placed beneath the care of a far worthier protector."

"Bid Sir Walter Manny hither," cried King Edward, looking joyfully around. "Good Matthias of Toledo, ten thousand thanks to you: brave Sir Johan de Boteler, whatever ye wish is granted: my worthy Sir Nicholas de Farendone, ye must forgive my harshness—it was my own error; but from this time forth ye shall have no reason to complain. And you, my tried and true friend," and his voice faltered, "what shall I say for my rash speech, Sir Walter? what shall I do for *you*?"

"Nought, my dear Sovereign," replied the chivalrous Manny, "save never to think of it again."

"Follow me, brave knights," cried the King, rising; "and you, too, good Matthias: we will hold high festival, and receive the gratulations of our faërie queen. And for this precious jewel, lest it should again be lost, I will place it in the keeping of my patron, St. George, for it shall be set in a chalice for his altar."

And so it was;—ere long a splendid gold chalice, executed under the superintendence of Sir Nicholas de Farendone, with "the great balas ruby" conspicuously set, was placed upon the high altar of St. George's Chapel, where for many generations it remained, challenging admiration from all, until that worthy Monarch Henry the VIII., with whom to see, to covet, and to take, were synonymous, caused the beautiful chalice to be coined into gold pieces, and placed the gem among the crown-jewels. Nor few were the after-vicissitudes of "the great balas ruby." It decked the bosom of the vain and hapless Anne Boleyn, when, unconscious of her short-lived regality, she moved in crowned and sceptred state from the Abbey to Westminster Hall; it blazed in the gorgeous stomacher of her more fortunate daughter, when, hailed as "goddess more than queen," she presided over the princely revels and dream-like pageants of Kenilworth ; it shone proudly on the threadbare grey hat of her sapient successor, when he edified the Star Chamber with lectures on theology, demonology, and that subject dearer than all, his divine right; and it glowed on the rich point collar of his unhappy son, when for the last time he quitted proud Whitehall, whither he was only to return a captive to his execution. At length, all its varied fortunes past, in the attempt to convey the crown-jewels to Holland, this splendid gem was lost: that deep depository of long accumulated treasure, that vast jewel-chamber of all past generations, the Ocean, finally engulfed " THE GREAT BALAS RUBY."

The City of the Desert.

ELEVEN days had I trodden these trackless solitudes: eleven times had I seen the sun rise from the vast level that stretched around me. It was now evening, and as the oblique rays shot athwart the desert, I fancied I descried the appearance of columns rising on the far horizon. I strained my aching eye-balls, to pierce, as it were, between the desert and the sky, that I might be assured no moving pillars of sand had been mistaken for the vestiges of human labour; but the appearances continued immovable. This, then, was the City of the Desert; here it was that, on the morning of the twelfth day, as my vision had revealed, I should obtain the promised gift—contentment! A thousand times had I bewailed the shortness of human life: "It is a worthless possession," I have exclaimed; "too brief for enjoyment: oh, that I might live for a thousand years!" "Go," said the vision; "go to the City of the Desert, and there learn contentment."

As the morning of the twelfth day dawned, it revealed

the object of my search. An irregular line of varied eleva-
tions, evidently the work of man, showed, either the existence or the remains of his habitation. As I approached,
the line grew into greater distinctness, and soon the uprisen
sun bathed in gold the pinnacles of a hundred temples! I
knew not if the City were inhabited; this, my vision had
not revealed; and I stopped to listen if any sound of life
came over the desert. The profoundest stillness reigned,—
the City was as silent as the wilderness that surrounded it;
and, as I passed within the walls, I believed myself to be
the only human being they enclosed. It was a solemn and
imposing spectacle. I wandered through long and spacious
streets all silent as the grave: palaces, temples, and private
dwellings, stood, some as if they were yet the habitations of
the living: some crumbling into ruins. Columns, upon
which the art of man had been exhausted, lay prostrate, or
stood yet erect, though mouldering away,—bright in the
rays of the morning sun, that for centuries had risen and
set upon their silent beauty. I was suddenly awakened
from a deep reverie by the sound of a footstep. An aged
man stood within a few paces of me; and, as I involuntarily
stepped back, somewhat awed by the presence of one whose .
appearance bespoke a nature if not different, yet less evanescent than my own: " Fear nothing," said he, in a tongue
that had long ceased to be the language of living lips, "fear
nothing: comest thou hither to learn, from one over whose
head centuries have passed, the misery of length of years?
Thou doest well: follow me, and thou shalt hear of the curse
that has rested upon me for a thousand years." I obeyed my

conductor, who led me into a garden, where, in the centre, shaded by date trees, stood a fountain, and on the ground a marble basin, into which the water fell, drop by drop. " See," said he, " there is only one pebble in this basin," and an exulting smile passed over his shrivelled countenance; " once there were a thousand,—but nine hundred and ninety-nine are resting on the ground: I have taken one from the heap each year of the nine hundred and ninety-nine that the curse has endured, that I might know my hour; to-night, when the moonbeam shall tip the date tree, I will throw this on the ground also. Sit down upon these steps," continued the patriarch, " and listen to the story of my life." I sat down beside the man of a thousand years, as thus he spoke :—

" The City which now contains but thee and me, and which has been for a thousand years the dwelling-place of only one, was once the habitation of a million of living men and women. Tens of thousands in lusty manhood once walked these silent streets; and the light glee of children who lived not to be men, mingled with the noise of the waters that once gushed from this fountain, and with the sounds of happy living creatures that filled the air, or gambolled on the earth. I see it all, but as yesterday. But a curse came upon the City; and the curse has rested upon me. Famine came first; many died—but they who had bread gave to them who had none—all, save me, and my kindred; we ate abundantly, while famished men fought with the dogs for putrid offals. Then came disease; thousands died in a day, and thousands were each day newly smitten; but no man refused to tend the sick—all were kind and compassionate, save me. When famine alone had visited us, I did not desert my kindred, because we had abundance; but now, I forsook all. My father was stricken, my mother—she who had so often watched over me—my mother was stricken—sisters, brethren, all were stricken; but I visited them not, nor helped them. I garnered my own dwelling with provisions and costly wines, and secluded myself from all intercourse with the diseased. There I prayed a selfish prayer for life: I said, 'Let all die; but grant life to me.' Alas! my prayer, my guilty prayer, was heard. 'Live!' said a voice, as my prayer expired on my lips; 'live, foolish Azib, be cursed with life—life for a thousand years!'

"I understood not then how life could be a curse. I exulted in the anticipation of length of years. Death, that to others was always near, to me was afar off. Life, that to others was uncertain, was to me assured—life for a thousand years. The period at which I was resolved to return to the world had not yet arrived; but the promise of life was sufficient security, even although disease should still be raging, and I came forth from my solitude. As I passed through this garden (for yonder, where that one column still stands, was my dwelling), I marvelled at the great stillness that filled the air; but I guessed not the curse that was upon me: that the City was half depeopled, I believed; that my friends, that my kindred had perished, might be; but not that all had perished. I entered the house of my kindred; I went into many chambers, but they were empty. I heard a noise in that which was my mother's; and as I approached the door, a hyæna came forth. Oh! what a spectacle was reserved for me! I passed quickly into the streets—they were silent and empty. I entered the houses;—in those that were shut I found the dead; in those that were open I found both the dead and the living—the dead of my own species, the living of another. Night came, and I again sought my dwelling. Now I prayed for death; but I heard the curse again pronounced—'Live! be cursed with life—life for a thousand years!' I again walked out into the streets, in search of death; but the hyæna and the wolf passed by, and avoided me. Now I knew that the curse was upon me, and that mine was a charmed life; and I returned to this garden, and sat down upon the marble steps where we now rest. I knew that life must endure for a thousand years, and I picked up a thousand peebles, and placed them in that marble basin, where now but one remains.

"Yet, hope had not entirely left me. I sought in the remotest and most obscure dwellings, if perchance I might find some human being—some child—whom disease, or at least death had not reached; but I found none; and when assured I had no living associate, I felt a strange consolation in the companionship of the dead. In their faces and forms there were recollections of living men; and I sat by them for hours and days, and disputed the possession of them with the wild beasts: but, one by one, they snatched them from me; and the traces of the living passed away, till nothing remained to remind me of my race. Next, the brute creation disappeared: during fifty years, birds and beasts some-

times visited the City; but at length they came no more.
The last creature I have seen was a pelican, that more than
nine hundred years ago sat one morning on the sun-dial
before the great temple.

"Dreadful has been the curse of life, and more dreadful
has it been every day. I would have made a companion
of the hyæna—I would have associated with anything
that had life. While watching the winged race, called into
existence by the sunbeams, I have felt less wretched; for,
like me, they were endued with life: but many centuries
have passed away since this small sympathy has been mine.
A curse is upon earth and air, as well as upon me; even the
insects that used to float in this basin, and with whose im-
perfect life I have felt some sympathy, have long been
extinct. I would have given—but what had I to give?
yet had I possessed one blessing, I would have resigned it,
to have heard even the cry of a jackal, or the scream of a
vulture!

"When life in animated beings could no longer be found,
I sought life or motion in inanimate things. I have sat on
these steps and listened for centuries to the gushing of that
fountain; but it has long ceased to afford this consolation,
for see, the water comes drop by drop. I have watched the
flowers that grew, watered by its spray, and the weeds that
sprung up among the ruins; but they are all withered, and
the country around is a desert: these date trees, that afford
me sustenance, alone survive. All this is the curse of
selfishness, the punishment of longing after length of years.
I might have given my sympathy, and died with my kindred;

but I refused it, and, lo! I have received none for a thousand years! A thousand years have I wandered, the sole tenant of these silent streets: I have seen the tooth of time gnaw the records of perishing men; its triumphs are the sole disturbers of the silence that reigns around, as columns fall to the earth, or dwellings crumble into dust."

The aged man paused for a moment. "It is now only mid-day," continued he; "go, walk through the City, meditate on what thou hast heard, and return hither at sunset."

I went into the City; I entered the habitations that had been tenantless a thousand years. I entered the dwelling of kings, and saw the vacant throne, and the enamelled floor, once swept by the purple of past ages. I stood among the ruins of temples, and stumbled over the mutilated idols that were mingling with the dust of those who had worshipped them; and I gazed on the sun-dial, that Time had spared, to be his chronicler.

At sunset I returned to the garden. The aged man still sat on the marble steps, and seemed to be watching the far horizon. I sat down beside him, and both were silent. The light of day was fast waning; the rosy hues of sunset died away; fainter grew the scene; at length a pale light on the horizon appeared, and grew, till the moon rose slowly up into the wide sky: soon, the date tree and the pinnacle of the fountain were tipped with silver: the aged man then arose, and taking the last pebble from the basin, threw it on the ground. One drop of water hung trembling from the fountain—it fell, but none other came; and when I raised my eyes to the countenance of the old man, I saw that his race was ended!

I quitted the garden to enter again upon my journey through the desert; and as I passed by the sun-dial, I saw that Time had no longer a record in the City of the Desert: the pedestal which had supported it had fallen!

The Princess of the West.

IT was in the latter end of the month of September that a solitary traveller in the interior of a North American forest found himself on the bank of one of those rapid streams near which the earlier settlers were accustomed to erect their log-houses, to plant the germs of a new growth of civilisation, and, amidst the hunting grounds of the Indian, to establish a fresh domain for man. The unpretending and hospitable board of the Dutch boor or the English puritan was always offered to a brother wanderer, not merely as a matter of bounty, but as a right to which his circumstances created an indisputable claim.

One of those primitive dwellings now invited the temporary sojourn of the travel-stained and almost exhausted subject of this narrative. It was not the residence of a modern squatter, a sturdy backwoodsman, a dealer in furs, or a fugitive from offended laws. The period in which these events occurred belongs to an earlier, and, if the phrase may be allowed, a more poetic age.

The inhabitant, or, properly speaking, the mistress of the mansion, was a lone female, unmarried, and still youthful, though the first bloom of early girlhood had passed from her fine countenance, with its usually evanescent character in the American hemisphere. Although the earlier transatlantic settlers despised the elegancies of profane learning, as they shunned the more imaginative adjuncts of religion, there were some among them who, partaking of the pedantry, and blind to the affectation then frequently found in Europe, conferred upon this remarkable woman the appellation of the *American Diana.*

Her aged father was the original planter of the settlement; and his daughter, by one of those rare chances, hardly probable enough for fiction, but more true than some of the relations of history, blended many, if not all, of the softer characteristics of her sex with great physical energy and moral hardihood. Familiar with every exercise of the woods, indifferent to their dangers, and inured to the climate, she had acquired an authority among the increasing community by whom she was surrounded, which, although it partook not of the forms, still less of the ostentatious splendours, of regality or chieftainship, possessed much of the substantial power occasionally denied to both.

To trace in detail the sources of that ascendency is beside the purpose of the present narrative; enough, that it was generously exercised, and never disputed. Her personal beauty and mental endowments; her pecuniary resources, rare in that age and country; her romantic disinterestedness and impartiality; and the influence of some predilections which she indulged in favour of Indian manners, enabled her to acquire this ascendency, which many qualities, intellectual and moral, that marked her extraordinary character, concurred to preserve.

The modern tourist in the United States will now find no remnant of the Indians of that district, though he may hear the tradition that such a race once existed, and be shown in evidence the treasured relic of some antique weapon which they wielded. Years have rolled on; the white man is lord of the soil; many millions of a commercial population swarm over the land; and the echoing sound of the axe adds, every succeeding year, hundreds of square miles to the domains of civilisation; while the rapid disappearance of the original inhabitants signalizes and disgraces the progress of refinement. In the busy streets of a trading town all remembrance is lost of that being whose gifts of nature, of fortune, and of education, raised her to the power of a princess, and to some of the honours of a goddess.

Though History will not condescend to record, and marbles and medals do not transmit to a remote age, events which in no degree influenced the scenes enacted on the great theatre of human affairs, yet another art, not always humbler in its pretensions, though generally more domestic in its subjects, has furnished one memorial, now occupying a place on the walls of my apartment, in which the exterior characteristics of this almost poetical creation have been faithfully preserved, in combination with accidents and adjuncts proper to her habits and illustrative of her character. Frequently as I have gazed on this exquisite, and, to me, invaluable production of art, have I become sensible of the intuitive perception of truth and nature which restrained the artist's pencil from giving to that pensive and almost divine countenance the common-place beauty of glowing roseate hues; for the freshness of the breeze seldom imparted to her cheek its bloom of joyousness; and art, by its immortal touches, tells, in that portrait, the oft repeated tale of—

"The grief of hearts forsaken."

The sun cannot revive the flower whose root is cankered, neither can the dews restore freshness to the plant whose principle of vitality is extinguished: so in human affections, as in the physical structure of man, there is no second Spring. The beauty of intense feeling rests on those faultless classic features; but their marble paleness shows that feeling's early blight.

The origin of her settled melancholy, the cause of such total retirement from society, the motives which drew her sire into the fastnesses of an unexplored region, were alike hidden in mystery and regarded with wonder. Of their native land nothing was known among the tribes excepting this—they came across the great river (the Atlantic) from a distant island, and they did not speak the same tongue as the other pale faces (the Dutch).

But to return to our more immediate subject. The solitary traveller, excited by the near prospect of rest and refreshment which the proximity of this lone dwelling presented, vigorously, as compared with his former pace, commenced ascending the elevation on which it was built, and quickly

found himself in the presence of its owner. After the dignified but unceremonious and hospitable welcome with which
he was received, the new acquaintances conversed with ease;
for they fluently spoke the language of Shakspeare and
Milton.

When the stranger had taken the requisite rest and refreshment, the conversation naturally turned on the peculiar
manners and habits of the people among whom the lady
resided; for these were some of the leading objects of the
traveller's curiosity.

The descriptions of modern tourists, and even the dramatic
novels of the present day, have conveyed no unfaithful repre-
sentation of the great outlines which mark the character of
the North American Indian; still they are but outlines, and,
at best, those writers deal in generalities. However true it
may be that hospitality, generosity, courage, fidelity, nay,
that every savage virtue adorned the red man, yet some
tribes, and especially some subdivisions of tribes, offered an
exception to the general rule; hence it was that the Princess,
as the Indians were accustomed to style her, cautioned the
traveller neither to place implicit reliance on his own estimate of the character of the Indian tribes then in their immediate vicinity; nor to imagine that he might, otherwise
than after many precautions, and by great good fortune,
hope to penetrate into and return from the hunting grounds
of that tribe whose village stood at the head of the stream
which wound its way round her dwelling.

"Beware," said she, "of disregarding the admonitions of
one long familiar with these scenes, who has no interest in

advising you to adopt caution, and who shudders at the thought that the spirit of research of her fellow-countryman may meet a sad reward in death by treachery. Return, since the purposes of your journey are now, to a certain extent, accomplished; proceed, and, without any prospect of benefit to science, you may perhaps leave no memorial behind, excepting those of violence, to indicate the route you have taken, or to communicate the fate which may have befallen you."

"Pardon me," replied the ardent traveller, his eyes lighted with the spirit of enterprise, the almost maddening desire of change, the insatiable curiosity that grows on that which feeds it, the love of hazard which makes some men feel—

That danger's self is lure alone—

"pardon me, lady, I am not quite so ignorant of those red men as your very kind, but (give me leave to say) feminine fears, lead you to apprehend. I have already journeyed far; I think I know when I need fear danger: the natives, if trusted, are true."

"If wholly trusted," she replied, "the tribe of which we are speaking may have sometimes proved not absolutely false. Coming as you do from the land of my forefathers, I cannot consider you as a stranger;—but, as a friend and countryman, once more I adjure you to beware! I have sojourned long in these regions; I have studied the people. I have made a woman's wit awe their bolder natures; and I have found it a painful lesson to observe how deeply duplicity is seated in the human heart. Manifold benefits, time, counsel, have not been spared; all that intellect and wealth could accomplish for their advantage—that have I done. The power that I enjoy has been the work of years of toil and vigilance, and is such as no European could be supposed capable of acquiring. But I sleep on a volcano; I grasp the slippery snake; I move as on the surface of a quagmire. The fire may slumber, but the principle of combustion is beneath; the trembling morass may sustain me for a season, but the least false movement plunges me into its depths. The snake may sleep and my grasp may be firm; but momentary relaxation is instant death. Dream not that there exists any state of society, civilized or barbarous, in which the evil passions of our nature are not found; social treachery masked under friendship is the bane of our fatherland: in savage life the principle is the same, the effects more immediately dangerous.

"These considerations, however, which should govern *your* conduct as a wanderer among those who are not bound to you by interest or gratitude, are not such as ought to induce *me* to change my abode, or to withdraw the benefits that I have the power to confer on these children of darkness. The ingratitude of the savage occasionally demands precaution. In guarding against it, I remember in mitigation that there is ignorance to be urged in its favour; while the hypocrisy of civilisation, as frequent as it is unpardonable, I could not encounter again, after it had poisoned the fresh springs of my youth!"

The surpassing quietude of her deportment, the calmness, approaching to apathy, which characterized a voice melodious, soothing, and dignified, and to which long intercourse with the Indians had imparted much of the solemn and romantic tones of the red man, made a deep impression on her guest—an impression materially enhanced by the evident absence of every feeling of our nature, excepting those which are connected with benevolence, in one so gifted with every charm of her sex.

"Come forth with me," she continued, with a sweet sad smile, "and look from my domicile on the wide field of creation. Let us mitigate the disapprobation within which this anatomizing of the weakness or wickedness of our fellow-creatures may lead us to indulge, by looking on Nature as she was designed for man, ever varying, yet still harmonizing in her minutest points."

The place to which they retired was a green sloping lawn, spreading over a wide expanse, and decorated with a few of the giants of the forest, allowed to remain for beauty after their companions had yielded to the purposes of utility. Numerous evergreens, sweetly scented, grew around; and the flowers of many a clime added their varied beauty to the scene. Far could the eye trace the productions with which Nature in this country teemed; then, roving further, it gradually lost the perception of objects in the dim haze of the horizon, where the blue sky and the green earth were blended into one indistinct line.

In a half dreamy, half meditative mood, the traveller enjoyed that happy, vision-like chain of feeling, when, the mind at rest, and care forgotten, man luxuriates in all the refined powers of a poetic imagination.

The interest unconsciously excited by his fair companion, whose sequestered position had a mystic charm for his romantic nature, was increased as the elevation of her mind was displayed: pure, unworldly, noble, profound, her thoughts were graced by feminine softness, and conveyed with a refined choice of expression, in a voice whose sad sweetness charmed the more for being devoid of effort or art. Her placid, resigned manner, was almost like self-communing, and proved that the wish to make a favourable impression was extinct in this early-chastened heart.

Much conversation passed; both were deeply-versed enthusiasts in the standard poetry of their native land; a community of literary taste is the earliest bond of intimacy, and their interchange of ideas was an unaffected display of riches in two highly gifted though strongly contrasted minds.

As the intellect of the enterprising traveller shone before her, the lady felt increased solicitude that so valuable a member of society should not be lost. She therefore renewed her endeavours to prevail on him to turn his footsteps to some other path. She failed in dissuading him from the enterprise, but eventually succeeded in obtaining a promise that he would use some portion of the circumspection which she recommended.

They parted, mutually pleased with each other. Both had taken their part in furnishing mental entertainment; and and here, amid the wilds of nature, intellect was a jewel that could be doubly appreciated, surrounded by the darkness which ignorance had spread abroad.

Weeks rolled on: the lady, in the routine of her solitary life, was accustomed to the casual passing visits of strangers; she adapted herself speedily to the conversation most interesting to her visitors; and, when they departed, she returned, as readily as before, to her own peculiar pursuits. Yet, at times, the remembrance of one so highly gifted as the traveller came across her mind, and perhaps carried her thoughts back to those earlier days when intellectual companionship had for her peculiar charms; when life was green, and the world was seen through the vista of hope. Then silently would the emotions of woman overcome her more stoical spirit, and the outpourings of a broken heart melt the icy casket in which she had sealed up Nature's feelings. These moments were not common—better far had they been so.

One day, an itinerant vender of the products and curiosities of distant climes, half hunter, half merchant, who at rare and distant intervals penetrated into these regions, called at the hermitage, and displayed, among other articles, a small compass, which the Princess immediately recognised as having belonged to the traveller.

"Whence did you procure this?" was the natural question.

"At the Clearing, near the mouth of the stream, from one of the Indians of the Black River, who had come down to make the annual purchases for his tribe, and to exchange his peltry for hatchets, gunpowder, rifles, nails, &c."

If her fears wanted corroboration, she had it in the cap

and the curiously carved staff, which she particularly remembered from their design, and the antique mounting of the
latter.

The habit of controlling emotion and masking anxiety
enabled her to put such questions as too clearly brought a
sad conviction to her mind respecting the death of the
traveller, so lately her guest; and she succeeded in drawing
forth such additional information as might lead to a more
full and detailed account of the affair. Having done this,
and purchased the necessary articles, she dismissed the
trader, without exciting his suspicions, or causing him to
imagine that anything beyond curiosity had led to her
inquiries.

Quick in resolve, decided in execution, her plans for
obtaining information were soon effective. She learned that
the traveller, after parting from her, had been tempted to
proceed on his purposed route, and had been murdered by
some of "the sons of the Black River," who, it appeared,
had been tempted by his imagined wealth.

The particulars and proofs of this atrocious crime were
reduced to writing, and forwarded to the colonial authorities';
but all this was infinitely easier to the energetic Englishwoman than to effect such a disturbance of Dutch apathy
as would be necessary for avenging the wrong. Perhaps
the authorities had not the power—they certainly manifested
very little of the inclination—requisite for bringing the murderers to justice; and in that quarter the earnest and
anxious entreaties of this extraordinary woman proved
unavailing.

Behold her now, seated under a forest pine : deep thought furrowed her brow, giving increased dignity to her appearance, while she reflected on the means of exacting that retributive justice which she had been unable to obtain from the government.   Like all persons of high resolve, the idea of failure—eventual failure—she never permitted herself to entertain.   With her mental eye fixed on the goal, she paused but to consider the best course by which it could be reached.

"I have governed tribes who never before acknowledged any law; I have exacted homage, where even respect was seldom before given ; and now I have asked redress from both the chief of the tribe and the authorities that here represent one of the European Powers, and they cannot give it! Am I, after all, the poor helpless being to rest contented here; and cannot I penetrate a few miles further amid these forests for an act of justice, when I could have braved all I have done for selfishness, to escape from odious and hypocritical society—ay, when I could even persuade my dear father to quit his country, and seek with me peace among less civilized nations ? Away with the idea of doubt ! I have resolved, and I will accomplish; ay, all !—these murderers shall know how deep is the determination of an Englishwoman! My people shall see that they yield obedience to no tinsel sovereignty. Mountains and rocks shall bear my name; and, if I reign, it shall be both with the power of a Queen and the dignity of a Woman."

Within a few hours after this determination, her table was loaded with jewels, trinkets, plate; and the general preparations indicated that all available means were to be employed in order to obtain a considerable sum of money as speedily as possible.

A small force was soon afterwards raised on the coast; auxiliaries were added from among her Indian neighbours; and, in a little time, an armed body of sufficient strength to venture upon penetrating into the interior of the forest was collected, and this intrepid woman proceeded to fulfil her determination by placing herself at its head.

Slowly and cautiously they advanced, molesting no one— nay, even conferring, where possible, benefit on any occasional wanderer whom they encountered; and thus intelligence of their progress was rapidly diffused by the scouts of the several tribes.

Alarmed at the formidable invasion now threatened, and not ignorant of the fame of its conductress, the menaced tribe sent to arrange terms; but a stern and peremptory repulse, coupled with a declaration that no conference could be held until the murderer was given up unconditionally, struck terror to their hearts; and the invaders uninterruptedly continued their march. The tedious march was now accomplished; and before them lay some of the devoted dwellings. Then, and not till then, was the murderer given up; and this influential and determined woman returned to her home without committing any injury in her progress; then, proceeding with the prisoner to the nearest point where European authorities were established, she delivered him to their charge, disbanded her troops, and once more sought the beloved quiet of her woodland recess.

It is our province to leave her here, and bend our steps to the place where preparations were to be made for the trial of the murderer. The authorities determined, as they had proved unequal to the task of seizing the culprit, at least to make up in parade, when he was in custody, for their previous indolence or impotence. They gave notice to the various parties holding jurisdiction in the neighbourhood, whether European or Indian, and also intimated to the sylvan Princess that they were willing to follow any directions which she might give. She replied, "that all she asked was justice; that she trusted they would inquire fairly into the case, and adjudge according to the evidence."

As the time for the trial approached, the utmost interest was excited throughout the whole district, and an immense concourse of spectators was attracted, both from the novelty of a criminal being so taken, and also from curiosity to see the famed Princess, who was expected to attend the trial. The wild and fanciful dresses of the chiefs, the heavier and more voluminous cloaks in which the wealthy inhabitants of the town and its environs were wrapped, and the calm looks of the more peaceful burghers, gave a varied and picturesque interest to the scene.

Arriving, with her customary simplicity and absence of parade, in the midst of this assemblage, the Princess graciously saluted those who were known to her, and passed forward to the house of a burgher with whom her father had long been acquainted, and whose residence she proposed to honour with a temporary occupation. Immediately on entering this plain, substantial dwelling, and being left in a room by herself, the written evidence connected with the impending inquiry engaged her attention; which, in a short time, was interrupted by the entrance of an attendant, ushering in a young Indian female, whose age just bordered on the earliest dawn of womanhood, and whose appearance, if it had all the wildness, wanted nothing of the interest that attached to her tribe—the children of the Black River.

The Princess intuitively perceived the errand of her visitor, and motioned her to be seated. The poor girl turned inquiringly to the attendant in waiting, as if to ask whether he were to remain. The lady, without hesitation, dismissed him; for she did not dream of the possibility of the least danger from the interesting-looking being who stood before her, and who, after a short pause, thus began :—

"Princess! I come to you as the sun of my destiny! you can wither and destroy, or you can shed the light of heaven over the desolate wigwam of the Son of the Black River. See you these hands, they have toiled; these feet, they have trodden many a day's journey, that the treasures I have obtained might be laid at your feet;" and she produced a small pouch, filled with silver coins. She then continued: "I seek my father; *you* may save him. I know that the Great Spirit at present hides his face from us; I know that my father has offended; I saw it all!" and she dropped her head on her knees: "ALL!" she repeated in an almost stifled voice.

The lady shuddered; but subduing her emotion, she said, "Tell me then all! but let it be the truth, for you know I cannot be deceived."

"Princess," replied the girl, proudly raising her head, 'I never deceived." Then sinking again into her former position, she added, "But time passes, and I have not yet spoken of my father. It was on a bright moonlight night that the stranger applied to my father to become his guide on that journey which he wished to make to the shores of the Upper Lake; and he offered for this service powder and lead, with these beads, a hammer, and a hatchet.

"We were without food; other tribes had wrested from us some of our best hunting-grounds; our men seldom went out upon the war-path, and the pale faces, from day to day, were gaining upon the slender possessions that remained. My father agreed to be his guide; and taking his rifle, prepared for the journey. He soon departed, leaving me alone; for my poor mother sleeps quietly by the shore of the lake. The door of our dwelling lay open; I could not sleep, so I passed through the open grounds along the bank of the stream, towards its source, till the clear lake lay in all its calmness at my feet.

"Dark seemed the little mound of earth raised over the grave in which my mother lay; and a deeper sense of loneliness than usual came over me. Perhaps, thought I, the spirit of my dear mother hovers not over me; I have been long absent, and she will not meet me, but will withdraw her welcome on account of my neglect. The flowers, too, droop their heads, and the pines frown on me. Well! perhaps my dearest mother will forgive me, and come to breathe the balmy odour of peace across my brow. I will lay myself down, and sleep with my mother! And I wept, and was happy; for then my cheek touched the sod, and the tears sank into the earth, and I thought if they moistened her cheek that her spirit would forgive me! Thus I lay I know not how long, when steps approached, and a voice strange to me asked if this was the lake? My father's voice replied that it was.

"The stranger then gave my father charge of his cloak, and slowly moved along the shore to a considerable distance. Why he came so far to visit this spot I know not. At length the sound of his steps gradually died away, and I knew that my father alone was near; but fearing lest he might chide me for my wanderings, I crept in among the underwood and lay still. Presently he came near the grave, and as he laid down the cloak, something dropping from the pocket struck against the ground: it sounded like money;— he started—and I soon heard him as if numbering the coins. Then he said to himself: 'Had I had this wealth, the wife of my bosom had not died; and the want of these base aids may cause my beloved child to follow her to the grave. Would that this treasure were mine! but it is another's, and confided to me. I ought not ever to have remembered it, or even to have touched it!'

"Then he seemed to be gathering it in his hand to put it again into the pocket of the cloak; when a hurried step approached, and the stranger passed quickly up the track ;— before the purse was replaced, he confronted my father. The light of the moon strongly fell on his features, and I saw them marked by the expression of distrust.

"'Give me,' he said, 'my cloak and my purse; what have

you taken? fool that I was to have trusted them out of my own possession; but I had forgotten that my money was there.' 'Trust!' replied my father, 'dare you doubt me? here is your purse.' The stranger took it in silence and counted the contents. 'The numbers are not right,' he added; 'you have taken more than the sum promised you; our bargain is at an end.'

"My father is, of all created men, the most prompt to feel bitterly any imputation upon his good faith, and I saw that his hand was on his knife. The stranger started, but my father answered, 'Fear not; you have trusted me: I cannot harm you; but you have yourself broken our bargain: we are for the future strangers.'—'Not so quick,' angrily replied the traveller; 'you have taken more than your pay.'—'I have taken nothing,' was the answer.—'It is false,' was responded.

"The knife gleamed in the moonlight; the stranger dropped: he uttered no sound; the spouting blood rushed upward, and fell on the grave of my mother! My father shuddered, and, looking round, stooped to raise the fallen man; but it was useless—life was now extinct.

"For a time he stood gazing at the corpse, until at last, like one roused from a trance, he took up the cloak, threw it across the body, and then, stooping down, leant for a time over the grave, as though communing with the spirit of my departed parent. He groaned bitterly; then, suddenly rising, he lifted up the cloak, opened the pocket, and took out the money: at that moment his foot struck against something, and stooping to pick it up, he found several of the coins, which he had dropped while returning the stranger's purse.

"'It is too late,' he sighed; 'I may as well take this treasure—*he* cannot want it, I do—he doubted me, and he fell.' So spoke my father, lady—need I proceed? I will die for my father, if you wish, but oh! save him; spare my only friend, or kill me too."

The Princess had not interrupted the poor girl's narration; but her deep breathing spoke the interest which it had excited. Taking the hand of the supplicant, she said: "I will be your friend."

"*You* my friend?" was all that the child of the woods could utter, and the poor girl sunk on the floor.

On the following day the Indian culprit was brought to trial. The proofs were clear against him, and the case was very speedily concluded. He was liable to receive sentence of death.

The proceedings were closed: the judges had but to fix the punishment, and the guilty man awaited in silence the fiat that should declare in what manner his life should be closed.

Intently gazing at the lady, as if to read her countenance, and see what feeling stirred her soul, the friends of the prisoner watched each movement she might make. Not a sound escaped from her lips, calmly pressed together; her brow was knit, but the expression of her eye rendered the frown doubtful. The judges inquired if she had any suggestions to offer; "for," said they, "to your heroism and love of justice may be attributed much of the merit of this conviction."

Who that has witnessed the awful moment when sentence is to be pronounced but must remember how much import-ance seems to attach to the tone in which the first accents are uttered. In this case, however, there was nothing left for hope. The president of the court made known the de-cision, and had pronounced the sentence in the usual form; yet the Princess still remained silent.

In that colony, as well as in every other wherein a shadow of sound jurisprudence exists, the executive power enjoyed the prerogative of mercy. However extraordinary such a step would have appeared under other circumstances, yet the governor of the colony, taking into consideration the peculiar incidents of this trial, signified his willingness to assent to any mitigation of the punishment that the lady who exercised the strange and anomalous sovereignty which has been already described might propose, resolving, on that individual occasion, to invest her with his own authority, and let her deal as she might think proper with the criminal. To this he was the more readily moved, from her having communicated to him the narrative of the Indian girl, ratified with all the solemnities of an oath, and bearing upon its face so many evidences of probability.

Like one, then, to whom sovereignty was familiar, she proceeded to its instant exercise. She spoke, and breathless attention hung on her words, while every anxious eye was turned to that form of majestic and surpassing beauty, as she thus addressed the prisoner:—"Your life has been for-feited, though I have not borne witness against you: my part in your prosecution was the collection and arrangement of facts, which spoke for themselves. True, I penetrated into your fastnesses, where you thought man, much less woman, dared not enter; and the secret murder in the prairie of one whom you considered friendless is revealed within a few moons after its perpetration. The laws of the pale-faces condemn you; the red man breathes not a word against the justice of that condemnation; nay, even your friends and the conscience within you speak to the truth of the charge.

"But *I*, an Englishwoman, *bid you live!* I have scrutinized your motives, and seen that you were not under the influence of deliberate malice, whatever feelings of offended pride, or powerful temptations of want, caused your dark crime. You thought that an Englishman might be destroyed with impunity. Of the contrary you have now been convinced. Learn also that England can practise mercy as well as justice. Behold! you are free. Henceforth, if an Englishman should cross your path, be his friend. Tell your brethren what you have seen; and when you wish for a blessing on your children, pray that they may be the friends of Englishmen, and that your country may become *another* ENGLAND."

The Indian Girl's Lament.*

THE moons of Autumn wax and wane ;—
    The hollow sound of floods
Is borne upon the mournful wind ;
    And broadly on the woods
The changes of the changeful leaves—
Those painted flowers of frost—
Before the round and yellow sun,
    How beautiful, are tossed !
The morning breaketh with the same
    Broad pencilling of sky,
And blushes through its golden clouds,
    As the great sun goes by ;
And evening lingers in the west,
    More beautiful than dreams
That whisper of the Spirit Land—
    Its wilderness and streams !

* An Indian girl, the last of the Red Indians, or Bœothwicks, died some years ago at St. John's, Newfoundland.   Her tribe, the aborigines of that Island, never held intercourse with any other tribe, or with the Europeans around them.

A little time—another moon—
  The forests will be sad;
The streams will mourn the pleasant light
  That made their journey glad;
The moon will faintly lighten up,
  The sunlight glisten cold,
And wane into the western sky,
  Without its Autumn gold:
And yet I weep not for the signs
  Of Desolation near—
The ruin of my Hunter-race
  May only ask a tear.
The wailing streams will laugh again;
  The naked trees put on
The beauty of their summer-green,
  Beneath the summer sun;
The morning clouds will yet again
  Their crimson draperies fold;
The star of sunset smile once more—
  A diamond set in gold!
But never for the forest path,
  Or for the mountain's breath,
The mighty of our race shall leave
  The Hunting-ground of Death.

I know the tale my fathers told—
  The legend of our fame—
The glory of our spotless race,
  Before the " Pale ones" came;

When, asking fellowship with none,
  By turns the foe of all,
With Ocean rearing up around
  Its dark eternal wall,
Companionless and terrible,
  Our warriors stood alone,
And from the Big Lake to the sea,
  The green earth was their own.

Where are they now?—Around the changed
  And stranger-peopled isle
A thousand graves are strewn beneath
  The mournful Autumn's smile;
The bow of strength is buried
  With the calumet and spear,
And the spent arrow slumbereth,
  Forgetful of the deer;
The last canoe is rotting by
  The lake it glided o'er,
When dark-eyed maidens sweetly sang
  Its welcome from the shore:
The foot-prints of the Hunter-race
  From all the hills are gone,—
Their offering to the Spirit Land
  Hath left the altar-stone;
The ashes of the Council-fire
  Have no abiding token;
The song of War hath died away—
  The Pow-wah's charm is broken;—

The startling war-whoop cometh not
    Upon the loud clear air,—
The ancient woods are vanishing—
    The Pale ones gather there !

And who is left to mourn for this ?—
    A solitary one,
Whose life is waning into death,
    Like yonder sinking sun !
A broken reed—a blighted flower—
    That lingereth still behind,
To mourn its faded sisterhood,
    And wrestle with the wind.
Lo! from the Spirit Land I hear
    The music of the blest ;
The pleasant faces of the loved
    Are beaming from the west ;
A voice is on th' autumnal wind—
    It calleth me away!
Ere the cheek hath lost its freshness,
    And the raven tress is gray ;—
Ere the weight of years hath bowed me,
    Or the sunny eye is dim,
The Father of my People
    Is calling me to him !

Scottish Haymakers.

THERE is no employment in Scotland so sweet as working in a hay-field on a fine summer day. Indeed, it is only on a fine summer day that the youths and maidens of this northern clime can work at the hay. But then the scent of the new hay, which of all others in the world is the most delicious and healthful; the handsome dress of the girls, which is uniformly the same, consisting of a snow-white bedgown and white or red striped petticoat—the dress that Wilkie is so fond of, and certainly the most lovely and becoming dress that ever was or ever will be worn by woman; and then the rosy flush of healthful exercise on the cheeks of the maidens, with their merry jibes and smiles of innocent delight! Well do I know, from long and well tried experience, that it is impossible for any man with the true feelings of a man to work with them, or even to stand and look on—both of which I have done a thousand times, first as a servant, and afterwards as a master —I say it is impossible to be among them and not to be in love with some one or other of them.

But this simple prologue was merely meant to introduce
a singular adventure I met with a good many years ago.
Mr. Terry the player, his father and brother-in-law, the two
celebrated Naesmiths, and some others, among whom was
Monsieur Alexandre, the most wonderful ventriloquist that
I believe ever was born, and I think Grieve and Scott, but
at this distance of time I am uncertain, were of the party.
However, we met by appointment; and, as the weather was
remarkably fine, agreed to take a walk into the country and
dine at "The Hunter's Tryste," a little, neat, cleanly, well-
kept inn, about two miles to the southward of Edinburgh.
We left the city by the hills of Braid, and there went into a hay-
field. The scene certainly was quite delightful, what with the
scent of the hay, the beauty of the day, and the rural group
of haymakers.   Some were working hard, some wooing, and
some tousling, as we call it, when Alexander Naesmith, who
was always on the look-out for any striking scene of nature,
called to his son—"Come here, Peter, and look at this scene.
Did you ever see aught equal to this? Look at those happy
haymakers on the foreground; that fine old ash tree and the
castle between us and the clear blue sky. I declare I have
hardly ever seen such a landscape! And if you had not
been a perfect stump as you are, you would have noticed it
before me. If you had, I would have set ten times more
value on it."

"Oh! I saw it well enough," said Peter, "and have been
taking a peep at it this while past, but I have some other
thing to think of and look at just now. Do you see that
girl standing there with the hay-rake in her hand?"

"Ay now, Peter, that's some sense," said the veteran artist. "I excuse you for not looking at the scene I was sketching. Do you know, man, that is the only sensible speech I ever heard you make in my life."

There were three men and a very handsome girl loading an immense cart of hay. We walked on, and at length this moving hay-stack overtook us. I remember it well, with a black horse in the shafts and a fine light grey one in the traces. We made very slow progress; for Naesmith would never cease either sketching, or stopping us to admire the scenery of nature: and I remember he made a remark to me that day which I think neither he nor his most ingenious son, now no more, ever attended much to; for they have often drawn most extensive vistas, the truest to nature of anything I ever saw, in my uncultivated judgment, which can only discern what is accordant with nature by looking on nature itself; but if a hundred years hence the pictures of the Naesmiths are not held invaluable, I am no judge of true natural scenery. But I have forgotten myself. The remark that he made to me was this: "It is amazing how little makes a good picture; and frequently the less that is taken in the better." Some of the ladies of the family seem to have improved greatly on this hint.

But to return to my story. We made such slow progress on account of Naesmith, that up came the great cart-load of hay on one side of us, with a great burly Lothian peasant sitting upon the hay, lashing on his team and whistling his tune. We walked on, side by side, for a while, I think about half a mile, when all at once a child began to cry in the middle of the cart-load of hay! I declare I was cheated myself; for, though I was walking alongside of Alexandre, I thought there was a child among the hay; for it cried with a kind of half-smothered breath, that I am sure there never was such a deception practised in this world. Peter Naesmith was leaning on the cart-shaft at the time, and conversing with the driver about the beautiful girl he had seen in the hay-field. But Peter was rather deaf, and, not hearing the screaming of the child, looked up in astonishment, when the driver of the cart began to stare around him like a man bereaved of his senses.

"What is the meaning of this?" said Terry. "You are smothering a child among your hay."

The poor fellow, rough and burly as was his outer man, was so much appalled at the idea of taking infant life, that he exclaimed, in a half-articulate voice: "I wonder how they could fork a bairn up to me frae the meadow, an' me never ken!" And without taking time to descend to loose his cart-ropes, he cut them through the middle, and turned off his hay, roll after roll, with the utmost expedition; and still the child kept crying almost under his hands and feet. He was even obliged to set his feet on each side of the cart, for fear of trampling the poor infant to death. At length, when he had turned the greater part of the hay off upon the road, the child fell a-crying most bitterly amongst the hay; on which the poor fellow (his name was Sandy Burnet), jumped off the cart in the greatest trepidation. "Bless me! I hae thrawn the poor thing ower!" exclaimed he. "I's warrant it's killed"—and he began to shake out the hay with the greatest

caution. I and one of my companions went forward to assist him. "Stand back! stand back!" cried he. "Ye'll
maybe tramp its life out. I'll look for't mysel'." But
after he had shaken out the whole of the hay, no child was
to be found! I never saw looks of such amazement as
Sandy Burnet's then were. He seemed to have lost all
comprehension of everything in this world. I was obliged
myself to go on to the brow of the hill and call on some of
the haymakers to come and load the cart again.

Mr. Scott and I stripped off our coats, and assisted; and,
as we were busy loading the cart, I said to Sandy, seeing
him always turning the hay over and over for fear of running the fork through a child, "What can hae become o' the
creature, Sandy?—for you must be sensible that there was
a bairn among this hay."

"I dinna ken, sir," said Sandy.

"Where could the bairn come frae?"

"I canna tell, sir," said Sandy. "That there was a bairn,
or the semblance o' ane, naebody can doubt; but I'm thinkin'
it was a fairy, an' that I'm huntit."

"Did you ever murder any bairns, Sandy?"

"Oh, no, no! I wadna murder a bairn for the hale world."

"Then where could the bairn come frae? for you are
sensible that there is or was a bairn among your hay. It
is rather a bad-looking job, Sandy, and I wish you were
quit of it."

"I wish the same, sir. But there can be nae doubt that
the craitur among the hay was either a fairy or the ghaist
o' a bairn, for the hay was a' forkit off the swathe on the

meadow. An' how could onybody fork up a bairn, an' neither him nor me ken?"

We got the cart loaded once more, knitted the ropes firmly, and set out; but we had not proceeded a hundred yards before the child fell a-crying again among the hay with more vehemence and with more choking screams than ever! Bless my heart! heard ever ony leevin the like o' that! I declare the craitur's there again!" cried Sandy; and flinging himself from the cart with a summer-set, he ran off, and never once looked over his shoulder as long as he was in our sight. We were very sorry to hear afterwards that he fled all the way to the Highlands of Perthshire, where he still lives in a deranged state of mind.

We dined at "The Hunter's Tryste," and spent the after-noon in hilarity; but such a night of fun as Monsieur Alexandre made us I never witnessed, and never shall again. On the stage, where I had often seen him, his powers were extraordinary, and altogether unequalled—that was allowed by every one; but the effect there was not to be compared with that which he produced in a private party. The family at the inn consisted of the landlord, his wife, and her daughter, who was the the landlord's step-daughter—a very pretty girl, and dressed like a lady; but I am sure that family never spent an afternoon of such astonishment and terror from the day they were united until death parted them—though they may be all living yet, for anything that I know, for I have never been there since. But Alexandre made people of all ages and sexes speak from every part of the house—from under the beds, from the basin-stands, and from the garret, where a dreadful quarrel took place. And then he placed a bottle on the top of the clock, and made a child scream out of it, and declare that the mistress had corked it in there to murder it! The young lady ran, opened the bottle, and looked into it, and then, losing all power with amazement, she let it fall from her hand and smashed it to pieces. He made a bee buzz round my head and face until I struck at it several times and had nearly felled myself. Then there was a drunken man came to the door, and insisted, in a rough, obstreperous manner, on being let in to shoot Mr. Hogg! on which the landlord ran to the door and bolted it, and ordered the man to go about his business for there was no room in the house, and there he should not enter on any account. We all heard the voice of the man going round and round the house, grumbling, swearing, and threatening; and all the while Alexandre was just standing with his back to us at the room-door, always holding his hand to his mouth, but nothing else. The people ran to the windows to see the drunken man going by, and Miss Jane even ventured to the corner of the house to look after him; but neither drunken man nor any other man was to be seen. At length, on calling her in to serve us with some wine and toddy, we heard the drunken man's voice coming in at the top of the chimney! Such a state of amazement as Jane was in I never beheld. " But ye needna be feared, gentlemen," said she, " for I'll defy him to win down. The door's boltit an' lockit, an' the vent o' the lum is no sae wide as that jug."

" However, down he came, and down he came, until his voice actually seemed to be coming out of the grate. Jane ran for it, saying, " He is winnin' down, I believe, after a'. He is surely the deil !"

Alexandre went to the chimney, and, in his own natural voice, ordered the fellow to go about his business, for into our party he should not be admitted, and if he forced himself in he would shoot him through the heart. The voice went again grumbling and swearing up the chimney. We actually heard him hurling down over the slates, and afterwards his voice dying away in the distance as he vanished into Mr. Trotter's plantations. We drank freely, and paid liberally, that afternoon; but I am sure the family never were so glad to get quit of a party in all their lives.

To prove the authenticity of this story, I may just mention that Peter Naesmith and Alexandre ran a race in going home, for half a dozen of wine, and, it being down hill, Peter fell and hurt his breast very badly. I have been told that that fall ultimately occasioned his death. I hope it was not so; for, though a perfect simpleton, he was a great man in his art.

The Wife's First Grief.

THE day had closed around me,
    The vapoury sun had set,
And evening shadows found me
    Lone waiting for him yet :
    Still waiting by the cottage-gate,
His faithful hounds and I ;
Whilst gloomy grew the hour, and late,
    And yet he came not nigh !

The old house echoed dreary—
    Its darkness awed my sight ;
So by the gate, all weary,
    I told the hours of night.
I listened—till new life would start
    At every step or word ;—
But the hope within my own sad heart
    Was evermore deferred !

The *Sister-stars* moved slowly
  Along the heaven's blue breast;
The clouds, like something holy
  Rose in the quiet west.
I watched from every casement fade
  The friendly taper's ray;
And with the shade grew more afraid,
  And anxious at his stay.

Ah! 'twas not when a maiden,
  Within my mother's cot,
Time came with tears o'erladen
  To mar my tranquil lot.
I deemed a maiden's bridal
  Made ever blest her brow;
But *maiden* griefs are idle
  To that *a wife* feels now.

I thought upon the wild wood,
  The home-flowers blowing free,
The school where we in childhood
  Went little *sisters three!*—
Now one her quiet grave doth keep—
  The other dwells afar;
And I am left to think, and weep,
  And watch each *Sister-star!*

The wings of eve departed,
  The dewy dawn smiled sweet,

Ere first, half broken-hearted,
  I heard his welcome feet.
He came—but with no kind reply
  To all my doubts and fears ;
Sharp was the word, and cold the eye,
  Which chid my weary tears.

The Forest of Sant' Eufemia.

ON a beautiful little rising ground between the shores of the Gulf of Sant' Eufemia and the forest of the same name, in the eventful years that succeeded the French occupation of the kingdom of Naples, there stood a solitary cottage nestled in the midst of groves of olive and orange trees, which, together with a screen of festooned vines, so much concealed it, that it was only visible from a neighbouring and a loftier hill.

This cottage was inhabited by a young girl of eighteen, an old woman, and an old peasant, and was the occasional retreat of one of a band of robbers that harboured in the forest, whose deeds had for years been marked with all the energy of fearless villany, and whose cunning and dexterity had hitherto baffled the pursuit of the French. It had been chosen by the brigand as a secure abode in seasons of idleness, and as a convenient spot in which to conceal his youthful dependant from the eyes of his ferocious and dissolute companions. The existence of this young creature

was scarcely known, excepting to the two old people who lived with her, to a monk from a convent hard by, and to the robber and three or four of his aged and confidential associates. Who she was, was known to still fewer ; but they all knew, and she knew herself, that she was not the daughter of the brigand Peppè Tosco. It was a strange caprice of fortune, to bring two beings so different together. Antonietta was guileless, mild and beautiful : Peppè Tosco was crafty and savage above the rest of his gang, and ugly as the distorting hand of crime could render him; yet Antonietta loved the only protector she had ever known, and Peppè Tosco with her could at times subdue the demon within him, and treat her with a kindness that seemed entirely foreign to his nature.

It was on a fine evening in the autumn of 1809 that Peppè Tosco and Antonietta had wandered a little way from the cottage, and found themselves, towards sunset, pausing by the ruins of a fallen watch-tower, whence the view was wide and beautiful in the extreme. The plain of Sant' Eufemia lay before them, chequered with white villages and farm houses, and traversed by two loitering rivers, the Angitola and the Amato. The Gulf of Sant' Eufemia opened beyond the plain, enclosing in its bosom the rocky islets of Ithacesiæ and a few white sails. Far over the sea, some specks dotted the dubious horizon,— these were the Lipari Islands; and another spot to the right of them, darker and higher, and which emitted a light blue smoke, was the volcanic island of Stromboli. The back-ground of the plain was formed by the dark waving

forest, and the wide rushy marshes, which presented an
almost impassable fosse to it; as though destined to
augment its mysteries, and " make security doubly sure " to
the desperate bandits who then haunted its mazes. To all
the beauties of linear landscape, to the variety of wood and
water, mountain and plain, was added the indescribable
charm of the colouring of a southern autumn evening : the
sky and the waves, in which the sun was sinking, glowed
with a refulgence that only Claude Lorraine, in a few
instances, has been able to imitate. Receding from that
line of glory, the peaceful level of the sea was like a fairy
carpet of orange and purple; the capes of the gulf, and the
mountains around, glowed with hues that might suit the
unfading roses of an eastern paradise; the broad shades in
the plain were of the deepest purple; but where they did
not fall, the vegetation, the trees, the rivers, the white
churches and cottages, were brought out with a warmth
and transparency which an untravelled inhabitant of the
North can never hope to conceive. But it was not the eye
merely that had a banquet to feast upon,—the air was
charged with an odour so sweet, so luxurious, so penetrating, that it went to the very heart; at the same time that
the ear was charmed by those sounds which seem the
cherished favourites of solitude. The bell of a monastery
on the hills sent forth a slow, melancholy tolling; some
oxen in the plain returning from labour, and some buffaloes
that were ranging in the black marshes, tinkled their dull
bells as they moved along; a shepherd boy was playing
upon a rustic pipe, made by his own hands from a reed of

the marsh; and a woodman afar off, blew his equally primitive *zampogna*, the sound of which, softened by distance, was pleasant and soothing. The querulous voice of the cicala, the croaking of frogs, the chirp of birds repairing to the wood, and the stilly flutter of the wings of the rapid bat, were also among the sounds of that quiet hour,—their union was sweet, and formed a tranquil symphony that harmonized with the scene.

Poor Antonietta felt it as became her;—her heart melted within her,—her frame quivered with delicious emotion,— her large black eyes filled with tears; and, by a natural impulse which disposes us to seek participation in every deep feeling, she turned to her wretched companion. Alas! in him such sympathies had never existed, or were for ever dried up: he gazed upon the scene, it is true; his senses imbibed the sweetness of odour and sound; but with as much indifference as the wolf of his native forest: his brows were knit into their habitual frown; his eyes scowled as though he saw an enemy or a victim before him; and his hands were unconsciously playing with the haft of the dagger, and the butt end of the pistols that were fastened in his girdle. Antonietta retreated several paces from him. Anon the church bells in the plain chimed the *Ave Maria:* the robber shook himself as the sound reached his ear, and began fervently to mutter his prayer to the Virgin Mother of God: Antonietta followed him,—but oh! with what different feelings. A few minutes afterwards, Peppè Tosco called her to hasten home. "I must have my supper betimes," said he; "when the moon rises, I must to the forest—my comrades expect me."

"But why away so soon;" said Antonietta: "it was but yester-night that you returned so sadly harassed and fatigued ?"

"Ask no questions! Here we must meet, and meet again, and consult;—and for what, in sooth ? why, not to secure booty, or plan expeditions; but to contrive our own safety—how to escape the pursuit of French blood-hounds. I tell you there will be no peace for us until the last of these accursed strangers is sent out of the world with a bandit's knife in his heart !"

Antonietta shuddered, accustomed as she was to similar horrors, though she considered the French as merciless invaders, and thought as firmly that her foster-parent's occupation was justifiable, as the mofe refined daughter of a licensed hero thinks that of her father glorious. She had hitherto possessed no means of correcting her mistake, as the people she had seen had all a fellow-feeling with Peppè Tosco; and even the old monk was too much devoted to his interests, to unveil to her the calling of his best customers, in its real deformity.

As they descended the hill, Antonietta's eye was arrested by a trim vessel, then doubling the romantic Cape of Suvero, one of the extreme points of the gulf.

"Oh, see!" said she, catching the arm of the impatient Peppè Tosco, "see that beautiful white sail there, which is not quite white now, but the colour of the violets I gather in the spring;—see there ! how it hurries along on the evening breeze ;—and look! close under the cape comes another,— 'tis larger, but not so pretty."

Peppè Tosco looked, and immediately recognised a French gun-boat, convoying a large transport. "Now may every curse," cried he, striking his dagger hilt,—" may every curse light upon these invaders! They are come to hunt us like bears, in our fastnesses ;—but let them come, band after band; our marshes are wide and treacherous; none but a brigand can thread our forest: Calabrian cunning, and bold hearts and sure shots, and ague and fever await them—they will yet rue the Forest of Sant' Eufemia!"

The robber hastened on : as they drew near the cottage they saw an old man seated at the door, who arose hurriedly as Peppè Tosco approached, and beckoning him aside, began a conversation in a whisper, the interest of which was plainly betrayed by the violence of his gestures. A more appalling figure than this veteran villain never occupied the pencil of Salvator Rosa, or of our own countryman, Eastlake or Uwins. He was short in stature, but most robustly knit; his round head, with its straggling grey locks, was sunk between his broad shoulders; and his body, and arms, and legs, seemed to have been shortened expressly to give them more strength. His hat was high and sugar-loafed, with broad flapping brims, that shaded the upper part of his face, but could not deaden his eye, which shone from under his snowy eye-brow like a burning coal. He wore a coarse velveteen jacket, covered with silver Spanish buttons, which being open at the breast, discovered a medal of the Virgin, and a little silk bag containing an esteemed relic: a broad leathern belt around his waist, supported a dagger, a large *couteau de chasse*, and a brace of pistols; a long heavy Spanish gun, that showed by the polish of its stock how familiar it was to his hand, was flung over his shoulder. His feet and legs were cased in a sort of sandal, made of strips of untanned hide, fastened under the knee with a silver buckle. Such was the exterior of Benincasa, the captain of the Sant' Eufemia banditti,— of the successful monster, whose atrocities had been the subject of dread and astonishment for so many years.

The dialogue between the two brigands soon ended. "Away! let us away!" cried Benincasa aloud.

"But my supper," expostulated Peppè Tosco, hesitatingly.

"Your supper, Peppè, must be eaten elsewhere to-night," retorted his captain. "Our legs and our hands must be tried ere our stomachs be satisfied;—if we succeed, our supper shall be a feast ; but if we fail, I believe some of us will 'have small need of food !—Come, come !—your gun, your powder-flask—haste !"

"Girl," cried Tosco to Antonietta, "bring here my gun and horn, and the knife that's under my pillow ;—Pasquale, Annarella, bear in mind my orders ; remember what I told you last night, or I'll ——."

With these words, and while his submissive underlings exclaimed, "The Madonna accompany you!—the Madonna bring you safe back!"—Peppè Tosco strode after his leader, who was already out of sight among the trees. After he had proceeded a few paces, however, he turned his head to look at Antonietta, and seeing her fixed as a statue, with her arms stretched forward, and her eyes bent upon him, he walked back,

"What, child!" said he; "you let me go away without saying a word to me?—Ah! 'tis well! you care not about my coming in or my going out; you care not if I never return—if the bullet of one of these French murderers!—well, well! who will take care of you then?"

"Oh, father!" replied the poor girl, "you set out so suddenly, I had not time to say what is here in my heart,—I never can do so!"

"Farewell then, now," said the robber, softened;—"fare you well; and if I return in safety, I will give you a new rosary, with pearl beads and a gold cross; and I will give you—but hark! old Benincasa is shouting after me—Sant' Antonio remain with you." He then kissed her, and in a minute was by the side of his impatient captain.

The tenderness Peppè Tosco had unwillingly allowed to escape him was of rare occurrence; but the expedition on which he was setting out was one of unusual danger, its object being nothing less than to destroy the French soldiers in Nicastro, and to liberate a number of brigands who had been surprised, and were then confined in the public prison. The watchful Benincasa had learned that the military force in the town was at that moment very weak, as several detachments had been drawn off to escort the receivers' money-chests, and one the preceding day, to accompany an *aide-de-camp*, who was repairing from the army at Reggio to the capital. These circumstances seemed to promise success to the project Benincasa had for some time meditated, and he had given, consequently, a rendezvous to the best part of his band.

By the clear light of the moon these determined men began their march: they kept near the borders of the wood until within a short distance of Nicastro, when they crossed some little hills, and concealed themselves in a thicket, while two of the most adroit went into the town to reconnoitre. The spies presently returned with the information that the town was wrapped in sleep; that no sentinel was before the barrack; and that only three men, who were smoking cigars, were near the prison. Benincasa led on his troop in death-like silence: they entered the town unperceived, they traversed several streets, and were in sight of the prison and of the sentinels, who, with an imprudence which had become habitual to the French from a long series of good fortune, were smoking and singing over a jug of wine, when one of the robbers stumbled over a stone in his way, and in falling let his cocked gun go off. This alarmed the soldiers;—in a moment they were on their arms, and were joined by several half-naked comrades, who had been sleeping in a hovel under the prison walls. The first impulse of Benincasa, on seeing his treacherous surprise thus frustrated, was to stab the fallen wretch; he was, however, withheld by considerations of a more weighty nature; and turning round, cried, "Forward! forward !— after all, they are but a handful; we have a dozen shots for each ;—take your aims, —down with the bloodhounds,—then your hands to your axes, and break the prison doors for your brethren, before a new force arrive."

The brigands obeyed his orders, by rushing forward with a fiendish yell, and firing on the sentinels ; but the mishap had thrown them into confusion, and it was no part of their system, excepting in cases of vital importance, to fight with a prepared enemy : their fire had no visible effect, while two of the gang fell, wounded by the French. Still, however, they remained firm by their leader, and were about to throw themselves on the sentinels, when a murderous discharge from an unseen enemy was opened upon their rear : the robbers, baffled and panic-struck, then took to flight, leaving several wounded and dead behind them.

The timely assistance which thus saved the sentinels from being massacred proceeded from the rest of the French in the town, who, having reflected on their exposed situation, had that same night left their separate quarters and united together, officers and men, to the number of twenty-eight, in an old church near the prison : they were on the alert immediately on hearing the fire ; and a few steps brought them in sight of their enemy.

The day after this affair, a detachment of light troops, that had come round in the transport the evening before, reached Nicastro. The French commandant, exasperated at the late attempt, determined to despatch them immediately to scour the country, and to attempt the forest in search of the brigands ; and the already harassed men were accordingly sent off, after a few hours' repose. The adventures they met with, and the hardships they suffered, might be found interesting ; but they do not come within the scope of our narrative, and we must rather confine ourselves to one of the hapless band,—a young officer of the name of Vernet.

This young man was said to be of a noble family, which had perished during the cruel excesses of the French Revolution. In the helpless age of childhood he was left alone in the world, and might have begged by the road-side, had not his beauty and ingenuity attracted the attention of an old officer, who had him placed in a military school. From this establishment he had emerged while yet a boy, full of lofty republican sentiments, of enthusiasm for glory, and of a restless desire to see the different countries of the world; and with many hundreds not older than himself, had been marched off in the ranks, to meet the assailing or assailed enemies of France. With the swelling fulness of heart that youth only knows, he had coasted the romantic shores of the Rhine; he had crossed the lofty, frozen barrier of the Alps; he had seen his enemy retreat before him, almost wherever they had met, and the French banner fly like a meteor (as brilliant, indeed, and almost as transient!) from the summit of the Grand Saint Bernard to the furthest shores of Lower Italy; he had traversed the land of ancient heroism and of genius, and had revelled on the feast she presented to all his stronger sympathies. At the moment we are about to bring him under notice his feelings had been considerably depressed: he had seen his darling republic distracted by weak and bad men, and at last evaporate before the dazzling beams of a fortunate conqueror: he had met with those, once his bosom friends, who a few years before had entered Italy with him ragged and barefoot—who had many times shared his bed of straw—now in command, and fluttering about, the ornaments of courts, the favourites of the kings and queens of a new dynasty! Perhaps he had felt that an unbending spirit, and contempt of flattery and intrigue, had kept him a subaltern in the most laborious corps of the army. The mistaken but noble principles, that had animated him in the beginning of his career, had died away, and their absence went well-nigh to make him quit the service ; to which, however, he was chained by the consciousness of obstacles to every other profession, by his unsatisfied curiosity, and a lingering fondness for change and adventure. Vernet was not altogether without the vices of his class : he was eager after pleasure, when his relaxation from danger and fatigue permitted its pursuit, and was not over discriminating in its quality : he was extravagant, imprudent, and headstrong; yet his redeeming virtues were many, and his experience in the unprofitable scenes of the world, and even the chilling dereliction from his high sentiments, which is generally a perilous fall, had not depraved the natural goodness of his heart.

On the evening on which our history begins, Vernet left Nicastro with his company.

"Well, here I am," said he, as he followed his men across the plain of Sant' Eufemia; "here I am, and truly in a glorious calling! I little thought, when I saw the plains of Italy from the Alps—when I saw the enemy leaving the field of Marengo—that after a few years I should be chasing dastardly robbers in the wilds of Calabria ;—but no matter, 'tis destiny,—all destiny; Napoleon was born to be the

Emperor of France, and to command Europe ; and I to do the biddings of some hundreds of my superiors. I must say, however, I should like a better field than this—'twould be humiliating to fall by the shot or the knife of a thief."

The soldiers slept that night at a largè *masseria* or farmhouse, not far from Nicastro ; and Vernet forgot, over a cheering bottle of Calabrian wine, the melancholy reflections of the evening. They began their route early the next morning, to reconnoitre the hamlets on the edge of the forest ; the men rambled on in the straggling manner usual with light troops, and Vernet imprudently enough, in such a country and on such an occasion, frequently strayed apart with a brother officer. As the day advanced, the sun became intensely hot, and they suffered greatly from thirst. About eleven o'clock Vernet found himself with a friend of the name of Beauchamp on the side of a hill, whence piercing a thick grove of trees, they descried a white cottage, superior in its aspect to the few wretched hovels they had hitherto passed.

"*Allons*, Beauchamp," cried Vernet, "there's a snug house, which seems by the smoke ascending from its chimney to have an inhabitant ; perhaps it may afford us a glass of wine and water."

They ordered their men to halt, and soon reached the open door of the cottage :—it was the house of Peppè Tosco, and on entering it they found Antonietta and the old man and woman at their early dinner.

"What, ho !" exclaimed Vernet to his companion, as he perceived the lovely and blushing Antonietta, "what have we here? is it Proserpine, or one of her nymphs, returned from the valleys of Etna to gather flowers in the plains of Calabria?"

The sudden entrance of the two strangers occasioned considerable disturbance to the party: Pasquale started to his legs, the old woman turned pale, and Antonietta hung down her head; she would have escaped, but Vernet detained her.

."Fear not, lovely girl," said he; "you have nothing to fear from us—we may have to fear you rather. Come, come, sit down! we want to partake of this repast, and 'twould be all unsavoury should the queen of the feast leave the table;—and you, good dame, don't look so alarmed, I pray you; and you, old gentleman, pray sit down, and leave off chafing about the room in this manner;—come, a jug of wine to our better acquaintance, and a little water here, good mother; your Calabrian suns make a man thirsty."

The frank manners of the intruders re-assured the suspicious Pasquale and Annarella; and Antonietta, though she had been taught to consider every Frenchman as a near relation of the devil, could not help stealing an occasional glance at the handsome soldier who sat by her side. She had never before seen any object so interesting; the feelings of nature triumphed over an artificial and unfounded dislike, and if she was not actually in love with him in this first short interview, she at least felt (without knowing it) the precursors of that tender passion, preparing her heart for its reception. Vernet on his part was enchanted with her beauty and artlessness, and his warm feelings of adoration threw an eloquence, in his manner and in the expression of his face, and in the few words he said to her, that made her heart palpitate with delight.   When the young Frenchmen had satisfied their thirst, and partaken of what was on the table, they had no longer any pretext for remaining: Beauchamp arose, and pulled Vernet by the sleeve; and he, too, though most unwillingly, prepared to depart.

"Adieu, my pretty maid," said he, patting her on her cheek, half playfully, half mournfully, "Adieu! thanks for your hospitality—and here's something by which to remember me."

Antonietta refused the dollar with something like offended dignity; the old woman, however, sprang forward and clutched it, and kept it in spite of her mistress's frown.

"Farewell, sirs," said Antonietta, "farewell!" She would have said something else, but old Pasquale watched her narrowly, and seemed to intimidate her. She followed Vernet to the door, and with her eyes until he was out of sight, and then sat down on the stone bench before the cottage.

"Well, Beauchamp," said Vernet, as they hastened on to join their men, "what think you of this rencontre?"

"My faith! she's an angel," cried Beauchamp.—"Who would ever have expected to unnest such a bird, and in such regions as these! Did you ever see so lovely a Grecian face, such swimming black eyes, under such narrow little arches of eyebrows—such a mouth—such lips—such teeth! —and then, such a transparent complexion, and such a rosy blush as now and then flowed over her cheeks, her forehead, her neck—even to her finger ends;—how she came by it, I can't conceive, in this burning country, where everybody we meet is almost as black as our Martinique cymbal-player."

"And her figure!" rejoined Beauchamp: "her neck—her waist—I'm sure I could span it! and her arms, her round, finely-turned arms—her white tapering hand—her feet! I never saw such feet but once—those belonging to the little Venus with the funny name at Naples." *

"She's a riddle, Beauchamp, that's certain. How came she by those elegant manners, and that pretty way of speaking? I suppose, at most, she's the daughter of some little farmer or buffalo driver; but how such a father should have such a daughter, quite passes my comprehension."

"But did you observe the old man and woman?" said Beauchamp.

"I can't say I did, very particularly."

"They have both certainly most sinister physiognomies—the countenance of the old fellow would sign his death-warrant before any of our military tribunals. I didn't much like his long knife, and that old gun in the corner. I think he's a dangerous rogue."

"Be he what he may, he shall not hinder me from repeating my visit as soon as our present chase is over."

"What! to get a knife in your back, or a bullet from

* The Venus Callipiga, which has been attributed to Praxiteles, and considered as a rival to the Venus de Medici.

behind a tree—eh, Vernet? He scowled at you most horribly when you patted the little girl on the cheek."

"Oh, nonsense! these people have all an instinctive hatred of us; and, as we run such pretty risks in our bounden duty, surely it may be permitted to us to get into a little amateur scrape, just on one's own account. The fact is, the girl has interested me more than I should be willing to confess to any one but you; and so, see her again I will, whatever be the consequences."

Here they joined their company, and soon had to attend to other matters. In this expedition they suffered severely: a pitiless sirocco, with its dull, red atmosphere, that lasted the whole time, depressed their spirits, and choked them with thirst; the marshes they had to sweep round exhaled fœtid vapours, which, combined with the impure water the soldiers drank in their maddening drought, proved fatal to many. To these serious discomforts was added the mortifying result of their expedition: the robbers were nowhere to be traced, and the shepherds and country people they interrogated seemed rather anxious to delude them than to direct them aright. Two of their men were killed, and another wounded, at the edge of the wood, without their being able to reach, or even to see the assassins; and, after two days of extreme fatigue and vexation, Vernet was fain to withdraw his detachment to the town of Maida. In this agreeable sojourn they had but short leisure to repose, for just before their arrival the commandant of the place had arrested an emissary of the brigands, who had visited the town to treat with a rich proprietor about the ransom of a drove of oxen, which had been carried off into the forest. This wretch, who was in fact one of Benincasa's gang, was induced by the fear of being shot, and by the promise of a considerable reward, to undertake to lead a body of soldiers to the robbers' haunt, and to surprise them in an unsuspecting and defenceless moment. Vernet was appointed to this expedition; and the following night, guided by the traitor, with his arms tied behind him, the little band left Maida for the wood. They traversed the plain by the side of the Amato, which river they forded at a short distance from the wood. After cutting their way, with great labour, through a thick copse, they entered the forest, favoured by a clear moonlight. They had to wade knee-deep through a pestilent marsh, at the edge of which they found their progress arrested by a wide and deep ditch; their guide, however, and two of their men, contrived to cross it. The robber now began to search in the thickets around, for some beams of wood which the brigands were accustomed to make use of as a bridge to pass the fosse: these were so well concealed, and he was so long in finding them, that when they were arranged, and the French crawled over, day began to dawn. They had not got many paces from the ditch when the barking of a number of dogs was heard, apparently a little further in the wood. A few minutes afterwards, the advanced guard, which had gained a narrow uncovered ridge, was saluted by a sharp running fire, accompanied by horrid shrieks and yells: no time was to be lost—the whole body rushed on; and, by the first bright rays of the sun, advanced into the thickest of the forest. Their rapid pace soon brought them to a large, natural circus, surrounded by thick, matted bushes, and shaded by huge cork trees : this they understood to be the brigands' head-quarters. A large fire burned in the centre, at which were roasting the quarters of a bullock and a sheep; a number of sacks full of bread and cheese, and ham, and several skins of wine, were scattered within the circle ; around which were tied to the trunks of trees, horses, asses, and mules, while the branches were decorated with the spare wardrobe of the robbers. The goodly smell of the meats, and the tempting aspect of the wine-skins, would have brought the fatigued soldiers to an agreeable full stop, had it not been for the voice of their leader :—" Run on, my brave boys ! the villains can't have had a long warning of our approach ; they can't have got far yet ;—let us, at least, secure a few of them ; it will give those nice joints time to roast, and we shall relish our feast the better after a bit of fighting."

Vernet halted for a few moments, to see that no loiterers evaded his commands. As he was proceeding on his way, his eye was attracted by an old brigand, who slunk from behind a bush, and unhooked a sort of knapsack that hung to a tree. Before he could get without the circle, Vernet's shot was after him; the robber, however, apparently untouched, leaped into the thicket and escaped. The soldiers followed the traces of the brigands through the thick wood: they found here and there fragments of their clothes torn in their flight, and hats hooked off by the hanging branches ; but their owners had been more fortunate,—not one could be seen, and at last their traces were entirely lost in a wide marsh, through which their guide could not, or would not, conduct them. On their return towards the circus, the men were in part reconciled to the escape of the brigands, by the discovery of a number of oxen and a herd of sheep, which they drove before them as their legitimate prize. To the banquet of Benincasa, which by this time was well cooked, they did infinite honour. Vernet and Beauchamp presided with all the joviality of adventurous soldiers ; but they were obliged to interrupt the festivity (somewhat prematurely, as the men thought), fearing the effects of intoxication, in case the robbers should make an attack on them during their retreat. The jolly band, however, emerged from the mysterious labyrinths of the wood in safety; and in its novel, pastoral capacity, driving its flocks and herds before it, reached Maida in the evening, covered with mud, and with the glory of having been the first to penetrate the Forest of Sant' Eufemia.

A few days after this adventure, Vernet removed from Maida to a masseria between Sant' Eufemia and Nicastro. Here he was not more than two or three miles from the cottage of Antonietta, and so warm was the interest she had excited, that he took the first opportunity of visiting it. Beauchamp, who had in vain attempted to dissuade him, determined to accompany him. On their arrival, they found Antonietta alone. She rushed forward to meet Vernet with pleasure glowing in her eyes and on her cheek; but this immediately gave way to an expression of fear and anxiety, and the words she was about to pronounce died away on her lips.

"Well, my mysterious fair one, here we are again; we found your sweet eyes and your sweeter tattle so enticing, that we have hastened to enjoy them once more."

"Oh," said Antonietta, blushing, "you are come again because you are thirsty,—a good welcome to you, gentlemen; here is a wine-flask, and here is water—but your pardon! I must call Annarella—she is hard by."

"Oh, no," said Vernet, holding her by the arm; "there's no need of that ugly old woman. Don't frown! No offence; but we really can do without her. Come, sit down here; there's no one will harm you. I would not hurt a lock of that flowing hair for all the riches of the two Calabrias: come,—why are you alarmed?"

"You are Frenchmen," said Antonietta confusedly.

"And what then, fair Calabrian?"

"You are the enemies of my country,—the foes of my friends, and—;" she hesitated, and blushed deeper than before. In a moment her eagerness to go after Annarella returned; but her search was anticipated by the old woman herself, who hobbled in, in great confusion, muttering maledictions on the visitors. She said something to Antonietta, in an under voice, and in so barbarous a dialect that the young men did not understand her; but Antonietta replied aloud, "Oh, no, no; the gentlemen have only come again because they are in need of refreshment."

Annarella at length became pacified. Beauchamp occupied her attention as well as he could, to prevent her from inter-rupting Vernet, who had taken possession of a stool at Antonietta's feet, and had begun an affecting little dialogue, the purport of which it will scarcely be necessary to explain. Thanks to the liberality of Beauchamp, and to his unfailing loquacity (which was for the greater part unintelligible to the old woman), half an hour passed away. The hag then began to murmur, "Do they never mean to go? Pasquale will be here in a moment: do you hear, Antonietta! If Peppè should return, you will rue this wrong-headedness!"

"Oh! go,—fly, dear stranger, fly!" said Antonietta, as soon as she heard Peppè named,—"fly, and never come here again!"

"We will depart instantly," replied Vernet, astonished at her eagerness,—" we go, fair stranger! But really, I, on my part, cannot promise to come here no more. Can you, on yours, wish it—wish that we may never meet again?"

"Oh, I wish—I wish—I cannot say what I wish; but only go now, and the blessing of the Holy Virgin go with you! Now, you are at the door,—adieu! adieu!"

Vernet grasped her hand,—a flush, like that of anger, overspread her face, and old Annarella swelled with rage at this familiarity. Antonietta tried to withdraw her hand: Vernet, who was unconscious of the dreadful punctilios of Calabrian propriety on this head, raised it, and kissed it: he kissed it again, and again,—and his heart was drowned with a flood of rapture, when he felt, or fancied he felt, the last time he kissed it, that the gentle girl pressed it softly against his lips.

As the two friends were returning to their quarters, Vernet could talk of nothing but the beautiful Calabrian; he declared he loved her,—loved her desperately; at which his companion laughed very heartily. He regretted he had not asked something of her history,—how she had obtained even a shadow of her acquirements, in the midst of such brute ignorance—who, what was her father, and several other interesting queries, which now came into his mind with great force, but had never presented themselves while he was in her company. At this, Beauchamp, who had more of French effrontery than his friend, and was not in love, very much marvelled, and thought he had made an ill use of the long intercourse his kindness had managed to procure for him. When Vernet talked of returning again in a day or two, Beauchamp became serious, and showed him the futility of such a course, and the risk that attended it: he again suggested the villanous appearance of the old people, and gave an interpretation to the alarm of the girl at the mention of Peppè's name, that might probably never have presented itself to his friend.

Vernet was not to be diverted from his object: he, however, felt the force of what Beauchamp urged, and it was agreed that they should return, accompanied by a few of their men, who might easily be concealed near the house. This being settled, Vernet counted impatiently the tedious hours of duty that intervened.

In the cottage of Peppè Tosco matters were not quite so tranquil. The brigand returned on the day after the Frenchmen's last visit, almost dead with fatigue, and smarting with a shot-wound in his arm : he was savagely morose : he flung Antonietta from him when she flew to embrace him, and he spoke neither to Pasquale nor the old woman.

It was not until he had cheered himself with long and repeated draughts of wine, that, with horrid imprecations, he related the disasters of the band at Nicastro,—his danger, wound, and fatigue in the forest (for he was with Benincasa at the time of the surprise), and the loss of his baggage and his share of the live stock. When he paused from his recital, Pasquale and Annarella, in that spirit which seeks to heap horror upon horror, began to relate the visit of Beauchamp and Vernet at length, without concealing the attentions the latter had paid to Antonietta, the liberties he had taken with her, and the great complacency she had manifested towards him. The ferocious mood of Peppè Tosco, at this information, rose to so frantic an excess, that he struck the meek, unoffending girl, to the ground; and raving over her, as she lay senseless and bleeding before him, declared he would make an end of her, for seeking to betray him to his enemies.

"How, girl!" cried he,—"is it thus you reward me for having preserved your life years ago,—for having kept you,—for having defended and cherished you? You open my doors to the dogs that thirst for my blood!— You display that pallid face and bedecked form, which my care has guarded from the scorching sun and cutting blast— which my hard-earned money has been spent to adorn!— You flaunt them before the eternal enemies of me, of my band, and my country!—You smile on them!—You play with their hands—their lips!—You deserve instant death!"

The necessity of consulting his safety, rather than the

deprecating, touching looks of the reviving Antonietta, re-called him to his senses. To remain on a spot that had been visited, and probably would soon be visited again, by French officers, seemed to him an excess of imprudence; particularly as he had lately learned, that, from an unfortu-nate celebrity he had acquired, he was—Benincasa, his chief, excepted—the brigand the most eagerly sought after. The solitudes of the forest offered a sure refuge; and thither, accordingly, he determined to repair with Antonietta, Pas-quale, and the old woman, that very night. His prompt plan was, however, frustrated; for as he was making pre-parations for the journey, Vernet and Beauchamp were seen approaching the house. The deadly hate and rage which then filled the heart of Peppè Tosco were measureless; and the expression that convulsed his face might have paralyzed for a moment the boldest heart.

"If you speak a word of warning," said he, in a sepulchral tone, to Antonietta; "if you speak one word, if you make one sign, my first shot shall be at you!"

He flew to his gun,—Pasquale did the same, and they both escaped through the back-door as the Frenchmen were about entering by the front. Who can describe the minute that ensued! Antonietta stood—with her long black hair hanging loose, and soiled with the dust of the floor—the blood streaming from her nose and mouth—trembling, and unable to speak one word, or move one step! One little word she had on her tongue—" Fly," but a suffocating force repressed it! One little sign she would have made, but her arm and hand were palsied! A minute more of that dreadful state of anxiety—a minute more, and her life's strings must have burst!—A gun was fired into the room: then she breathed and moved,—and rushing forward, clung around him whom all unwittingly she adored.

"A deadly shot that," said Vernet, who, from a long familiarity with scenes of danger, could trifle in the very worst of them,—"a deadly shot, indeed! It has carried away the gold tassel of my cap, that Giulietta of Ancona gave me when we parted."

"Ay, we're in a pretty wasp's nest, as I thought," said Beauchamp, who had placed himself under cover by one side of the window, and was preparing his pistols; "but, quick, come here, or you're a dead man,—quick! quick! our merry lads will be at our backs in a moment."

But Vernet had not time to move: Peppè Tosco had already fixed him with his murderous long gun: he had been indeed a dead man (for it was almost impossible that so sure a shot, though blinded with fury, should miss twice), but a sudden and violent return of old feelings, a momentary softening of the heart, seized Peppè: his Antonietta shielded the Frenchman with her body,—her cheek lay against his,— and there was scarcely enough of his person exposed, to plant a bullet: he could not kill her,—he could not draw the trigger: that momentary delay saved Vernet,—for, as the demon got the upperhand, and he was pressing the lock with his finger, a chasseur reached him, struck down the butt of his gun, and the bullet lodged in the cottage ceiling. When Vernet and Beauchamp ran out, their men had already secured Peppè Tosco and Pasquale. Vernet, on looking at the former, recognised him as the brigand he had fired at in the forest.

"What, old Grim!" cried he, "I believe you and I are old acquaintances. Oh, ho! your arm is wounded, eh? What, then, I hit you? I thought, by the nimbleness of your flight, that I had missed you as scandalously as you did me just now; but I find you owe me a shot. And pray who cut your head in this way?"

"That I did for him," said one of the soldiers; "for the dog wouldn't surrender."

"Well, well, we must keep him from giving and receiving such compliments for the future. Home to quarters with him."

The brigands were carried bound into the cottage. The feelings of Antonietta, which had been distracted by a variety of fears and interests, were now entirely concentrated in one point. She ran to Peppè Tosco; she wept over him, and stanched the blood that streamed down his face in torrents, with a handkerchief she tore from her neck. Some time passed ere Vernet could gain her attention; and when he informed her that she must be removed with her companions, she silently placed herself by the side of her foster-father, and only by a sign expressed her readiness to depart. The old woman, who had looked upon the fearful scene with the most perfect apathy, when she found that she too was arrested, shrieked dreadfully, and called upon the Madonna to protect her innocence. The doors of the cottage were secured, and the procession moved off. On the road, Vernet tried to reassure and console Antonietta; but she answered not a word—proceeding by the side of Peppè, with her eyes bent upon the ground.

When they arrived at the masseria, Vernet ordered that Peppè Tosco, Pasquale, and the old woman, should be confined bound as they were, in a strong room in the under part of the building. As they were proceeding thither, Antonietta supplicated to share the imprisonment of her foster-father; and he, on his part, gazed at her with commiseration, fearing, perhaps, the effects of French licentiousness, to which she was thus left exposed. If so, his fears were unfounded, for Vernet treated her with all the respect due to a young and innocent female: he assigned her a room apart from the rest, and made a country girl of the house attend upon her.

The next morning, the officers summoned Peppè Tosco before them, as they were anxious to examine him, before they committed him to the prison of Nicastro. He appeared in their presence, sullen and determined: he refused to answer their interrogations, and only protested that he attempted to defend his house and the honour of his daughter, from their assaults; that the wound in his arm, and an imagined likeness to a brigand in the forest, proved nothing; and that they, in justice, ought to release him immediately. Pasquale and Annarella were then questioned, and with more success : their feebler spirits were dashed; and hoping to obtain pardon as the price of evidence against their superior, they made an ample confession. It principally imported that Peppè Tosco was one of the leaders of Benincasa's horde; that he had been a brigand from his boyhood; that he was stained with several murders and robberies; and that Antonietta was not his daughter, but the child of a gentleman and lady, who had been destroyed as they were travelling through Calabria fourteen or fifteen years before.

The latter part of the confession was what most interested Vernet, and his eager questions elicited further details. Pasquale related circumstantially the attack made on a foreigner's family on the skirts of the forest; the discharge of one gun killed husband and wife, and a wretch had pointed his pistol at the child, when the youthful wife of one of the robbers rushed forward and saved it. The helpless orphan was conveyed with the plunder into a cave (one of the secret resorts of the banditti), and brought up as the child of the bandit by whose wife she had been preserved.

The unfortunate Antonietta, in the meantime, had recovered from her stupefaction, and dwelt with agonizing fear on the fate of Peppè Tosco. When Vernet visited her, he found her walking hurriedly about the room, and tracing her steps with her fast-falling tears. She instantly turned to him, and, without answering his kind inquiries, began to supplicate for the brigand: she threw herself on the ground, and, clinging to his knees, begged, with heart-searching fervour, that he would not kill him. Vernet endeavoured to make her comprehend that his fate did not depend upon him; that it was his duty to consign him to the prison at Nicastro, and that he would there be disposed of by justice. To her mind, however, prison and justice conveyed the idea of tyranny and murder; and she continued to implore that Vernet would set him at liberty. The young Frenchman explained the enormity of his offences; but she would not give credit to the greater part, and for the rest, as we have already said, she had been precluded, by her mode of life, from learning to estimate them aright. A feeling of horror prevented him then from acquainting her with the mystery he had discovered—that the wretch whose cause she advocated was one of the murderers of her parents; and besides, he feared the effect such a disclosure might have, on a brain that seemed already well-nigh distraught. She continued to pray, and it was not easy to resist her prayers.

"You told me, in the cottage," said she, "that I was pretty, and that you loved me—that you would die for me. Now I only ask you this favour—grant it, and I will follow you to the end of the world,—*I* will die for *you!*"

All that he could he promised, namely, that if Peppè Tosco should show signs of repentance, and give hopes of amendment, he would interest himself in his favour, and endeavour to save his life. Her gratitude knew no bounds. She, on her part, undertook (if Vernet would permit her to visit Tosco) to induce him to abandon his evil calling, and never to carry a gun again : the permission was given, and they separated.

To second, as it seemed, the fulfilment of Vernet's promise, an order arrived from Nicastro, to detain the persons arrested where they were, until further directions; the prison of the town being already too much crowded. On the return of Antonietta from the chamber in which Peppè

Tosco was confined, she acquainted Vernet that he had solemnly promised, on his being pardoned, to relinquish all connection with his band ; and then she began to conjure Vernet anew, to redeem his pledge.

Vernet acquainted her with the atrocities of her former associates—that Peppè Tosco was one of a band of assassins who had deprived her of her parents when she was an infant; and by the favour of her natural good sense, they soon enabled her to form those ideas of social right and propriety, from which she had been precluded by the singularity of her fortune.   Still she was eager for the life of the robber.

"I must yet supplicate for that unhappy man," said she. "I will never see him more !   I had a father and a mother, and he perhaps killed them.   Oh! his sight would now kill me !—but he saved my life,—he reared me under his roof,—he supported me, and delicately too,—and sometimes he would be kind to me—so kind!   Oh, he must not die ! he must not !"

Vernet again pledged himself to do all he could to save his life, and gave her to hope that his endeavours would be successful.

It was then agreed that Antonietta should seek a temporary shelter in the house of a respectable inhabitant of a neighbouring town; and Vernet left his lovely *protégée* to enjoyments of which she had till then had no experience,— a participation in the harmony and repose of a virtuous family circle.   An unwonted sadness fell upon his heart as he was leaving her,—a sadness he could not account for, as he knew he left her in safety and might soon see her again. Poor Antonietta was equally depressed, and perhaps with as little apparent reason : she accompanied him to the door, she returned the grasp of his hand, and when he ventured to press her cheek to his lips, her tears flowed down it.

Vernet, anxious to fulfil his promise to Antonietta, and to dismiss the revolting subject for ever from his mind, repaired the next morning to Nicastro. He succeeded in obtaining a sentence condemning Peppè Tosco and his two associates to solitary confinement in a fortress on the coast ; and, full of joy, and picturing to himself a sunny futurity, he mounted his horse to return.

A short time after the departure of Vernet from his quarters, a little old man, in the dress of a mendicant friar, arrived at the masseria, and asked to speak with the officer. He was admitted to Beauchamp, to whom, after numerous salutations and *benedicite*, he revealed that he could conduct him to a spot, three or four miles off, on the skirts of the wood, where a small body of robbers, rich with booty they had just captured, might be easily surprised by his troop. He pretended to be very anxious for his own safety, and begged he might be disguised as a French soldier, and mixed with the men, to avoid being seen acting as a guide by any of the country people, who would not fail to inform the brigands, and so bring down certain destruction upon him. All this deceived Beauchamp : he unreflectingly fell into the snare, and leaving six or seven men to guard the house, prepared to march with the rest of his company. Accordingly, to the great amusement of the soldiers, the guide's " holy wool" was stripped off, and after a deal of trying on and fitting, his droll figure was equipped in a chasseur's uniform, and his burly person placed between two soldiers. They set out at full speed : in the course of an hour, they reached the spot referred to by the priest, panting from the rapidity of their movements—for the pseudo-friar had made them race like a pack of hounds—where the reverend gentleman came to a serious halt, and told Beauchamp that as they were within a few shots of the brigands, he must go forward in his monastic dress to lure them into the toils. "Do you, meanwhile," said he, "keep yourself concealed among this brushwood, and do not move until you hear my shrill whistle ;—in ten minutes you will have them, and the whole of their booty in your hands." He now resumed his former toilette, retaining only the good blue breeches—part of his military disguise that could not be seen under his monk's garments—and advanced at an exceedingly brisk pace into the wood.

The soldiers followed his advice, and lay down without moving or speaking : ten minutes passed away—a quarter of an hour—half an hour ; but when nearly an hour had elapsed, and no other sounds were heard than the chirping of the little birds that were flitting about in the woods, Beauchamp arrived at the very mortifying conclusion that he had been duped, and with many invectives on the fugitive friar, ordered his men homeward. When he approached the outward gate of the masseria, he perceived, to his great dismay, that the ground was in several places stained with blood ; and hastening on to the house, he soon learned the

object of the trick that had been played upon him. The
room where Peppè Tosco and his companions had been confined was broken open, and two of his men were lying dead
near the doorway. Beauchamp was now informed by a
wounded soldier, who had just descended the stairs, that
soon after he had set out with the monk, the masseria was
surrounded by a number of robbers, who advanced and
attacked the prison and the few French that remained : they
had defended the prison as long as they could, and after two
of them had been killed the others retreated, with the
people of the house, to the upper part of a small square
tower, in which they had barricaded themselves, and whence
they had seen the brigands carry off the prisoners in
triumph.

"Truly," said Beauchamp to himself, when he recovered
from the excess of his rage and mortification,—"truly I
have got myself into a pretty scrape. How shall I answer
for this to Vernet ? He will call me a madman, for having
trusted to anything in the shape of a monk ! Oh, I shall
be ashamed to see his face !"—But that face he had never
to see again lit up with life!—He had nothing more to fear
from its biting, sarcastic air,—or to hope from its commiserating and friendly expression !—Its muscles had moved for
the last time, and were now fixed in the rigid languor of
death !

Poor Vernet, cantering gaily homeward, attended by only
one soldier, had reached a little thicket not far from his
quarters, when a shot, from an unseen hand, laid his
attendant upon the earth. The next instant he saw Peppè

Tosco by the side of a tree, aiming at him,—and in another moment, the villain's shot had pierced his heart! When the brigands rushed on the body of the unfortunate young man, in search of plunder, they found three or four dollars —the whole of his worldly wealth,—an edition of Horace, a lock of Antonietta's hair, and a pardon for his assassin, Peppè Tosco! The bodies were discovered in the evening by some soldiers returning with forage: the orderly-man was not dead, and had just breath enough to relate the above particulars.

The sad news soon reached Antonietta : it almost killed her. Indeed her real existence ended at that moment; for she was soon induced to bury herself in the deadening monotony and unserviceable sanctity of a monastery, with all her youth and beauty, and disposition for the loftiest virtues.

[This narrative was written at Naples, after a tour in the Calabrias, and while the scenes described were fresh in the mind of the writer. The whole of the story, with a very slight exception, is matter of fact. The attacks and decoys of the brigands were related by an eye-witness,—an officer in the French service.]

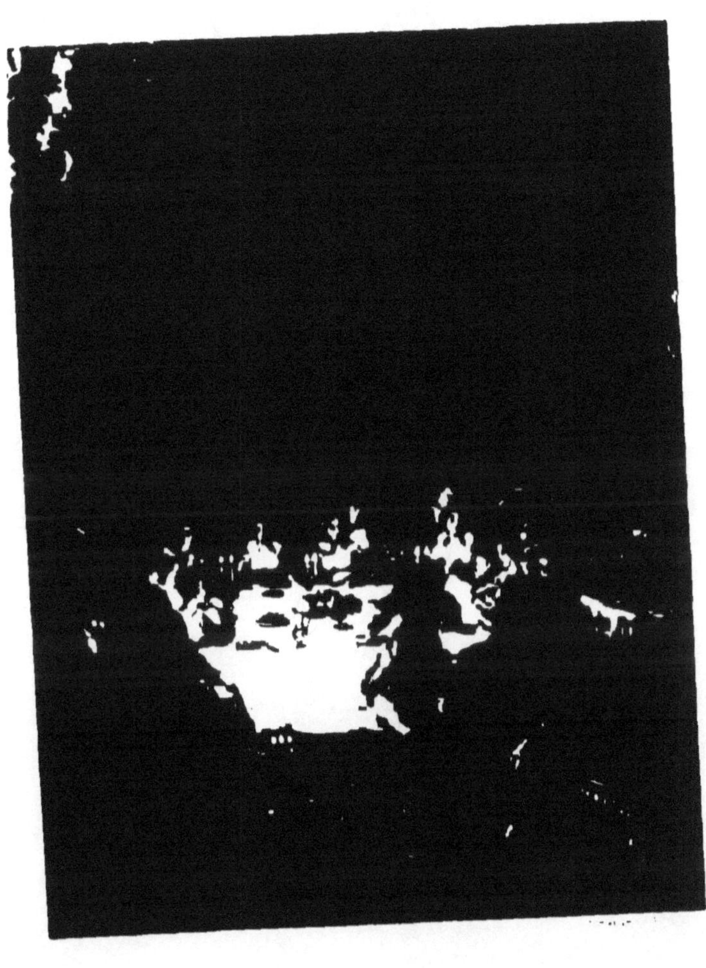

Sans Souci.

OME ye forth to our revel by moonlight,
   With your lutes and your spirits in tune;
The dew falls to-night like an odour—
   Stars weep o'er our last day in June.

Come, maids, leave the loom and its purple,
   Though the robe of a monarch were there;
Seek your mirror, I know 'tis your dearest,
   And be it to-night your sole care.

Braid ye your curls in their thousands,
   Whether dark as the raven's dark wing,
Or bright as that clear summer colour,
   When sunshine lights every ring.

On each snow ankle lace silken sandal,
   Don the robes like the neck they hide white;
Then come forth like planets from darkness,
   Or like lilies at day-break's first light.

Is there one who half regal in beauty,
  Would be regal in pearl and in gem ;
Let her wreathe her a crown of red roses—
  No rubies are equal to them.

Is there one who sits languid and lonely,
  With her fair face bowed down on her hand,
With a pale cheek and glittering eyelash,
  And careless locks 'scaped from their band,

For a lover not worth that eye's tear-drop,
  Not worth that sweet mouth's rosy kiss,
Nor that cheek though 'tis faded to paleness ;—
  I know not the lover that is :

Let her bind up her beautiful tresses,
  Call her wandering rose back again ;
And for one prisoner 'scaping her bondage,
  A hundred shall carry her chain !

Come, gallants, the gay and the graceful,
  With hearts like the light plumes ye wear ;
Eyes all but divine light our revel—
  Like the stars in whose beauty they share.

Come ye, for the wine cups are mantling ;
  Some clear as the morning's first light ;
Others touched with the evening's last crimson,
  Or the blush that may meet you to-night.

There are plenty of sorrows to chill us,
  And troubles last on to the grave;
But the coldest glacier has its rose-tint,
  And forth rides the stormiest wave.

Oh! Hope will spring up from its ashes,
  With plumage as bright as before;
And pleasures like lamps in a palace—
  If extinct, you need only light more.

When one vein of silver's exhausted,
  'Tis easy another to try;
There are fountains enough in the desert,
  Though that by your palm-tree be dry.

When an India of gems is around you,
  Why ask for the one you have not?
Though the roc in your hall may be wanting,
  Be contented with what you have got.

Come to-night, for the white blossomed myrtle
  Is flinging its love-sighs around;
And beneath, like the veiled eastern beauties,
  The violets peep from the ground.

Seek ye for gold and for silver—
  There are both on these bright orange-trees
And never in Persia the moonlight
  Wept o'er roses more blushing than these.

There are fireflies sparkling by myriads,
  The fountain-wave dances in light ;
Hark ! the mandolin's first notes are waking,
  And soft steps break the sleeping of night.

Then come all the young and the graceful,
  Come gay as the lovely should be ;
'Tis much, in this world's toil and trouble,
  To let one midnight pass *Sans Souci.*

A Tragedy of Other Times,

IN the year 1805, while General Junot was governor of Paris, as a poor mason inhabiting that city was returning one evening from his day's work through the Champs Elysées, he was accosted by three men, whose features the darkness of the evening prevented him from distinguishing. They asked him if he was willing to come with them forthwith, for the purpose of executing a work in masonry, which it was necessary should be completed before the morning. He expressed his readiness to do so, provided he was well paid for it. They then promised him five and twenty Napoleons as his reward, on condition that he would consent to have his eyes blinded, and would come with them without an instant's delay.

The mason acceded to the proposal, and a handkerchief was bound over his eyes. The men then led him along at a quick pace for some time. At length they stopped, and

* The following relation of a true story was given to the author in conversation at Paris, in 1816, by General Hulot, who was aid-de-camp to Marshal Junot, Duke of Abrantes, at the time it happened.

told him he was now to get into a carriage. Having placed him in it, and got in themselves, the carriage drove off with rapidity. For a considerable space of time they rolled over the stones, but afterwards left them, and appeared to be passing along a cross road. About an hour's drive brought them to the end of their journey. The carriage halted, and the mason was taken out of it. He was then led through various passages, and up and down staircases; probably for the purpose of rendering it the more difficult for him upon any future occasion to trace his way.

When the bandage was taken from his eyes he found himself in a room illuminated with many wax candles, and hung with black cloth. The floor, the walls, and the ceiling were alike covered with these mournful hangings; and no part of the apartment was without them, except one large niche in the wall, near which were placed stones and mortar, and the necessary implements for making use of them. The mason was astonished and alarmed at all he saw: he turned round to seek explanation of it, but found himself entirely alone.

He had full leisure to examine the funeral decorations by which he was surrounded: but at length he heard a noise, and a portion of the hanging being lifted up, discovered a door, which was thrown open. Through this entered a number of men in black cloaks, and whose faces were concealed by masks. They entered dragging with them a beautiful young woman, whose dishevelled black hair, streaming eyes, and disordered dress, proved, at the same time, her misery, and the compulsion under which she was suffering.

As soon as she was in the room, she sunk on her knees before her masked conductors, and implored them in the most moving manner to have pity on her; but they only replied by shaking their heads. She particularly addressed herself to one of them, who, from his gray hairs, appeared to be older than the rest. She embraced his knees, and, with sobs and tears, besought his mercy. To these supplications no answer was given; but upon a signal made, she was again dragged forward, and, in spite of her screams and resistance, was forced into the niche, where she was bound with cords.

The gray-haired mask then desired the mason to begin his work, and to wall her up. But the poor man, horror-struck with what he had seen, and affected beyond measure with the imploring lamentations of the lady, who besought him not to be an accessary to so foul a murder, refused to proceed. Upon this the masks began to threaten him. The mason fell on his knees, and entreated to be permitted to depart. But the masks drew their swords from beneath their cloaks, and told him, with imprecations, that if he continued to refuse to perform what he had promised, instant death should be his portion; while, on the other hand, if he obeyed, his reward should be doubled.

The poor man, thus intimidated, commenced unwillingly his horrible task, but stopped from time to time, and requested to be permitted to desist. The masks, however, stood over him the whole time with drawn swords, and obliged him to proceed; till at length, while the shrieks of the victim became every instant more dreadfully piercing, as the wall rose upon her which was to shut her out from life, the tragedy was completed, and the niche was hermetically sealed with solid masonry.

The mason threw down his trowel more dead than alive—the gray-haired mask put fifty Napoleons into his hand, his eyes were again covered, and he was hurried from the room in which this tremendous scene had taken place. As on his arrival, he was led up and down through various passages, and then put into a carriage. The carriage was whirled along as rapidly as before; and after the stated period, the mason found himself with his eyes uncovered on the spot in the Champs Elysées where he had first been met, and alone!

The night was now far advanced, or rather, the morning was approaching. The man was stunned and bewildered with what he had witnessed; but, after a short time, he recovered the use of his intellect so far as to determine to go forthwith to the governor of Paris. Having with difficulty got admission to Junot, his tale was at first disbelieved; but the fifty Napoleons which he produced, and still more, the unvarying accuracy with which he related the different circumstances of that dreadful night, at length gained him entire credit.

The police employed themselves very diligently for some weeks in tracing the scene of the crime, and the perpetrators of it. Various houses within a certain distance of the capital were searched, and the walls of rooms were inspected, to see if any marks of new made stone-work could be discovered. The principal house-agents of Paris, the coach-hirers, the guards at the *barrières*, &c., were examined, in the hopes of finding some clue ; but entirely without success.

This mysterious murder remained, and still remains, unexplained and unpunished; but conjecture imagined it to have been an act of family vengeance. According to this solution, the masks were the father and brothers of the unfortunate lady, who was considered in some way or other to have dishonoured her race. They were also supposed to have been strangers from some distant part of the country, who had come to the neighbourhood of Paris for the purpose of completing this vindictive act, and had gone away again after its perpetration.

One Peep was Enough.

ALL places have their peculiarities: now that of Dalton was discourse—that species of discourse which Johnson's Dictionary entitles "conversation on whatever does not concern ourselves." Everybody knew what everybody did, and a little more. Eatings, drinkings, wakings, sleepings, walkings, talkings, sayings, doings—all were for the good of the public; there was not such a thing as a secret in the town.

There was a story of Mrs. Mary Smith, an ancient dame who lived on an annuity, and boasted the gentility of a back and front parlour, that she once asked a few friends to dinner. The usual heavy antecedent half-hour really passed quite pleasantly; for Mrs. Mary's windows overlooked the market-place, and not a scrag of mutton could leave it unobserved; so that the extravagance or the meanness of the various buyers furnished a copious theme for dialogue. Still, in spite of Mr. A.'s pair of fowls, and Mrs. B.'s round of beef, the time seemed long, and the guests found hunger

growing more potent than curiosity. They waited and waited; at length the fatal discovery took place—that in the hurry of observing her neighbours' dinners, Mrs. Smith had forgotten to order her own!

It was in the month of March that an event happened which put the whole town in a commotion—the arrival of a stranger, who took up his abode at the White Hart: not that there was anything remarkable about the stranger; he was a plain, middle-aged, respectable-looking man, and the nicest scrutiny (and oh how narrowly he was watched!) failed to discover anything odd about him. It was ascertained that he rose at eight, breakfasted at nine, ate two eggs and a piece of broiled bacon, sat in his room at the window, read a little, wrote a little, and looked out upon the road a good deal; he then strolled out, returned home, dined at five, smoked two cigars, read the Morning Herald (for the post came in of an evening), and went to bed at ten. Nothing could be more regular or unexceptionable than his habits; still it was most extraordinary what could have brought him to Dalton. There were no chalybeate springs, warranted to cure every disease under the sun ; no ruins in the neighbourhood, left expressly for antiquarians and picnic parties ; no fine prospects, which, like music, people make it matter of conscience to admire; no celebrated person had ever been born or buried in its environs; there were no races, no assizes—in short, there was "no nothing." It was not even summer; so country air and fine weather were not the inducements. The stranger's name was Mr. Williams, but that was the extent of their knowledge ; and

shy and silent, there seemed no probability of learning anything more from himself.　Conjecture, like Shakspeare,
" exhausted worlds, and then imagined new."　Some supposed he was hiding from his creditors, others that he had
committed forgery; one suggested that he had escaped from
a mad-house, a second that he had killed some one in a duel;
but all agreed that he came there for no good.

It was the 23rd of March, when a triad of gossips were
assembled at their temple, the post-office.　The affairs of Dalton and the nation were settled together; newspapers were
slipped from their covers, and not an epistle but yielded
a portion of its contents.　But on this night all attention
was concentrated upon one, directed to "John Williams,
Esq., at the White Hart, Dalton."　Eagerly was it com-
pressed in the long fingers of Mrs. Mary Smith of dinner-
less memory; the fat landlady of the White Hart was on
tip-toe to peep; while the post-mistress, whose curiosity took
a semblance of official dignity, raised a warning hand against
any overt act of violence.　The paper was closely folded,
and closely written in a cramped and illegible hand; suddenly Mrs. Mary Smith's look grew more intent—she had
succeeded in deciphering a sentence; the letter dropped
from her hand.　"Oh, the monster!" shrieked the horri-
fied peeper.　Landlady and post-mistress both snatched at
the terrible scroll, and they equally succeeded in reading the
following words :—" We will settle the matter to-morrow at
dinner; but I am sorry you persist in poisoning your wife,
the horror is too great."　Not a syllable more could they
make out; but what they had read was enough.　" He told

me," gasped the landlady, "that he expected a lady and gentleman to dinner—oh, the villain! to think of poisoning any lady at the White Hart; and his wife, too!—I should like to see my husband poisoning me!" Our hostess became quite personal in her indignation.

"I always thought there was something suspicious about him; people don't come and live where nobody knows them, for nothing," observed Mrs. Mary Smith.

"I dare say," returned the post-mistress, "Williams is not his real name."

"I don't know that," interrupted the landlady; "Williams is a good hanging name: there was Williams who murdered the Marr's family, and Williams who burked all those poor dear children; I dare say he is some relation of theirs: but to think of his coming to the White Hart!—it's no place for his doings, I can tell him: he sha'n't poison his wife in my house;—out he goes this very night—I'll take the letter to him myself."

"Bless me! I shall be ruined, if it comes to be known that we take a look into the letters;" and the post-mistress thought in her heart that she had better let Mr. Williams poison his wife at his leisure. Mrs. Mary Smith, too, reprobated any violent measures;—the truth is, she did not wish to be mixed up in the matter; a gentlewoman with an annuity and a front and back parlour was rather ashamed of being detected in such close intimacy with the post-mistress and the landlady. It seemed likely that poor Mrs. Williams would be left to her miserable fate.

"Murder will out," said the landlord, the following morning, as he mounted the piebald pony, which, like Tom Tough, had seen a deal of service ; and hurried off in search of Mr. Crampton, the nearest magistrate.

Their perceptions assisted by brandy and water, he and his wife had sat up long past "the witching hour of night," deliberating on what line of conduct would be most efficacious in preserving the life of the unfortunate Mrs. Williams ; and the result of their deliberation was, to fetch the justice, and have the delinquent taken into custody at the very dinner-table which was intended to be the scene of his crime. "He has ordered soup to-day for the first time ; he thinks he could so easily slip poison into the liquid. There he goes ; he looks like a man who has got something on his conscience," pointing to Mr. Williams, who was walking up and down at his usual slow pace. Two o'clock arrived, and with it a chaise. Out of it stepped, sure enough, a lady and gentleman. The landlady's pity redoubled—"Such a pretty young creature, not above nineteen !"—" I see how it is," thought she ; " the old wretch is jealous." All efforts to catch her eye were in vain, the dinner was ready, and down they sat. The hostess of the White Hart looked alternately out of the window, like sister Ann, to see if any one was coming, and at the table, to see that nothing was doing. To her dismay she observed the young lady lifting a spoonful of soup to her mouth ! She could restrain herself no longer ; but catching her hand, exclaimed, "Poor dear innocent, the soup is poisoned !" All started from the table in confusion, which was yet to be increased : a bustle was heard in the passage—in rushed a whole party, two of whom, each catching an arm of Mr. Williams, pinioned them down to his seat!

"I am happy, madam," said the little bustling magistrate, "to have been, under Heaven, the humble instrument of preserving your life from the nefarious designs of that disgrace to humanity." Mr. Crampton paused in consequence of three wants—want of words, breath, and ideas.

"My life!" ejaculated the astonished lady.

"Yes, madam; the ways of Providence are inscrutable—the vain curiosity of three idle women has been turned to good account." And the eloquent magistrate proceeded to detail the process of inspection to which the fatal letter had been subjected; but when he came to the terrible words—"We will settle the matter to-morrow at dinner; but I am sorry you persist in poisoning your wife"—he was interrupted by bursts of laughter from the gentleman, from the injured wife, and even from the prisoner himself! One fit of merriment was followed by another, till it became contagious, and the very constables began to laugh too.

"I can explain all," at last interrupted the visitor. "Mr. Williams came here for that quiet so necessary for the labours of genius: he is writing a melodrame called 'My Wife'—he submitted the last Act to me, and I rather objected to the poisoning of the heroine. This young lady is my daughter, and we are on our way to the sea-coast. Mr. Williams is only wedded to the Muses."

The disconcerted magistrate shook his head, and muttered something about theatres being very immoral.

"Quite mistaken, sir," said Mr. Williams. "Our soup is cold; but our worthy landlady roasts fowls to a turn—we will have them and the veal cutlets up. You will stay and dine with us; and, afterward, I shall be proud to read 'My Wife' aloud, in the hope of your approval, at least, of your indulgence;"—and with the same hope I bid farewell to my readers.